# The Last Illusion
# of Paige White

# The Last Illusion of Paige White

*A Novel*

Vanessa McCausland

CROWN
NEW YORK

CROWN
An imprint of the Crown Publishing Group
A division of Penguin Random House LLC
1745 Broadway
New York, NY 10019
crownpublishing.com
penguinrandomhouse.com

Originally published in Australia by HarperCollins Australia in 2024.

Library of Congress Cataloging-in-Publication Data
Names: McCausland, Vanessa, author. Title: The last illusion of Paige White : a novel / Vanessa McCausland.
Identifiers: LCCN 2024021669 | ISBN 9780593799949 (hardcover) |
ISBN 9780593799963 (trade paperback) | ISBN 9780593799956 (ebook)
Subjects: LCGFT: Detective and mystery fiction. | Thrillers (Fiction) | Novels.
Classification: LCC PR9619.4.M3793 L37 2025 | DDC 823/.92—dc23/eng/20240812
LC record available at https://lccn.loc.gov/2024021669

Hardcover ISBN 978-0-593-79994-9
Ebook ISBN 978-0-593-79995-6

Printed in the United States of America on acid-free paper

Editor: Lori Kusatzky
Production editor: Serena Wang
Text designer: Amani Shakrah
Production: Heather Williamson
Copy editor: Tom Pitoniak
Proofreaders: Barbara Greenberg, Nicole Celli
Publicist: Tammy Blake
Marketer: Hannah Perrin

9 8 7 6 5 4 3 2 1

First US Edition

The authorized representative in the EU for product safety and compliance is Penguin Random House Ireland, Morrison Chambers, 32 Nassau Street, Dublin D02 YH68, Ireland, https://eu-contact.penguin.ie.

*To Soph*

"The desire to be loved is the last illusion. Give it up and you will be free."

—Margaret Atwood, "A Sunday Drive"

# The Last Illusion
# of Paige White

# Prologue

They weren't all sisters, but they looked the same. Dark-haired, as though they had somehow resisted the warm north-coast sunshine that honeyed the locks of the other girls. As though they had resisted the light that seeped into everything here, bleached the blinds, squinted the skin around eyes. They dressed differently too. Some said it was because they were religious, but really, wouldn't that make them more like everyone else, not less? They wore kohl on their eyes, flowers in their hair, nothing on their feet. And they moved as though they already knew the secrets of the world at sixteen, as though they floated above the backyard barbecues and the beach days. These girls were of another place, or maybe they just wished they were. And I wished I was like them.

# CHAPTER 1

# Jane

She traced the outline of the woman's face on her screen. Dark hair strewn like seagrass across pale skin. Sticks and foam and flowers in the sand.

*It couldn't be her.*

Jane closed the browser window, her hand reacting before her mind could fully make sense of the image.

Sometimes at low tide, the water was so shallow you could wade out to the middle, and when the sun hit at a certain angle it was like a mirror, like walking on water. When Jane thought of her childhood, she always thought of this mirror place. And the tree cathedral on the lip of the lake, branches stretching toward the low, hot sky in worship. The briny water, warm around her ankles.

She willed her eyes to focus on her desktop, to reconnect with the thread of her news story. She was meant to be writing about locals protesting the development of a huge shopping mall on their street. Her editors were pestering her for copy but she was still waiting on a quote from the council. She straightened her back and took a sip of water. Her eyes wouldn't focus on the words in front of her. Everything was hazy, like the morning mist that veiled the water at dawn.

A message pinged on her screen. URGENT.

*Masters. Drop the development story and get this Instagram woman one up now.*

Jane's hands were shaking. *It can't be her. Surely someone would have told me.*

She studied her hands as though they were someone else's. Blue veins that threaded under her skin like estuaries. *Does a home etch itself into a body?*

She pressed her palms onto her desk, took a deep breath. She had to focus. She was a journalist. She lived in Sydney now. She had built a life here, a career. That shallow lake didn't have any purchase over her anymore.

And yet.

Jane hovered over the link her editor had sent, hesitating. It felt like holding her breath underwater. The call of the wetland birds at dawn. The flash of silverfish just pulled from the water. The sound of her dad's voice.

She pressed the link and the image slid onto the screen again. The woman's eyes were closed, wet hair fanned out in the shallows. Jane felt the lukewarm water on her own skin. She touched her face as if expecting to find moisture.

*No. No. No.*

She felt the surge of nostalgia, of longing, at the same time as the awful wash of recognition hit her. She read the headline.

HAUNTING LAST POST BEFORE WOMAN FOUND DEAD

Jane drew in a deep breath, and it felt like breathing in water. She continued reading.

*Tragic last social media picture posted only hours before her body was found in the lake.*

The white curve of her arm cradled her head as though she were sleeping. As though she were one of those archetypal women reclining in a Renaissance painting. The tree cathedral above her like a green crown. *Their place.* The place where everyone played as children, drank as teenagers, and then got married. Jane was the one who got out.

Her eyes skimmed the story, as though, by only half-reading it, it would only be half-true. The haunting photo seemed a harbinger of things to come only hours later.

*Paige White led an idyllic lake-side life . . . Tragedy struck one morning on a lake near her home . . . She was turning thirty-five that day . . . It seemed she might have been leaving a message in her last Instagram photo. Police are still investigating the cause of death, and are asking the public for help.*

Jane stood. She didn't know why, but she couldn't look at the words, the pictures, couldn't compute what they meant. She felt herself moving away from her desk. Suddenly Jackson was beside her.

"Hey, Masters, did you get the breaking Instagrammer story? Can you get something up ASAP for online?"

She turned to him. He looked calm. She noticed a small brown stain just below his collar, the tiny threads of silver at his temples. The faint line between his eyebrows creased deeper.

"Are you okay, Jane?"

She reached out for him, gripped his arm. "I can't."

He shook his head. "What's going on?"

"It's Paige."

He took a step toward her. "You knew this girl? The influencer?"

She tried to speak but her mouth, her lungs, felt flooded.

"Bloody hell. A mate from back home? Were you two close?" He rubbed his chin. He hadn't shaved this morning and his eyes were slightly red. She wondered if he'd been out again last night and who he'd been with.

He took her hand and squeezed it, but it was subtle, hidden between their bodies. That was the thing about Jackson. He could read people. That's what made him so good at his job. He bit his bottom lip. He always did that when he was excited, or nervous. She'd seen him both ways, but mainly excited.

He spoke slowly. "I know you'll need a moment. I'm going to get you a glass of water. Actually, I'll make you a nice cup of tea, that will help, yeah? And I want you to take a walk around the block while I make it."

"No, not tea, I don't drink tea," she said, annoyed he didn't know that.

His voice was calm, composed. "Coffee. I'll get you some coffee. And then I'd like you to come back and just get this story up for the online team now, but then maybe you could look at writing something more in-depth about Paige down the line. Do you think you could do that? To, you know, to honor her?"

Jane felt bile rise in her throat. "I . . ."

"I know you can do this, Jane. You're one of our best feature writers. You're the only one who can do this story justice. It's a really great story. She has . . . had a lot of followers. Her body was found a few hours after she posted that image on socials. No words, just a photo of herself lying in the shallows of the lake. She's not dead in this photo, despite what it might look like, lying there like that. She's got a smile on her lips if you look closely. Apparently dead bodies don't . . . can't smile naturally like that. But then she was dead a short time later." He paused, his fingers drumming on the desk. "That picture and the timing is eerie. It implies it might have been suicide, but we know the police wouldn't issue a press release and ask for help if there weren't suspicious circumstances."

He leaned forward to study the image on her computer screen. "Chilling. You can't help but feel there's more to this story."

*This isn't just another story to churn out.*

Jackson squeezed her shoulders. It was something he did. This had been the first thing that had made her think there might be something more between them. He was touchy-feely with people, but the way his hands had lingered so close to her neck . . .

He ran his thumbs down her bare arms now and she shivered. It was so rare he showed her overt affection in the office. "You can do this."

Jane looked around but everyone was continuing as though nothing had happened. She turned to the screen.

*I've written stories about dead girls before. It's another story. I just have to get something up fast. I can do this.*

She felt herself nodding slowly.

"That's my girl."

She felt discomfort skittle across her skin.

*Paige isn't just another dead girl. She was your friend.*

Maybe she could write something beautiful. A personal eulogy from someone who had grown up with her. But she opened the new story template and waited for something to click over, for the words to flow. The thing she had spent years honing, the muscle that flexed when she was on deadline, felt stiff, unresponsive. The words didn't come.

She thought of the usual intense, yet somehow distant pity she felt for the people whose tragedies she covered for the news every day.

*You need to disconnect emotionally from this if you're going to do your job.*

Jane read the police press release. The media had picked up on Paige's popularity online, found that last image on Instagram and gone nuts. She could call police media, try to get more details, but she didn't want to, she couldn't. Besides, she didn't have time. The online team just needed a straight news story replicating the press release and the same angle the other publications had taken.

She heard whispers from the desks surrounding her. Their words sounded like they were in an echo chamber.

"Never heard of her. Bloody influencers. Who even cares? It's just 'cause she's beautiful."

The room had begun to spin. She put her head in her hands.

*You are stronger than this. You're a professional. You've got to finish the story. Just finish the story.*

She bit her lip until she tasted blood. She looked at the pictures on Paige's Instagram account. Ones where she looked happy and smiling and beautiful and alive. *A perfect charmed life.* She filed the bare bones of a story, a carbon copy of all the others, and then found herself on her knees beside her desk. People were looking at her with odd expressions on their faces. Someone had their hand on her back. She couldn't speak but she saw a single tear drip off her nose, and soak into the ugly gray carpet. She looked at her trash bin and wondered if she was going to be sick.

Jackson was heading toward her across the newsroom. Others were backing away as though not wanting to catch whatever she had. What did she have? She felt her body rise and move toward the elevators. She wasn't in control of herself. She needed to see the sky. She had to get out of here.

⁓

Outside on the street a light rain grazed her skin. She began to walk. She didn't know where she was going, but some small part of her was screaming that she couldn't do this. She had worked so hard to get here, she couldn't just walk away like this. And she needed an umbrella. But her legs wouldn't stop.

Then she heard a voice she hadn't heard in a long time. She looked down and her phone was in her hand.

*Paige.*

Her voice had always been one of the things that made her powerful. It had a huskiness to it, a sweet grit. She had inherited it from her father. A preacher's daughter. The voice was telling her to leave a message.

God, she'd called Paige's number accidentally. And then there was another call coming in. She answered it. His voice was low and grounding.

"Dad?" Her own voice sounded too high, like a child's. She could almost feel his coarse, warm hands in hers. "What's happened? Has something happened to Paige?"

But even as she said it, even after she'd written and filed a story about it, it didn't seem possible. Paige was always the incandescent one. She was always the one who was meant to get out. She was the one with the charisma, the loving supportive family, that house.

"Jane." He had used her proper name instead of Janie, so she knew it must be true, it must be real.

She closed her eyes, and she could almost hear the swamp that edged his house breathing. Because on that side of the lake it was really half swamp. Sometimes you could smell the salt, the clean eucalypts that lined the shore, hear the bellbirds tinkling in the forest. Other times all you could smell was mangrove mud and egret shit, and all you could hear were the eels squirming just below the surface.

She knew what he was going to say, and she didn't want him to say it. She had the urge to run inside the building, back to Jackson, to this safe, solid, successful life she'd built around herself to keep that seeping lake water out.

"Janie, I think you'd better come home."

CHAPTER 2

# Paige

I was raised thinking the beginning and end of things looked like the Garden of Eden, and then the gates of heaven. I know I'm not in heaven. I'm in an old caravan, late afternoon, summertime. I can smell everything, feel everything, but I'm stuck here. Trapped. I've tried to open the door and it won't budge, as though it's locked from the outside. The windows won't open. They won't even break when I smash the coffee percolator against them over and over again.

The thing is, where I am is beautiful. The sun is streaming through the windows, turning everything golden. Like an Instagram filter. *Valencia, Gingham, Sierra.* Andy used to call it the golden hour. There are small potted cactuses lined up on the windowsill, their tiny hairs illuminated. I touch them and I can feel their unexpected soft down. I touch them so that I know I still exist. The warmth of the sun on my arms when I sit at the slide-in table. The smell of ripe fruit and the baby wipes we used for Viv comforts me.

I call for Andy, for Viv, but the silence of stale sunshine and dust answers me. It never gets dark. The sun never fades. It's so hot in here. I can't breathe, I can't get out. I feel like I'm in the "live" setting on a photo on a phone, where mere moments are recorded, where everything is moving and alive and then, suddenly, still. Captured. Frozen in time. That's what it feels like, where I am.

It's as though I'm trapped in my own Instagram photo. The one with the most likes. Everyone loved our little retro caravan. I suppose it's not all that surprising that I'm here—everything reduced to tiny little squares, compartmentalized. It's what I spent a good chunk of my life doing—trying to put neat parameters around myself. Whatever I was trying to do didn't work. I've been thinking a lot about this since I've been here.

I spent my time looking at other people's perfect tiny pictures. Beach vistas and plates of pasta, fluffy cats on sofas, smiling dogs, bright cocktails and beautiful dresses. I sieved my reality through artful angles and filters that made everything look like nostalgia. I spent my life dissecting camera angles and ways to make my nose look less bulbous in selfies, my eyes brighter.

I compared myself to the stream of images coming at me, their pings like small alarm bells in my body. I suppose I was trying to make things beautiful. Or not even. I was just on there. Doing what? I wasn't living. I was filling in time. Waiting for what? Scanning for something that never came. Or maybe it did. That little hit that I got with a flattering new comment, new likes, new followers. It felt like that was all there was. I forgot what it was like to exist in the world without recording it, massaging it, curating it for the other world. The other world became my real world.

And now I'm there. I'm here. I have been for a while, but I don't know how long. I have no concept of time. I've been sucked into this strange and yet strangely familiar ether.

My father always says that hell is a place of our own making. Not the fire and brimstone of the Old Testament, not being thrown into the lake of fire to burn—the dramatic stuff I always loved reading— but our own personalized worst nightmare. A place without god's presence. There is no god here except the god of hedonism. And there would probably be people who would tell you I was going to hell.

But I wasn't a bad person, was I? If I did things that hurt others it was because I was trying to survive. I was muddling my way through like the rest of us. Trying to be loved. Trying to be accepted. Trying to be happy. But I can't get out of here. It won't stop. When we lived in the caravan, Andy would set up a sheet strung between the gum trees and we'd put down a picnic rug and cushions and project movies onto this makeshift screen. Everyone loved that on my feed. I guess it did look pretty idyllic. But now that sheet is all I can see out the window of the van. The Disney movies we once watched with Viv have been replaced by images from my social feed. All I can see is other people's lives projected onto it, going on and on, like I'm scrolling through the apps just before bedtime and I can't stop, even though I know I won't sleep for hours. It's interminable. Don't get me wrong, it's beautiful. It was always fucking beautiful. That was never the problem. But god, the beauty hurts, not because I'm not there to see the sunsets or drink the wine, but because I'm not there to bury my nose in my little girl's hair.

Viv. I was not a bad person before you came to me, but I was self- ish. Surely I didn't need to be stuck here to see that you changed me. I can see the account, the feed I made for you. It keeps on going. Why aren't I with you? Where the hell am I?

Life just keeps going on and on and on, an endless feed that never, ever has an end. Here's something that never occurred to me—it never stopped. The feed never ended. I never found that place, the endpoint, to get off the apps, off social media. And even when I'm not living in the real world anymore, I am here, still, suspended in this twilight of warped beauty. Without my baby. I don't know how I left my darling girl.

Maybe God has given me this time—maybe I'm suspended between heaven and hell. To reflect on all the things I did wrong in life. The people I hurt. I used to love reading the Book of Revelation and all those Bible verses about hell when I was little. I don't know why. I guess growing up with your father being a minister does that to a person. All those Bible passages.

*The sea gave up the dead that were in it, and death and Hades gave up the dead that were in them, and each person was judged according to what they had done. Then death and Hades were thrown into the lake of fire. The lake of fire is the second death.* (Revelation 20:13–14)

I miss my family. I miss when we used to hold hands around the dinner table and pray, even though it was lame and I hated it at the time. I miss the times I didn't record in pretty pictures, the stop gaps of life. The way the screen door slammed every time it shut, morning breath, car trips home after a holiday, sleep. *Sleep.*

Maybe I'm looking at this wrong. Maybe this limbo I'm in is me needing to atone for my sins. Maybe it's like the confession booth in church. Maybe I need to go back and remember my life but be more honest with myself this time.

Because, stuck in this hazy perfect world of my own creation, I know that I haven't been all that honest.

# CHAPTER 3

# Jane

Jane pulled into the parking lot edging the forest and killed the engine. The scent of lukewarm lake water seeped through the crack in the car window. Through the trees the lake was turning silver in the late afternoon. Nothing had changed. It had been nineteen years since she'd left for good. She felt a deep nostalgic pang coupled with mild panic as she opened the car door and hesitated. She had worked so hard to leave this place behind. The reason she was back returned to her like a slap.

An image of Paige's face, veiled and upturned to Andy's as they took their wedding vows under the arch of the trees, came into her mind. What was it—three years ago they were married here? Was that really the last time she'd been back? It was easy to tell herself, and everyone else, that she was too busy at the paper, and she had been. She'd only stayed for the reception and then driven back to the city the next day.

She reached for her phone on the passenger seat. She'd put it on silent after Jackson's first message. More had come in since.

*I'm so sorry, Masters, I didn't realize you were that close to her, that you'd just walk out of the office and not come back. I had my deputy editor's hat on, not my friend hat.*

*You know how crazy I get on deadline. Please call, worried.*

*Friend.* Interesting choice of words. *Worried.* That wasn't his style. He must be feeling really bad. Jane put her phone in her pocket and got out of the car.

The track was still here, a pathway through the leaf litter, through tall, thick-trunked palms, but now there was a concrete parking lot and a sign. The air was sweet, sharp, like crushed ants and gumtree sap. She stood at the start of the track, the scent of damp leaf litter rising. She thought of those shaded places under the palm canopy that didn't let in any light.

*Don't go in there.*

She remembered the dusty, dank smell of churches, and the tree cathedral had that same scent, dwelling there just below the sunlight. She could feel the pull of it under her skin. She found herself moving toward the path. She was still wearing her heels from the office.

Her body and mind felt numb—was it shock, or the drone of hours of concrete speeding past on the freeway? She had acted on pure instinct. She'd just walked out of the office, gone home, thrown a few things in a bag, and left. And now she was here. *Why are you here?* This was Janie kind of behavior—erratic, spontaneous. She was still wearing her suit. Why hadn't she changed? She was usually much more centered, sensible.

She slipped off her heels and her feet sank into the spongy forest floor. How many times had they walked this track barefoot? Now it felt dangerous, and she thought about snakes and spiders, things hiding under leaves and logs, and wondered if she might tread on something poisonous. But she couldn't stop herself. It felt like this place was drawing her in, and some distant flicker of happiness wafted past her like a gust of wind.

She followed the track until she came to a small clearing. Pews fashioned from tree trunks, cut down the middle and halved. A dirt floor netted with roots. The place where Paige was married, and her father preached each Sunday. The forest forming the ceiling and the walls. Tall palms and gums and soft paperbarks slowly shedding their skins. She was alone. She approached a small stone altar that bore witness to the vast body of water beyond the forest. The lake.

She could hear the soft wash of the shoreline, the lone call of a single bird echoing across the water. *Why were you here, Paige, the morning you died? What did your final post mean?*

A voice, one she had ignored for so long, whispered softly, *Were you trying to tell us something?* Though it could have been the wind in the leaves. She didn't trust her mind. She didn't trust her body.

Her hands were shaking as she took her phone out of her pocket. She sat down on a log. It was cold and covered in a thin layer of moss. She found Paige's final picture. It felt too intimate, this image, as though the viewer was witnessing something they weren't meant to. Is that what gave it a haunting quality? It was striking, strangely beautiful. There was such an interplay of light and dark. The body in repose. The hollows of her cheekbones, her black hair, the white sand, the flowers. But if you looked closely, really looked, the hair was tangled, the skin blanched, the flowers bruised. Sodden, abandoned. A broken thing. *Soon to be dead.*

A branch snapped and Jane turned, but there was no one there. Only the shadowed trees stooped in silent worship to the lake. She shivered and drew her arms close. Dread moved through her, as though the cold had got into her bones. Had Paige referenced the thing they'd made a silent promise to never speak about again?

Jane shook her head, dislodging the thought. She squashed it down like the damp rotting leaves under her bare feet. No, all that was so long ago. They had been so young. She'd go to see her dad, attend the funeral, then return to Sydney. *The funeral.* Jackson was going to want her to write something. He'd said as much—something "more in-depth about Paige down the line." *How am I going to do that?*

A black swan landed on the thin surface of the lake and Jane was suddenly aware of how alone she was. And yet there was something here. The hollow rattle of the leaves. The fetid scent of the soil in the places the sunlight didn't penetrate. This was the last place Paige had been seen alive.

Jane couldn't stay here. She turned to leave, but as she walked down the silent aisle of the trees, a cry echoed over the water. Her breath hitched in her throat and her hand went to her mouth.

*It's a bird, not a woman,* she chided herself. She turned and saw that the lake had stilled, casting back the trees, the sky. *It doesn't reflect who you are anymore. You are not Janie. You're Jane. You're a journalist. You live a successful life in Sydney. You got out.*

But the wind in the trees was still whispering and the lake was still a mirror.

# CHAPTER 4

*It was much bigger than I expected. I'd expected a small cabin, I suppose. That's what it said on the website. Cabin implies compact to me. Anyway, it wasn't small. It was a sprawling wooden structure almost dipping its toe into the lake. I turned the rusty key in the lock and stepped inside. It smelled like it had been locked up for the summer. The weather was just turning, the leaves beginning to crisp, the air cooler at nights. But you could tell that this place had soaked summer's moisture into its timber walls. The room was large, sparse, with a fireplace and a lounge that looked over the water.*

*That was the appeal, how close it was to the water. That's why I came here. The lake. I needed to be close to the water. I didn't really know why I needed to be here now, after all these years, I just knew somehow that I needed to return.*

*I got a warning from my manager at work. A customer had made a complaint. Said I had "anger issues." Well, if only you knew the things I have to be angry about, I'd thought. But of course, I said nothing, didn't defend myself and left on the spot, walked right out of there. They hadn't expected that. I hadn't* expected that. But I couldn't let them have power over me. I couldn't bear it. And I hadn't taken a holiday in years, so, I guess that's what this was, in a strange way. A holiday from the everyday of my life. I wonder how many people step out of their lives entirely at some point? I can tell you, it's a scary thing to do. To let everything fall by the wayside and just leave.

But to be fair, many people can't do this because they have people to answer to, families. It's only me, and that's why I'd wanted something small, to keep me from realizing my own aloneness. I wandered through the wood-paneled halls. There were four bedrooms—too many, but I chose the master with the view onto the lake. I took my clothes out of my bag and hung them in the wardrobe, something I had never done on holidays, but it was to tell myself that I was here for the long haul, I think. The agent said it was available indefinitely and that I could stay longer, but I just paid for a few weeks.

I didn't have much. I used to have a lot. I suppose I was addicted to stuff like everyone else, once, but life taught me that you need very little. It's a hard teacher, life. But if you come out the other side of pain you are honed like a bone. You are back to your bare essentials, and that rarely means "things."

After I'd unpacked my clothes, I took the box of food out of the trunk. Simple things—crackers, bread, cereal. I don't really bother cooking anymore. Mostly it's crackers with cheese and a beer or a glass of wine, or several. Maybe a piece of fruit. I figured I'd go into town later to get fresh produce.

I looked out across the lake. There was a flock of white cockatoos adorning the trees on the other side like Christmas baubles. A fish jumped. I couldn't see any man-made structures or humans. Perfect. I poured myself a glass of red wine and took my book out onto the veranda. Everything was overlaid with a fine dusting of dirt, everything tarnished with rust from the salt-encrusted breeze that rattled the wind chimes above my head. I found a broom and swept and it felt like I was sweeping away all the other people who had stayed here. Making it my own.

And then the cockatoos rose suddenly from the trees in a screeching mass and my heart beat hard in my chest, like white wings on the air. And I thought, No, I'm somewhere else but I still can't escape it.

# CHAPTER 5

# Jane

Her father's house had sunk, like skin into old bones, though she didn't know whether it was under the weight of all his stuff or the marshlands slowly reclaiming what was theirs. Banana palms loped over the tin roof, their fibrous trunks muscled up against the fibro walls, and Jane wondered when the vegetation would win. The brown and orange canvas awnings had been saturated, stripped by the sun. The back veranda sat perilously close to the muddy shoreline, and she was sure the lake had crept closer since her last visit.

A squirm of shame made itself known in her stomach. She hadn't even stayed here when she was in town for Paige's wedding. She'd booked a motel on the road slightly out of town and left the next day with wedding-brunch prosecco probably still in her veins.

He must have heard her car because he was there with his slightly bowed legs and an arm in the air and she felt her throat thicken at the sight of him. *How have you made him wait so long to visit properly?* she thought.

"Long drive? You look just about ready to put your feet up." He came in for a hug when Jane was half out of the car, his beard brushing her cheek, the angle awkward. He still smelled like childhood mornings—instant coffee and toast mixed with mangrove mud.

"Hi, Dad."

"Hi, love. Look at you in your nice suit. Sorry, I didn't have much time to clean up."

She tried not to notice the rusting car against the fence, the old tires, the stacks of wire, the proliferation of water-filled bins.

"It's okay, I know it's a bit sudden. I didn't expect to be here . . ."

Her father gave her shoulder a squeeze and hung his head, silence opening between them, and she knew he was thinking of Paige too. He busied himself with removing her bag from the trunk and her chest ached as he led the way into the house. It had gotten worse. There had always been boxes lining the hallway, but now they were towers reaching to the ceiling, narrowing the entry passage like a hole a worm had burrowed into the core of an apple. A sweet rot that spoke of too much moisture and too little air.

Jane felt her vision narrowing, her throat closing. She fought the urge to leave.

"Just getting rid of some stuff," he said, even though that was clearly the opposite of what was happening. She wondered if he knew he had a problem, or if it seemed perfectly reasonable to him that his house was slowly filling up from the inside.

Guilt pinched her as she shifted sideways past the boxes. The weekly (or fortnightly if she was honest) chat wasn't enough. They came into the living and dining area, with low windows looking out through ferns to the lake beyond. It was like living in the rain forest, the thin walls and glass barely keeping the leaves and vines at bay, the water kicking light off the lake's surface. She noted that while there were stacks of books and newspapers pushed against the walls of the room, and the kitchen surfaces were hidden under mugs and pots and pans, there was at least a clear through path here.

She followed him down the hall off the living room and he put her bag in the doorway of her old room. Dusky salmon walls, faded band posters, the single bed with the brown Indian-style bedspread, the guitar in the corner. She was sure she could still smell the cheap perfume from the chemist lingering in the air. It was a time capsule of her youth. Love and despair all wrapped up in mothballs and dusty sunlight.

"I'll put the kettle on. You still a coffee drinker? Sorry, I only have instant. If I'd known when I did the last shop that you were coming . . ."

His thoughtfulness made her chest hurt. "That's fine," she said. She pictured all those unwashed mugs proliferating around the sink. She longed for her tiny, pristine apartment with her coffee machine.

There were so many unspoken things here, like the dust particles that only became apparent in the light. She sneezed. Now they could add Paige's death to the tally.

"Dad . . . sorry it's taken me so long to . . . have a proper visit."

Her father turned. "Well, you've got your busy job . . . I pick up the paper every morning and see your name. Show all the guys up at the club. Your old dad's proud of you."

Jane smiled, but it felt sad. "Be out in a minute."

She watched his slow shuffle down the hall. He had aged more than she'd expected. She sat on the bed, ran her fingers over the familiar rivulets of the bedspread as though feeling the knotty texture of her past.

Her phone pinged in her suit pocket.

*You're in town. We're having something tonight for her at the house. You should be there.*

Yas. Paige's sister. No greeting, no preamble, no emotion. Yet there was inherent familiarity, an inclusion, an offering, no matter how small or detached. Jane wondered how Yas already knew she was here. But that was the thing about small towns, wasn't it? People knew everything about each other's lives. She suddenly felt the stifling heat of her room and cracked open the window.

Her fingers moved over the phone.

*How is Paige gone? What happened? Not what the media headlines say happened. How the hell is Paige dead? And why don't you even sound upset???*

She stared at her words and deleted them. Yas didn't sound upset because that wasn't her way. She was the opposite of Paige. Where her sister behaved like she was an open book, Yas was shut off, always slightly detached, but still enigmatic in that White way. Where Paige was happy to live her life exposed to the internet, Yas wouldn't dream of that. She was practical where Paige was romantic. No "we're having a wake to celebrate Paigie." Just "we're having something." No "it would be really special if you came." Just "you should be there."

And she should. She knew that. That's why she was here, that's why she'd come back. She thought then of Jackson, of his expectations for her writing something. She knew she had an "in" with the family, but she wouldn't share that with him. It didn't matter that her and Paige's lives had diverged. They had just drifted apart, hadn't they? But it was still as though Paige was sewn into the fabric of who she had become, just like this place.

She thought of the Whites' sprawling lakeside house, its steepled roof and rambling gardens, polished floorboards, views from bay windows. That warm, charismatic family who had embraced her after everything had fallen apart, but who she had, deep down, never felt good enough, kind enough, beautiful enough around.

Jane changed out of her suit and went into the kitchen. Thank god her dad was on the deck outside. It was the only place in the house that wasn't jammed with stuff. He was sitting at the wooden table among his potted plants. They were in small ceramic pots and large plastic pots, suspended from the roof in baskets. But an abundance of plants didn't make her feel claustrophobic in the same way. He was pruning one absently, a cigarette dangling from his lips. Her mother had never allowed it in the house and now, nearly twenty years after she left, he still didn't smoke inside. Two mugs sat on the table. Jane picked one up and then put it back down. She reached for his pack of Dunhills, lit one, and breathed in.

His brow creased. "Janie, are you okay?"

She took a sip of the weak coffee and shook her head. "I'm not sure."

"It's a bit of a shock, isn't it?"

She looked down at his hand resting on the table. It was so familiar, and yet not. The age spots, the rough texture.

"Everyone in town is shocked. Everyone knew Paige. I still remember the two of you in primary school. It doesn't seem . . ." He shook his head.

"I wrote a story about it for the newspaper, about her last social media post, about how she was found dead a short time later. I don't even know how I was able to do that."

"You did your job."

"It didn't feel right."

"What didn't?"

"Writing that story . . . or . . . the police issued a statement, which means they're treating her death as suspicious. But who would want to hurt Paige White?"

She saw something cross her father's face. She had become good at reading body language. Her job relied on it. She cocked her head in question.

He stubbed out his cigarette in the green glass ashtray that was as old as her. "It's probably nothing."

"What? What have you heard?"

He picked up the spray bottle and began tending to a maidenhair fern. "Oh, it's just the fishing boys, you know, they talk."

"What did they say?"

"Well, they see things, you know. Paige was out on the water every morning at the same time, right on dawn. They'd see her sometimes in that old kayak, crossing the lake."

"She was always an early riser, and she loved the water . . . What's weird about that?"

"Well, a young girl, all alone on that lake . . ."

"Dad, she was hardly young. She was thirty-four—thirty-five," she corrected herself. *She only got one day of being thirty-five,* Jane thought. "And she grew up on that lake. She knew its rips and currents. It was probably the only peace she had in the whole day, what with a small child . . ."

"Well, I'm just sayin' there's unsavory types around—that's the case in every town."

"You really think the police are looking at homicide?" Jane felt a cool breeze across her skin.

"It was just something one of the boys said."

It felt like Jane had to use every one of her reporter's skills to get anything out of her dad. She stifled a sigh. "What?"

"Well, Kenny knows some of the guys down at the station . . . It could be just gossip. You know what the boys can be like."

"What did they say?"

He scratched behind his ear. "Are you sure you want to know this stuff, Janie? It's probably just local talk, and this isn't another one of your big-city-journalist jobs. This is your home."

It felt like a jab, or maybe it was just acknowledging the gap that was now between them. Jane was grateful that she'd changed out of her suit. She held his eye. "You can tell me, Dad."

A puff of air left his mouth. "There was a fellow, hanging around the camping area. Well, living out of his car. And there was some mention of a stalker, or something like that, in the mix."

Jane shook her head in disbelief. "Paige had a stalker?"

"I'm not sure. Just that the cops were looking at a few different angles."

"Maybe he followed her on socials." It came out of her mouth before her brain had even caught up. She took out her phone.

"Oh, I don't know about all that online hoo-ha. But someone said Paige was famous. Was it on Instagram? Or Facebook? I can't keep up. I don't really understand what that means. But I guess it's the world we live in now—everything photographed and put online. Ridiculous really. It's a whole other world going on that you young people seem to live half your lives in. What about good old plain reality, eh?"

Jane looked up from her phone, guilty. "Sorry," she said, putting it face down on the table. In the time it had taken her dad to finish his sentence, she'd opened Instagram to Paige's account and already located a picture of a young male follower who looked like he might live out of his car.

# CHAPTER 6

# Paige

I have a lot of time to think here in this strange half-life. Think is really all I can do. I think about the caravan I'm stuck in. We went away for four months with Mom and Dad's old van towed behind the 4WD. It was seventies-style, the kind that's now really hip—but ours was the real deal. Mom and Dad had taken it on religious missions back in the day, driving down the coast converting people, living by the beach in big tents, commune-style. I found a picture of them stuck to the mirror in the van wearing matching white robes, sandals, and huge brown sunglasses, as though they were living in biblical times or in fancy dress. They were smiling, so young, so carefree. That's how the van made us feel too. Viv was just a baby when we went and I guess it's how the whole thing really took off.

I wasn't trying to be famous or anything like that. Andy just liked taking photos and we wanted to get away. We couldn't afford to move out of Mom and Dad's place—Andy was freelancing, taking photos for marketing firms to get us by. He did friends' weddings too, but they only paid in wine. We had a dream of being a team—he'd do photos, I'd do hair and makeup. I'd always been good at that sort of thing, making people look nice. Making myself look nice. Andy said it was the pretty girls who got into makeup and style—but I disagreed and said that actually, it was the plain girls who needed to learn all the tricks. That's how I felt about myself. I don't think people always understand my fragility. It's hard to explain. I've only had some of these thoughts since I've been here. It's funny the perspective that's coming, having all this time to reflect. Also, the crushing loneliness.

But that was a time in my life when I never felt lonely. We thought of it as an adventure, a road trip. It took ages to clean out the old van. I washed down the brown vinyl seats with sugar soap and got the grime off the windows. I made thick cotton curtains with yellow daisies on them to keep out the light so that Viv could nap during the day. Andy fixed the sink and put in a new bar fridge, converted the back area into a bed with a thin mattress. We started in this big old-growth forest up north, the red gums as straight as matchsticks, moss like pincushions on the forest floor.

Anyway, I guess Viv and I were just there in some of the photos Andy took. It was that first year when she was so little, and to be honest, I was so tired I hardly even remember putting the photos up on social media. It was a way to document our trip, to keep in contact with friends and family. It felt more like archiving. It certainly wasn't meant to be an enterprise. But looking back, it was perfect and I was pretty naive. Every afternoon we would nap on the mattress in the sun that streamed into the back of the van, warming it like a tin can. We'd wake up sweaty and happy, her little body crammed against mine. Can a mother's body ever forget that half-sleep daze of those early years? I never thought I would not be tired. It was in those afternoon nap times that I told her stories of the forest gods. Since birth she had been taught about the Lord, but I wanted her to understand that appreciating nature was a form of worship and that there were other gods and goddesses who watched over the natural world: dryads, tree and forest nymphs in Greek mythology; Gaia, the primal mother goddess; and Selene, the goddess of the Moon. I know I sound like a hippy. I guess I was.

I blame my parents for raising us in nature, our church literally the trees above our heads. I wouldn't call it a conventional religious upbringing. No musty pews, hymn books, or stained-glass windows. Every Sunday morning my father would preach from the stone pulpit to an adoring congregation sitting on logs under a vault of trees. The light throwing off the lake was our stained glass. No mournful organ notes, only the sound of the breeze through the leaves. After the service we would stand ankle-deep in the warm lake water and talk, eating cake baked by my mother. Spirituality was the backbone of our lives. I was always going to go that way. It's another reason I'm so divided about this place I'm in.

My father taught me about limbo. In Catholic theology, it's a place between heaven and hell, where the souls who are not condemned to punishment and yet deprived of the joy of heaven linger.

*And besides all this, between us and you a great chasm has been set in place, so that those who want to go from here to you cannot, nor can anyone cross over from there to us* (Luke 16:26).

But then maybe this is meant to be heaven, because I'm suspended in one of the happiest times of my life. Isn't it funny how sometimes it's only in retrospect that we can truly see something for what it is? I think even then I knew, despite the exhaustion of new motherhood, that this was a special time. Andy and I were both doing what we loved—being in nature, being free. We would spend the mornings while Viv napped working—me reading or writing, him taking photos and fixing things, and then we'd sit outside in our canvas chairs under the shade of long tree trunks and eat a simple lunch of bread and cheese with fruit. In the afternoon we would walk along nearby beaches, wade in shallow waters, beachcomb shells to decorate the van. We gave each other space.

I didn't know that this would be the best time of my life. That I would cease to exist in the real world one day. I knew it intellectually, but I didn't know it in my body. I was still too young to think about the flip side of everything. You only have to look at a flower, cut from the stalk, as it slowly wilts into decay. I guess I have always been fascinated with the dark as well as the light. Maybe that's what set me apart from all the other voices, all the other images online. I've never been afraid to delve into the depths. I find it beautiful.

I have a lot of time to think back on all the photos, all the memories . . . suspended moments in time. They are so bright, but hazed in a kind of half-light ether. Filtered to reflect a perfection that reality could never really live up to completely. That's what people criticized me for—how flawless my life appeared, how romantic. Now, in hindsight, in many ways, maybe it was.

But no. I'm being disingenuous, seduced by my own story.

I started to get hundreds and then thousands of new followers after a few other #vanlife Instagrammers shared my stuff. They were living the same life as us, so it was a natural connection. I asked about practical stuff, and they were more than happy to share. And they said they loved our aesthetic. That's the first time I started to grasp what we were creating. I hadn't realized, but it turned out that connection and friendship are how it works, even on the apps. I can't say I wasn't elated by this new popularity. Who among us could deny how good it feels to be loved?

But that was the surface of my life. Underneath, things started to come apart. I guess when things got bad, I held on even tighter to the images of perfection I put up every day. It was comforting. Even if I felt bad, sad, lost, they were testament to the fact that I hadn't given up entirely, that life was still being good to me. Life was still beautiful. I had so many people saying how gorgeous my family was. In a way, maybe I thought of those photos as a type of gratitude. Because I did have Andy and Viv, I did live in an idyllic paradise. But deep down, I knew that beneath the shiny surface of my life, it was me who was probably broken. Me who wrecked things. And this place has not proven me wrong, because now I'm not with them anymore.

# CHAPTER 7

# Audrey

The first time I saw the White sisters they had bare feet and were picking up ice from our gas station. I'd already heard about them. I caught snippets of their conversation as they walked through the rows of motor oil, sweets, and freezers filled with ice cream and fish bait. I hid the cherry lollypop I'd been eating but I knew my lips were stained with it.

"We need a bag of ice. A couple of bottles of Coke? Is Vinnie bringing the vodka?" Paige asked.

Yas was only twelve months older than Paige but she had a sort of stoic composure that made her seem even more adult. "Yeah, but you know it's risky. Someone's parents will turn up," she said.

They brought the bottles of Coke to me at the counter. "Can we get a pack of Winnie Blues? For my dad," said Paige, tucking a strand of dark hair behind her ear innocently.

The way she looked at me, took in my faded brown T-shirt, my faded brown hair, she was daring me to believe her. Even after only a few weeks at The Lakes, I knew in the way teenagers assimilate such social knowledge that her dad was a preacher. There was no way he smoked. My eyes flicked to the back of the store to check that my parents weren't around.

"Sure," I said, handing over the cigarettes, hoping they wouldn't pick up on the tiny tremor in my voice, my hand.

Paige pocketed the smokes and smiled. She had the kind of teeth you only saw on TV—white and very straight. "I've seen you around. Do your parents own this place?" She indicated some dusty shelves filled with inflated bags of chips.

"Yeah, we just moved here." If only I could have left it at that, but then I added, "I'll be going to your school next term," like an utter try-hard.

My family moved to The Lakes after my dad had a midlife crisis and decided to indulge his love of cars and bikes and buy a small-town gas station with lodgings out in the back. The house smelled like gasoline, bait, and the tang of the nearby lake. It was a hard age to move schools, to move away from the city. But I'd grown out of my old friends. I knew I didn't fit in. I was a dreamer, I suppose, or that's what the teachers always called me in report cards. *Audrey could do even better if she spent more time looking at the board and less time looking out the window.*

Sometimes it's hard to articulate how you're different, or why. My mom always said it was because my imagination was too big for my brain, but all I saw was a body that was too big. I was tall, my arms and legs thick, whereas other girls were tiny, with their swishy hair and fragile limbs. I just felt giant and clumsy next to them.

"Cool. See you then, I guess," said Paige.

I had a strange feeling as they walked away. It was regret, a sadness that they hadn't invited me to their party, but also a kind of lightness, a relief.

But then Paige turned. She was a leader. Her straight teeth and hair, her clear skin and her charm. She wore her power lightly, and so it appeared that she wasn't one of *those* girls, not at all.

The cigarette packet was already opened in her hands. She put one behind her ear. "Hey, anyway, do you know many kids around here?"

I had the presence of mind to shrug, as though the potential of an invitation meant nothing to me.

"We're having a thing by the lake tonight. If you want to come. The little beach next to the tree cathedral. You'll see the fire."

My voice stuck in my throat. Sometimes you feel the sands of the desert of your life shift beneath you. You know that you're living a turning point, a slippage in time. And I knew then.

"Sure," I said, as though I would fit in with people like Paige and Yas White.

Mom came into the shop, passing them as the little bell clanged to signal their exit. "Who are they?" she asked, her eyes following their languid movement across the concrete, past the gas pumps.

"They're the cool girls," I said. "They invited me to a party."

I was lucky, I knew. I had the cool, pretty mom. She and Dad had been that perfect teen couple—the equivalent of a high school prom king and queen. But despite this (or perhaps because of it), Mom didn't want me to fit into any particular mold. She remembered what it was like to be sixteen, the agony of fitting in (even though I think she naturally did). So she didn't say what we were both thinking—*Do you want to be friends with girls like that?* Mom called it our special radar. She taught me to always listen to it, that slight shimmer under your skin, in your gut, that told you something you couldn't articulate out loud. Something you felt without fully understanding.

It was partly because we were both creatives, she said, that our radar was so attuned. But she also knew that I needed friends my own age. That having your mom as your best friend was not enough.

She looked at me, a question.

I rolled my eyes. It wasn't at her, it was at the situation. The look I gave her said, *I'm sixteen and desperate for friends. Of course I'm going to a lake party with the cool girls.*

# CHAPTER 8

# Jane

She was glad to get out of that house. Not to have to eat dinner made in that kitchen. *What did he even eat?* She pictured her dad's chair by the television. The sagging imprint of his body, the greasy spot where his head rested. It was like a sad throne in a crumbling castle. She imagined him balancing a bowl on his lap there every night, watching fishing documentaries and golf tournaments.

She felt her chest constrict the closer she got to the Whites' house, but it was preferable to staying at her dad's.

From the end of the drive it looked like a church. Jane wondered if she'd ever noticed that before. The way the roof steepled to a point, the symbolism implicit in this image. *Holy, untouchable.* The Whites had the nicest house on the lake. Three stories, climbing ivy, decorative eaves, and white French-style window frames. It sat just back from the lake, the water licking softly at the luminous grass that led up to carefully tended gardens, the chicken pen, the hammock strung between gums, the outdoor fire pit. From the kitchen and the wraparound veranda you could see all the way across to the tree cathedral on the other side.

It wasn't filled with stuff the way Jane's house was. It was quiet and tranquil, with framed inspirational sayings on the walls and lots of white, as though the people who lived in the house had rubbed off on its interiors. Because of this, Jane had always been nervous about sitting on the cream couches, of walking lake mud across the polished parquet floors with their plush rugs. To counter this, everyone had rubber boots, lined up like little sentinels on the back doorstep.

Now she got a strange feeling, steering her car up the drive lined with pines and white-trunked gums, peeling bark to their base. It was an old feeling, like that discarded bark. It was as though the parts of herself she'd left behind were humming at her edges. She was Jane Masters, a successful Sydney journalist, she reminded herself. She was dating the deputy editor of one of the biggest newspapers in the country. She went to restaurants with low lighting and vintage decor and lemon-infused cocktails. But as she stepped out of the car and smelled the salt from the lake mingle with the eucalyptus and pine, she was Janie Masters again, Paige's childhood best friend and the girl from the swampish side of the lake.

Penny White came out of the house. Even in the midst of her grief, Paige's mother's face was still soft; it hadn't hardened into bitterness. She waved, not necessarily because she could see who was getting out of the car, but because theirs had always been a house that welcomed everyone.

*Love is patient, love is kind. It does not envy, it does not boast, it is not proud* (1 Corinthians 13:4).

Jane hadn't been aware she still knew that. She saw the spark of recognition on Mrs. White's face. They would always be Mr. and Mrs. White to her. She couldn't help it.

She rushed over to the car and drew Jane into a hug. "Oh Janie, Paigie is so glad you're here. I can just feel her spirit singing."

Jane felt these words tangle in the fine hairs on her arms, but she forced a smile onto her lips. She wanted to say, *I'm so sorry, I'm in shock, I can't believe I'm here after all these years, and Paige is gone*, but Mrs. White was beaming at her, her white-blond hair falling softly to her shoulders, still angelic after all these years. Was Mrs. White rejoicing that Paige had entered the realm of the saved? It made Jane feel unaccountably sad, this relentless positivity in the face of death.

"Come inside. We're making food. Everyone's here. We thought . . ." Mrs. White paused, and Jane saw the crack in her beaming facade gape open. "Paigie would want everyone she loved to be together." She squeezed Jane's hand and led the way up the front steps into the house, where she turned. "Oh, why was I coming out the front? I don't know where my mind's at. That's right, to pick some rosemary. You go on inside with everybody—they'll be so happy to see you, Janie—and I'll join you shortly."

Jane wanted to grab Mrs. White by the shoulders and shake her. Tell her that Paige was dead. She wasn't floating in the ether, her spirit singing. She was gone and something bad might have happened to her.

But then she thought of all the ways she had seen people grieve over the years. As a cadet journalist, Jane had been made to do death knocks, going to the houses where families had only days before lost a loved one in a "newsworthy" way. Accidental electrocution, dog attack, helicopter crash. There were so many awful ways people could die. It felt so wrong, so intrusive to turn up and ask them to tell the story of how their child or their husband or mother had died. But more often than she expected, the door opened. Sometimes people wanted the story of their loved one recorded, known. Or maybe they just wanted someone to listen as the awful story poured out. Over abandoned cups of tea, they told her that she didn't seem like a journalist. That she seemed too nice, and her kind face was what had made them open the door. That's what this moment felt like—another death knock, another tragic story where people were behaving strangely, as people did when things like this happened.

She watched Mrs. White walk languidly into the garden, absently picking flowers, holding them to her nose. Jane wiped away the sheen of perspiration at her hairline. Where was the raw devastation? The somber shock? Was Jane missing something? She didn't want to go into this perfect house with its inspirational quotes and pretend that everything was okay. She stood at the front door, staring at the knocker, a bird in flight. Should she knock? Mrs. White had said just to go straight in, but that didn't feel right. Her knock was tentative, and she waited, listening for noise from inside the house.

The door swung open and Yas stood there. She was carrying a child, and another came racing toward her then attached to her leg. They had the same fine bone structure as their mother.

"Jane," she said. She had been the only one not to call her Janie. Yas was a full-name kind of person. She called herself Yasmine, but no one else had ever got the memo. "You came."

There were no hugs, no warmth, so unlike her mother. But somehow Jane found this reassuring, that at least Yas wasn't making light of her sister's death. She stepped aside to let Jane in. It was the same living room, as though frozen in time. Jane realized that this pinnacle of sophistication in her mind now looked a little tired, dated. She had once thought cream leather couches were so classy. Now they were graying and sagging at the places where bodies rubbed against them. Had it always been this way? Was it her own perception that had changed after being away for so long, or was it just the passage of time, simple wear and tear?

She followed Yas into the kitchen. It was filled with people. People taking food out of the oven, pouring drinks, sitting at the dining table talking. The doors to the veranda were open and she could smell the smoke from the fire someone had lit down near the water's edge. There was soft music playing somewhere, maybe acoustic guitar, threading under the hum of voices.

Jane stood awkwardly on the outskirts. She wanted to clap her hands and shout, *Hey! For fuck's sake, someone has died. This isn't a house party.* But then she saw Paige's dad. Stephen White was sitting in an armchair in the corner of the room. His face was in his hands. His shoulders were heaving. Jane realized that he was crying silently, that no one had noticed him, the town pastor, the bereaved father . . . which was strange and heartbreaking all at once. Here was someone behaving in a way she could understand. She found herself drawn to the sorrowful curve of his back, to the realness of this grief. She went and kneeled down next to him, feeling like they were the only two people in the room.

She didn't touch him, just spoke very softly. "I'm sorry, Mr. White."

He looked up and it took him a moment to focus on her. She knew grief transported people to places deep within themselves, places they had buried to be able to carry on with life, waking up, eating cereal as though they had an infinite number of days to wake up, an infinite number of days to eat corn flakes. It took them to the place in their own bodies where they knew in a kind of visceral way, a way discordant with bowls of cereal, that death was always close by, possible.

"Janie." He drew her into a hug. And this huge, enigmatic man, who preached at a church made of trees, whom people listened to as though it were the Lord Himself speaking, wept against her shoulder. Somehow it didn't feel strange or awkward, but like the thing she'd been waiting for—the dam wall of grief to break inside her.

Mr. White wiped his eyes with the crisp sleeve of his shirt. He might not have been coping but he still looked immaculate in that White way. He took Jane's hand between both of his. They were large hands, tanned against the thick gold of his wedding band. His eyes were the same blue as his daughter's had been, his dark hair now gray.

Jane remembered thinking as a girl how handsome Paige and Yas's dad was, how he carried himself with a confidence that people were so drawn to. The easy warmth of his manner, his voice. So unlike her own father.

"Bless you for coming. Paige loved you dearly, Janie Masters. When I think of Paige as a little girl, I can't see her without you by her side. Paigie and Janie. I'm so glad she had a friend like you."

His words felt like a soft ripple, a breeze across a flat expanse of water. She shivered. It was so easy to idealize the past. To fall into the trap of thinking that everything before was perfect, glossed in the sweet haze of nostalgia.

But that was a long time ago. Jane didn't know the Paige whose face glowed out at her from social media. She had never met her daughter, Viv. They had formed their own lives. Paige was a mother, a wife, living some idealized version of womanhood. Paige wearing a sheer white dress on a beach, the swell of her belly cradled in her arms. Paige with the sun haloing her and her tiny daughter, the light in their eyes. Paige on a date with her equally beautiful husband, smiling over glasses of wine, her top low-cut. The holy mother, but still sexy. Jane scanned the room for Andy or Viv, trying to make mental allowances for how people appeared online versus reality. But she couldn't seem to spot them.

Jane was none of the things Paige had been. She did not have a curated online life nor an aspirational reality. She dressed in navy blue suits. She spent her weekends recovering from the week, trying to sleep rather than turn over in her mind all the things she hadn't done right, and then reading newspapers, meeting colleagues in wine bars in the evenings where they complained about work. Waiting for Jackson to call.

The disappointment of last Friday night returned to her.

*Just finishing up at work. Will message which bar we go to x*

*Ok x*

She had kept her suit on. She didn't want to look like she was trying too hard. More like she'd just come home and then popped in at
the bar. She texted again at 9 p.m.

*You out yet?*

*Oh sorry, Masters . . . heading home now. We just went for a super quick one
down the road. Shit of a night. Hope you didn't stay up x*

*I did stay up. I always stay up. You know I always stay up.*

She didn't write that of course. Instead she wrote:

*No worries, just in bed reading x*

He sent a picture of himself in the cab, and she could tell he'd been
drinking more than "a quick one." But she didn't want to seem clingy.
They weren't official.

Why had he even singled her out? She wasn't beautiful—she was
a newspaper reporter, not TV. She was hardworking. She was passionate. There was a spark there, yes, but still, it felt somehow like a
hastily written article—he was the lead paragraph and she was buried at the bottom of the story. Sitting in her suit on the lounge, she
had poured a glass of wine and told herself that her life was not a
holding pattern.

Mr. White released her hand and she looked around the room.
There was a cake sitting on the kitchen counter. Chocolate icing covered with fresh flowers. Why was there a cake? Jane felt something
uncomfortable deep in her belly. The black of Paige's hair. The way it
had fanned out in the water in that final image, crowned in flowers.
The pulse points in her temples began to throb. What had happened
on the lake?

And who were all these people? Were they all Paige's friends?
Why was this feeling more and more like a party? Or a religious cere-
mony? Pastor White gave Jane's arm a squeeze and was now making
his way around the room, hugging people and pressing their hands
between his own, his eyes closed. Maybe it was some kind of blessing.
A woman knelt in front of him and he touched her head. An image

returned to Jane from long ago. The tree cathedral. A woman, arms crossed against her white dress, waist-deep in the lake. Pastor White touching her forehead and then tipping her backward. The complete trust, the adoration in her beaming smile as she broke the surface. The sound of singing coming from the trees. He was helping the woman to her feet now, that same look on her face.

Jane felt hot suddenly; the smiles, the smell of sausage rolls, discordant and strange. She passed Mrs. White floating in her haze of denial and handing around trays of food garnished with the rosemary she'd just picked from the garden. Jane needed air. She went outside, following the sound of children playing. They were running on the green lawn outside, the soft thwack of a tennis ball being hit around a stick. Squeals from an enclosed trampoline. Yas stood beyond them, ankle-deep in lake water. She was smoking a cigarette.

Jane stood at the shoreline. She wasn't sure she wanted to wade in. The sun had lost its sting and clouds were moving fast across a low sky. A cockatoo screeched in the trees. She slid off her shoes and felt the water cover her toes, the silky mud slip under her feet like slipping backward in time, warm and murky. She looked down and saw a face in the water, and her heart raced before she realized it was her own.

"Did you have some cake?" asked Yas without turning around.

Jane felt all her words whoosh out of her, like the birds in the distance swooping low on the lake, snaring fish.

"It's what I do now. Make cakes and care for children. The new domestic goddess." Yas turned and she had two perfect rivulets down her face where tears had run.

"I don't understand," Jane said, because she didn't, not any of it, and she felt a kind of helplessness envelop her. It made her want to sink into the tepid water at her ankles, like surrendering to a warm bath.

"None of us do. Do you want one?" Yas dug into a pocket in her dress and held up a single cigarette.

Jane wanted to, but two cigarettes in one day was almost a habit. Jackson hated smoking. She shook her head. "Why is everyone here, acting like this is a party?"

"It's what my family know how to do."

"But Paige only died two days ago."

"It's what their community does. They rally."

"And her husband? Andy?"

"He's taken off with Viv, to see his folks. They're up north."

"What? Why would he do that?"

"That's exactly what the police said when the car was gone, and Mom was in tears because Viv wasn't in her cot, and he just left a note on the bench and took all the spare diapers."

"Yas, what happened to her? I . . . I read the press release. The police . . . they weren't giving away much."

"You wrote a story. I saw it." Yas laughed without mirth and Jane felt her face burn with shame.

"I'm sorry. I was in shock. I didn't want to write it." But even as the words left her mouth she didn't entirely believe them.

"I suppose you think you got out? With your journalism career. I think deep down Paige was proud of you, you know? I'm surprised you came back."

"Yas, of course I came back."

"To get the scoop for the paper?"

Jane dropped her head. "Of course not," she said quietly.

"A journalist tried to call the house. I told him to fuck off. I saw all the headlines. Beautiful young influencer and all that. Why do they do that? Make the only bit about her how beautiful she was? Did you know the online British papers are running it?" Yas laughed. "Paige *would* have got a kick out of that."

"What they were saying, about her last Instagram photo . . . did she really post it just before she died? Did she drown? How could Paige have drowned? The police just said they found her body and were investigating . . ."

"All we know is that Paige went out on her kayak like she did every other morning at dawn before we all woke up. And this time, she never came back."

Jane felt the breeze brush the back of her neck. A fish jumped right in front of them, its eye silver, naked.

"And if you're wondering about the cake, about everyone being here, I made it for her birthday. Everyone was coming here today for her birthday party. And it turned out to be her death-day party."

CHAPTER 9

# Paige

After we got back from our caravan trip, things started to change. I'd open the app on my phone each morning and there would be more followers. That's the thing about influence—the more you have, the more you get. It's the same with money, I'm told. I had become a self-fulling prophecy. It felt like existing. Like I'd finally arrived in the world. Like I'd found a place. I'd found a vision for my life, for our life, and it was #dreamy #raw #nature.

We started with nothing and so it felt organic, like fate. And really, it was all because of Andy, his pictures. The texture in tree bark. The quality of the light falling through Viv's hair. It's what set what we did apart from all the others vying for space on the grid. What *we* did. It didn't feel like just me—it was both of us. I did my own hair and makeup and he took the photos. It was an artistic endeavor and we were living our small-business dream. We were getting some money too, which we needed. A computer company paid us to take photos of me working on their brand of laptop in an apricot bikini top, sipping tea out of a roughly hewn mug with the morning sun streaming into the van. I got to keep the laptop and got paid for the post. Companies sent samples for me and Viv, our exact sizes. All we had to do was wear the clothing that was in keeping with our aesthetic. It seemed too easy. I thought Andy was happy.

Andy has never been the jealous type. He's the type to pick up his surfboard when things get hard. He soothes himself the same way I do—in nature. We were sitting in a small cafe by the beach. Wildflowers sat in glass jugs, and fresh fruit and granola arrived at our table in pottery bowls. Andy's camera sat beside him. He took it everywhere, like a pet. His fingers would find the grooves in the lens and move over them unconsciously.

He was so beautiful when he took photographs. It was his confidence. He glowed. It was the color his skin turned under the hot sun, the way the bleached hairs on his arms caught the light. He spent all his time chasing the light, on his board, through his lens. Yet he was oblivious to how he emitted it. Is there anything more attractive than a man who isn't overly aware of his beauty?

I am, by contrast, acutely aware and without light. I'm pale, the purple of my veins apparent at my wrists. My hair is Purple Midnight, straight from the box. Blond never suited me the way it suits Andy. It felt too twee, too pretty, and I wanted to be something more interesting than pretty. I was my mother's child, but I wanted my sister's and my father's dark hair.

I asked Andy to take a photo. He knew by now it would be a good image for the grid. The wildflowers, the fruit, the light.

"And will you get me and Viv with the beach in the background?"

He put down his mug. "Can I finish my coffee?"

I shot him a small guilty smile. "It's just I want to get some pics of the food. And then we can eat."

There were expectations. That's what having an audience, having

followers, meant. I started to get pangs of regret that I'd missed a perfect shot. I guess it had started to feel like an itch that needed to be
scratched, a compulsion.

He shook his head, but it was subtle, as though he didn't have the
energy for it. "Viv, you can eat your breakfast, honey." He handed her
a piece of strawberry. She was eating finger food by then, just starting
to walk.

I read the subtext, I understood how he felt, what he was doing,
but it fired something in me. "I'm sorry to make this a photo opportunity but you know I need to post something today."

"*Need.* It's a funny word, isn't it? Enjoy your breakfast. Let your
daughter eat."

I guess *enjoy* was the word I missed . . . what it meant. I took out my
phone. I don't know why I did this. Maybe I didn't want him to be
right, or face what he was trying to tell me. I can be stubborn like that.
I took a selfie of me and Viv at an angle that showed the wildflowers,
the fruit, and the thin line of horizon in the background. It took ten
attempts, but I got it.

While my fingers moved over the screen, cutting and filtering and
hashtagging, Andy got up and left. He walked onto the sand. I picked
up his camera and took a photo of him, like that, with his back to us. I
didn't know it was an omen of what was to come, that photo. Relationships are flux, fluid, even the ones we think are static, safe. Because
at the heart of all relationships is power. Needs being met. Or not
being met . . . and what that ends up doing to a relationship.

# CHAPTER 10

# Audrey

I approached the bonfire slowly, trying to make out their faces in the flickering light. Paige was there, and Yas. They were laughing at something an older boy was saying. There was something tough about them, even though they were so pretty. They were a hardscrabble kind of angel, with long, knotty hair and bare feet. They wore leather jackets—but old ones, the kind that might have been hauled from a secondhand bin—over short floral dresses. Slashes of bright lipstick made their skin look even paler. They looked like they might have been vampires. Or maybe I'd been reading too many fantasy books. I loved the other worlds, the other creatures. I was always on the lookout for the thing that was going to allow me to escape my reality.

Maybe all those stories helped me find the thing that was tough inside me. I knew that deep down I was fucking strong, and I wasn't going to give over my power to just anyone. But these girls seemed different. They were like creatures I'd come up with in my imagination, flickering flames, bright illusions. These girls were raised in nature. We were in the middle of the forest at night without parents. I guess that was the toughness I was sensing.

They had built a bonfire at the altar of the forest church. It blazed like some strange violation, a sacrilege. The reflection of the flames made the lake look like fire and brimstone. But they were the pastor's daughters, so who was anyone to tell them they couldn't light a fire at this cathedral?

I felt shy suddenly, and self-conscious. I'd spent far too long in front of the mirror checking my outfit, trying to get my hair to look straight rather than frizzy. I had also overthought what time I should turn up. I hadn't wanted to be too early, too eager, but now that I was late, I wondered how I would assimilate into this bright fire tribe.

"Our cigarette girl!" Paige yelled and I actually jumped. She beckoned me over and I felt relief as she drew me into an embrace and pulled me down onto the dirty faded cushions. "You came!"

She introduced me to some of the people around the fire. The boys looked older than us, but I knew I wasn't on their radar. There was a girl on her other side whom I'd seen with them before. She was introduced to me as Janie. She had a softer face than the White sisters. She gave me a little wave and in that little wave, I knew I would like her.

A bottle of rum was being passed around and I took a swig and coughed as the liquor hit my throat.

"Here, have some of mine." Janie passed a bottle of some kind of mixer that was sweet and much better than straight rum.

"Thanks." I smiled.

Paige squealed and got up to greet someone else and Janie inched closer. "You just moved here?"

I nodded, played with the cheap chunky rings on my fingers.

"Paige told me your family owns the gas station."

I cringed. These kids all came from better-off families than mine. I could tell by their confidence.

"She's pretty happy about being able to get ciggies."

I shrugged.

"I mean, sorry, that sounded really rude. I don't mean that's the only reason . . ." Her eyes darted away.

I was sorry to make her uncomfortable. I waved my hand, trying to dismiss the sinking feeling in my stomach that this was just going to play out the same as all the other friendship groups. "That's okay, I get it."

"Sorry, I'm . . . I'm so awkward sometimes." Janie shook her head.

"Don't worry, awkward is *all* I am." I was glad of the warm firelight camouflaging my flaming face.

"You seem really confident."

I stared at her. "Me? Confident? Look at me!" I laughed, indicating my baggy sweater, baggy jeans.

Janie smiled. It was a nice smile. She didn't try to tell me that I was thin and beautiful. I could already tell she was too authentic for that. "No, you really do . . . I'm not just saying that. You have this calming, grounded air about you. Like you know what you're doing."

"I'm a sixteen-year-old with a fantasy-novel and red-lollipop addiction."

"You read?"

"It's all I do. Apart from serve in the shop. And school soon, obviously."

"Me too. I read everything I can get my hands on. I haven't read much fantasy though. You'll have to tell me what's good."

"Oh my god, I have so many books I can—"

Paige squished herself between us, hooking her arms around our necks. Her breath smelled like candy. She had a fluttery energy about her, like a moth. "Do you like our party? Audrey. Is it Audrey?"

"That's my name," I said.

"You're very cool. Isn't she cool, Janie?"

Janie nodded. "I was just telling her that."

"You seem way older than us. Like you've ... I don't know, seen things."

"A lot of dragons and magic lands. Vampires."

Paige looked puzzled but Janie smiled. She had charmingly sharp eyeteeth. And I realized that we already had an in-joke.

"Maybe it's coming from Sydney," said Paige.

I was about to tell her there were plenty of bloodsucking bitches in Sydney when there was a loud hiss, and we instinctively scrambled back from the fire as smoke issued into our eyes, our lungs. Mine were watering. We were all coughing. When the smoke cleared, I saw him. A tall man with an empty bucket in his hands. For a second it felt like something out of one of my stories.

"What on earth is going on here, Paige? Yas?" He shook his head and picked up an empty bottle then sniffed it. "Are you drinking? Smoking?" His voice cracked and I realized it must be their father, the preacher.

Several of the boys slunk off into the darkness like scared animals. It seemed very dark now that the fire was out.

"I got a call. Someone thought the tree cathedral was on fire."

"We were just having a party ... for Vinnie's birthday." Paige's voice was small.

"You told me and your mother you were going to Janie's place for a sleepover. And now to find out you've been drinking and smoking cigarettes?"

Paige kicked at the butts littering the ground. She looked so vulnerable beside me, with her mascara smudged around her eyes where she'd rubbed the smoke out. Perhaps I was buoyed by their compliments, by their sense that I was cool and somehow more worldly. Or maybe I just wanted them to like me even more. I don't know, but I felt myself getting to my feet.

"It wasn't their fault. I sold it all to them," I said.

I looked down to see Paige's and Janie's eyes huge in the dark.

"And who are you?" His voice boomed and I could imagine him delivering a sermon on sin right here.

"My parents own the gas station. I have access to cigarettes and alcohol." My voice was even, strong, not betraying the thundering of my pulse.

"Your family's new to town. Well, I don't know if this is what Sydney teenagers get up to on a Saturday night, but I can assure you it's not what lakeside teenagers do. I'll be talking to your parents. And you'll all be back here tomorrow morning to clean up before church. Yas and Paige, you'll be grounded for a week. Two."

As she slunk, head down, toward her father, Paige grabbed my hand, drew me to her, and whispered in my ear. "Owe you one."

I knew then that I was in, and that I was stronger than I even realized.

# CHAPTER 11

# Jane

Shep had once had a crush on her. He was the kind of boy she imagined mothers wanted their daughters to go out with. Gentle, kind, sort of scruffy, with a mop of hair that seemed to always get the better of him, falling in his eyes. It made sense he'd become a cop because his dad had been one. But after everything Jane had seen—all the police she'd spoken to in her years as a journalist, the stories she'd heard about what they went through—part of her worried for him.

She'd DM'd him on Facebook last night, unable to sleep, Yas's words buzzing in her head, her old bedroom triggering strange, nostalgic, peach-duvet dreams. She knew he'd meet her for a coffee in the way any girl who once had power over a boy knows.

The place was in a little line of local shops hedged by palm trees. There was a liquor store, a fish-and-chips shop that doubled as the cafe, and a small supermarket. She sat under the black umbrella outside and tried not to be snobby about the coffee. Sometimes she imagined there was more caffeine in her veins than blood, and she knew every good coffee shop within a kilometer of work and home. It wasn't really a fair comparison. At least there were cafes here now, and it was better than the out-of-date instant coffee at her dad's.

"Hey, stranger."

"Hey." She rose and they hugged with what felt like too many elbows. He was wearing civvies—shorts, a polo shirt, flip-flops. That made her feel better. She thought he might wear his uniform to announce his position, his power, but she realized she was thinking of the men in her office, not this small-town cop who used to make her laugh in math class.

"How long has it been?"

He raked his hand through his hair, which was still abundant. "I don't want to think about it, makes me feel fucking old."

"You've got kids?" She'd seen them on social media—two tiny things, also with impressive manes.

"Yeah, they're great. Not great sleepers though."

"That's what I hear from those deep in the young-kids stage."

"But how about you?" His smile was a nudge. "Big-city journalist. Saw your article."

Jane stiffened.

"Sorry. That was a bit insensitive. I'm sorry . . . about Paige. I know you two were close."

*Used to be*, she thought. "No, no, it's okay. She's the reason I'm back here." Jane shook her head. "Paige. I can't believe it."

"So, are you back here as Janie, Paige's friend, or Jane Masters the journalist? We're talking strictly as old friends, off the record here, right?"

Her face flushed, a sort of dread mixed with morbid curiosity churning in her gut. *What are you doing? Are you a journalist or Paige's friend? Are you Jane or Janie?* All she knew for sure was that she needed to know what really happened to Paige, for herself, and she had the tools at her disposal to find out. Shep could help her get a quick in-sight into what was really going on. She hadn't been sure whether he'd want to talk, or would even be able to talk to her about the case, but his whole body was pitched forward and she could feel the intensity of his gaze, his attention. She didn't know where to put the feeling it gave her.

"Of course, of course. One hundred percent here as a friend. Do you want a coffee? Here, I'll order you one." She stood. She needed to take a moment to sort out the strength of her feelings.

"Thanks, I'll have a flat white."

She counseled herself that anything he might offer up was his to offer. She didn't want to seem too eager for information, nor string him along too much. Given their history, she didn't want him to think she was using him, that the case was the only reason she'd wanted to meet for coffee. It was actually surprisingly nice seeing him after all this time.

She returned and sat down, taking a deep sip from her own cup. She knew by his posture, the soft tap of his fingers on the table, that he wanted to talk. She had good instincts like that. And she'd learned that sometimes silence was the best prompt.

He ran his hands over the table. "It's hard when it's someone you know."

"Yeah, it is. Writing that story about Paige . . ." She shook her head. "It didn't feel like the right thing to do."

"You were doing your job. Sometimes people don't understand that."

She looked into his eyes—still very blue—and saw that he got it. That he understood and that they were on the same side.

"Still, ethically it's a finer line for me," she said. *Covering a friend's death.*

"I wouldn't have been able to tell her family. I would've cried on the doorstep, I reckon. I got the other guys to do it. I remember going to the Whites' as a seven-year-old kid for birthday parties."

"They had the best parties. Remember that one where we all swam in the lake? There were inflatables we were jumping off. And roasted bananas with melted chocolate stuffed in them."

"Everyone wanted to be invited to those parties."

"That's why I'm a bit . . ." Jane pursed her lips. "Paige grew up swimming in that lake . . . Can you talk about it? As Paige's friend, promise."

He took a deep breath and laced his fingers together in front of him. "She . . . her kayak was found partially submerged. Her body was found not far from it."

"But Yas said she went out on that kayak every single morning. She was a strong swimmer."

Shep shook his head. "Small vessels in deep water are still a drowning risk. There are the conditions . . . weather . . . there was a bit of wind, choppy water that morning. Currents, submerged objects, other craft. She wasn't wearing a life vest."

"Yeah, she wouldn't have been. Not her style."

Shep raised an eyebrow and looked down at his hands. "Yeah."

His coffee arrived and he thanked the waitress by name. Everyone knew everyone here.

"So, why isn't it a simple case of an accident? Why are the police investigating further? I take it they'll know for sure after a post-mortem?"

Shep ran a thumb over his chin. "Definitely off the record."

"Yep."

"She'd recently been stalked by a guy staying at the campsite on the lake. Didn't notify police, mind you. Her sister told us. They're trying to track him down."

Her dad's buddies had been right about the campsite guy.

"And Andy, Paige's husband, took off up north that afternoon. Local police up there are ascertaining his whereabouts to let him know he might be required for a statement. Not the smartest move, especially taking their daughter."

"Okay, yeah, that's a lot. So, Andy?" All Jane could picture was the two of them at their wedding, deeply in love. "Maybe he was just shocked, grieving? People do weird things."

Shep scrunched his mouth to one side. "You know what it's like though. In our jobs you've seen everything so you need to look for everything. Nothing would surprise me anymore."

"So . . . they suspect what?"

"Well, with drowning, cause of death isn't simple or clear. They just want to rule out other possibilities. See if anyone saw anything that morning, any other craft on the lake, fishermen and the like, or early-morning walkers."

"I bet you didn't think it'd make international headlines."

"Yeah well, as for the 'haunting last Instagram post'—you'd know all about that. That's just the media putting spin on it 'cause Paige was good-looking. 'Cause it makes for a good story."

Jane grimaced. "I'm not going to disagree with you. And besides, she might not have even taken the photo that morning, just posted it. I know you can schedule pics you've taken earlier."

Something passed over his face then, a shadow of something, and Jane caught it. "What?" she asked.

"Except for two things. Not things the media knows." He said it pointedly. "She was wearing the same flowers in her hair, a flower crown I think they're called, that was in that last photo."

"What do you mean? It was—"

"Still on her when they found her. Just a bit odd, you know? Why would you take that picture and wear that sort of thing kayaking?"

Those bruised flowers in that final image. The warm breeze rustled the palm leaves above them and Jane shivered. She hoped Shep hadn't noticed. That was the thing about reporters and police—they could read all the subtle cues, the ways the body gave the mind away.

"And before you ask, they were the same flowers. We checked, obviously."

Jane swallowed, but the bitter coffee rose in her throat. "That is pretty weird," she said. "What was the second thing?"

"The shadow. Very hard to detect, but someone took that last photo of Paige. We'd like to know who that was so early in the morning in a remote location."

Jane took out her phone from her bag. "Sorry, I have to look at it again. I didn't see that." She opened the app, found the photo. Shook her head.

"Here." Shep leaned in and pointed to the lower left-hand corner.

"I would have never—"

"That's why they pay us the big bucks."

They both laughed. You didn't get into law enforcement or journalism for the money.

"Maybe someone leaked something to the media, about there being more to this story," she said.

"Doubt it. They just saw a beautiful dead girl and that final picture of her and ran with it. But people pick up on things. I don't know how but it's like something feels a bit off. You must get that. Reporters have a nose for that kind of thing. The instinct for a certain story? Not that this is—"

"Another story, no."

"Maybe it's not that different what you and I do," he said.

They caught each other's eye. She wondered if he had any remnant of the feelings he once had for her after all this time. He broke eye contact and drained his coffee.

"Seems like she was a big hit on Instagram. I didn't even realize. I'm only on Facebook. Don't get time for all that. I don't really get it to be honest," he said.

"I'm on Facebook and Twitter for work but I rarely post. I had no idea Paige was . . . I suppose you'd call it famous. All I knew was that she had a lot of followers. It's like another world. A world that's just going on silently parallel to ours, one that can make you a lot of money, I'm assuming. Her life looked pretty perfect though, I guess."

"I think you and I both know at this stage in our careers that no one's life is perfect."

"Yeah, just scrape away the surface . . ."

"And there's dirt," he finished.

Their eyes met again.

"When was the last time you saw her, anyway? You two were inseparable as kids."

Jane shrugged her shoulders to try to disguise her discomfort. "I hadn't seen her since her wedding to Andy. What was that—three years ago? God, where does time go? I guess with me moving to Sydney we just grew apart. A few times over the years we had a drink when she was in Sydney. And it was nice. You know, in that way it is with old friends who know you." It was only once and it was strange and awkward, but there was no point going into that with Shep.

"But you never wanted to come back here?" He chuckled. "Bigger dreams than the small-town newspaper, eh?"

"Lucky for that, or I'd be out of a job. It all went online and they cut staff years ago," she said. *And I couldn't bring myself to come back here.*

"I think people just grow apart, don't they. I've got friends from school who went to Sydney. It gets a bit hard. It's a different lifestyle," he said.

"We used to be so close, me and Paige. But when I look at her socials, I feel like I didn't know her much anymore. Or maybe I did. I'm not sure how to feel." Jane felt her cheeks warm. She hadn't intended to be so honest with Shep. But he had that quality about him, that gentle, nonjudgmental one. It made him a good cop.

As if sensing the shift, the intimacy, Shep squared his shoulders.

"Well, I'd better be off. Got to pick the kids up. They're at their mom's this week."

Their eyes met but his darted away. He was divorced. "Ah, sure, well, thanks for meeting me," she said. "Paige's family don't seem to know much and, well, you know how it is. I just needed to know."

Shep nodded. "Yep, we'll get to the bottom of it. Thanks for the coffee. I owe you one. I guess I'll see you round. If I hear anything . . . we'll—"

"Facebook," they both said in unison.

# CHAPTER 12

*It didn't take long for the cabin to cast its spell on me. My days were bookended by the rising and setting of the sun. From the front window I could see the morning mist that rose from the water, through the trees, and the blackbirds taking off in the evening, shrouding the low sun.*

*I wondered how I'd spent my days packing people's grocery orders in the fluorescent aisles of the supermarket, so far from nature for so many years. Did those coffee and cigarette breaks near the loading dock under the shade of the overhanging trees count? Their roots cracking the asphalt beneath our sneakers? The sweet, yeasty smell from the bakery next-door mingling with eucalyptus sap? Sometimes picking the pies from the top of the bins, thrown out in white paper bags, patches of cold oil pooling on the top? I still remember the pasty taste of the chicken and vegetable. I didn't miss anyone, even though we'd worked together for a long time. They were work friendships that didn't bleed outside those bright aisles and the small talk in between nicotine relief. But I've never really needed people that much, anyhow. Maybe they've hurt me too much in the past.*

Or maybe I'm just a closed kind of person. The price of loneliness is safety. But I'm not alone here, not entirely.

I saw the kayak on the second morning I arrived. It cut through the still glass of the water and I thought, what a perfect way to greet the day. It made me want to hire a kayak and do the same thing. Instead, I decided I'd get up early the next morning and walk the bush track that rimmed the lake. It became a ritual, it gave me purpose, a reason to get up and get on with my day when I could have stayed in bed. Nature, after all, has no reason for the sun to rise, for the dawn to break. The reason is implicit in existence, and that's what I felt this time was teaching me. That existence alone, as simple as it might be, is worthwhile. And every morning it was there at the same time, sliding through the still morning like a silent prayer.

I had woken early my whole life. It's funny how that has never changed. I was like that as a child and I'm like that now. That body clock seems built into our DNA. On the mornings I didn't walk I took to sitting up in bed and watching the cockatoos rise from the trees in a white sheet as the girl in the kayak drew near them. Somehow that lone presence on the lake comforted me. I couldn't say exactly why. Or maybe it wasn't the girl; maybe it was just the birds.

# CHAPTER 13

# Paige

A ndy had access to my apps, my socials, because they were originally his accounts. He was the one who started it—putting up
his photos. He never wrote anything, never added a hashtag. It was
just the image. Sometimes beauty doesn't need a context, it is its
own context. He didn't even understand how to do it at first. I remember setting it up for him, but he had never been good with
words. Maybe, in retrospect, that's why he found it hard, the trajectory I was on. Because he understood the world through images.
Maybe he felt like I'd taken over his world, the only power he felt
he had.

I never would have changed the passwords. It would have felt like
a betrayal. We were sitting on the veranda drinking beer, the sounds
of the water birds growing loud at dusk, the smell of Mom's chicken
roast coming through the open kitchen window. I picked up my

phone, an instinct, a tic, a reflex by then, as inevitable as breath. I saw the look he gave me.

I put the phone under my leg. "Do you want me to stop posting stuff? I will."

He shook his head. I could see the tan line of his sunglasses on the high plane of his cheekbone. I wanted to reach out and touch the pale, vulnerable skin. Maybe he saw that it was just me trying to placate him, that I wouldn't really be able to stop. My income was actually sustaining us. We'd been on a complimentary holiday because of it. Turquoise pool, striped navy towels, burgers in bed, a view over the city to the harbor. We'd been able to settle since coming back from our road trip. We could pay my family rent and we were thinking of maybe finally renting our own place near the beach so Andy could walk to the shoreline each morning to surf.

"I just feel like I'm doing something wrong, and I don't know how to fix it," I said.

"I've been on there recently. I've seen what men write to you."

I paused mid sip of my beer, laughed. "Oh yeah, at hotguy22 . . . you are sexy." I made my voice into that of a thug.

"No, in the spam, the hidden requests."

I waved my hand and took a sip of beer with swagger. "Oh, I haven't even gone looking in there." It was a lie. Of course I had. That's how I met Buckley. But at that point he was a fellow writer, nothing more. And to be fair, that's all he was at first.

Andy turned his whole body toward me. He'd finished his beer, so he took a sip of mine. It was a conciliatory gesture and I felt the muscles in my shoulders relax. Viv's and Mom's voices carried through the window and I was filled with a moment of brief peace.

Andy rubbed his hands over his knees. "I'm just not sure this is you, Paige. What about our wedding business? Hair and makeup, me taking pics. Where did all that go?"

I felt myself bristle but tried to hide it. "Well, I *am* technically doing hair and makeup. And you're taking pictures . . ."

"There are only so many pictures I can take of my wife's ass looking good in sweatpants on a beach."

"What?"

"I mean, it's not exactly creatively satisfying."

"What are you saying about my ass?" I tried to make him laugh. There was a time when he would have laughed at that, but this time he didn't.

"Are you jealous? Is that what all this is about?" There. I'd said the thing that had been building like an afternoon storm over the lake after a hot day. I knew there'd be lightning.

"Fuck off, Paige."

"No, you fuck off." I was surprised by the force of my repulsion for him in that moment.

I stood and went inside. I picked up my daughter and buried my nose in her salty hair and milky scalp to stem the tears. Mom said dinner was nearly ready.

Later in bed, after we'd had really good make-up sex—the kind that's extra good because there's that little bit more tension and passion—I said, "You've never sworn at me like that."

"You've never sworn at me either," he said, and I felt myself tense. But then he said, "Sorry. I was just upset that you'd think I was jealous of your success."

I wanted to say, *But you are, and what are we going to do about that? Maybe what you are saying is that you're unhappy working as a barista while I get paid for people clicking a little icon. But how are we going to get through this, because I love you and I don't want to lose you. I don't want to lose our little family.*

Instead I said, "It's fine if you want to stop taking the photos. I can take them on my phone, or hire someone or whatever."

He didn't reply at first, just stared at the ceiling, his face serious.

"Maybe we should go back on the road. Just the three of us again. We were happy then."

*We were happy then.* His words filled me with a silent grief, but I didn't want to ask permission from him—about whether I could keep posting if we did go back on the road, and if he'd take pictures like last time. I didn't think I should need to. What I was doing was for our family, it wasn't just about me.

It made me feel claustrophobic suddenly thinking about that van, in the middle of nowhere, how warm and airless it would get in the afternoons.

"Maybe," I said.

# CHAPTER 14

# Audrey

I got in trouble, of course. Dad's face looked like I'd taken a key to the side of one of his cars. Mum said she was disappointed in me, and her eyes looked glassy. They knew I hadn't taken the booze from the shop, but it was the lie that they didn't like. I think Mom understood, though, that I was trying to make friends. But it made them look like bad parents, they said. They were trying to establish themselves in a new community. They were small-business owners and now maybe people would get their cars fixed and buy their fuel at the bigger gas station closer to the highway. Now it looked like they had an out-of-control daughter.

I think that was a bit of a turning point for me. I started to believe the narrative that had been spun about me. It wove itself around me like a sticky cobweb that wouldn't come off. But after so many years of feeling invisible to people, to my peers, maybe part of me liked the feeling, the tingle of horror. At least I was visible.

At the new school I was the girl who had smuggled contra to the Whites' bonfire party at the end of the holidays. We sat in a big group in the playground eating lunch under these trees that would shed their blossoms and we'd spend the rest of the day picking tiny petals out of each other's hair. The feeling of that, of being groomed by my tribe, was so foreign, so beautiful. I used to get tingles in science, the feeling of soft fingers combing my scalp, brushing my shoulder. I got up from my place wedged between two girls whose faces were interchangeable in their prettiness, to put my lunch in the bin. I was determined to be thinner, to be more like all of them. Suddenly I felt my body pitch forward, a blow from behind. I turned my head, an instinct. My body felt sweaty, hot with humiliation.

Paige was on my back, her arms slung about my neck like a toddler hoisted on a parent. Even supporting her whole weight, she wasn't that heavy, but I stood there for a moment suspended in shock. There was a twitter of laughter around the group. I felt that thick familiar shame, imagined my large body bucking back like a horse. I tried to keep very still. I feared that's how the White sisters thought of me, as their pet, the person they had collected as you'd collect a weird puffer fish you found bloated on the beach among the sea debris.

"Cigarette Girl!" Paige cried and slid off me. "Can you get more for next weekend?"

I could feel eyes on me. Waiting. Watching. "Sure," I said, shrugging. I had no idea how, but I knew I'd find a way.

"What's Sydney like, anyhow? Did you and your friends hang out in the Cross? Darlinghurst? I have a friend in Sydney, Steph Hart—she lives in like, Paddington, and she said it's cool there. So many interesting characters, unlike here."

I felt the redness of a blush start at the base of my neck and I willed it not to creep into my face. "We used to hang out at the Rocks a lot. There's this cool park that looks over the harbor. Lots of old cobblestone streets and cafes and things."

"Do you miss it? You must miss your friends. Poor Auds." Paige hugged me. She smelled like those blossoms that fell from the trees. She was the one who christened me with a new name. Auds wasn't Audrey. Auds was someone who was *someone*, who meant something for the first time in her life. She was alien and so totally and utterly thrilling to me.

"Yeah, totally," I said, and all I could think was how well I was disguising the real me—who hadn't had friends. Who had walked the streets of the Rocks alone, sat overlooking the harbor reading books and imagining a better life. The girl who wouldn't dream of stealing from her parents or lying. I knew I couldn't show them who I really was.

Janie was different though. I'd felt it from the start, at the bonfire when we'd talked about books. We'd been paired together for a physics assignment. The way the teacher had looked at me when she saw my first test results. It was a weird feeling, a glimpse of the old Audrey coming through. She put me with the smartest person in the class.

We were at Janie's place finishing the assignment. I loved her house. It was palm-fringed and brimming with vegetation, inside and out. Her mom worked late, but when she was home she was always yelling at her dad to stop bringing home fucking plants. But I loved the plants. It felt as though the house was part of the forest. It didn't seem real. I always thought maybe the seven dwarves would come out of it carrying mushrooms. I guess that's what brought us together, as well as the love of reading. We were both from the wrong side of the lake, but it didn't feel like the wrong side if you were both on it.

"You're really good at this, Auds." Janie threw down her pen in exasperation. I wondered if I should try explaining it to her again. She narrowed her eyes. "You're actually really scarily smart, aren't you?"

I shrugged. No one here knew that I was as good with numbers as I was with words—that I had topped Year 10 back in Sydney. It wasn't cool to be smart. I'd learned that the hard way. "Only as smart as you, Miss 'I've read all the Brontë sisters.'"

"Yeah, but I'm just good at English. You're something else. What the hell is physics anyhow? But your brain gets atoms and stuff, science, math. That's too much. That's nuts." She shook her head and my stomach squirmed. I knew she was cool with me being good at English like her, it was kind of our thing. We sat in the back of the class with Paige and swung on our chairs pretending not to listen but really, we were listening. We finished the texts fast and discussed them as we sat on the back porch among the ferns. I guess part of us knew that it was better to do this alone rather than with the others, their judgment.

"I just did it at my other school already," I said, shrugging. It was an excuse I'd used lots of times. Other people seemed to buy it.

"That's bullshit. I saw you just work out that problem in ten seconds flat. I was still trying to understand the question. Are you some kind of . . ."

The word that came into my mind was *freak*. The look on her face made the squirming in my stomach become something sharper. Cold and hard and rising in my chest.

"Haha, yeah, you got me, I'm a bloody genius." I widened my eyes and stuck out my tongue as though I was mad, and she laughed.

But after that I could see her eyes flicking to me, watching me. I started to pretend that I took longer to understand things. At night lying in the tiny back bedroom that smelled like fuel and cherry candy, I dreamed of being average. Average height, average weight, average intelligence. What a gift that would be.

I think Janie knew. She was too smart herself not to see what I was doing. But she never mentioned it again. And I loved her so fiercely for that.

# CHAPTER 15

# Jane

Jane woke early, the dawn bird calls echoing across the water out her window. The air felt thick, humid and she threw the duvet off. It was hotter up here than Sydney, the crispness of autumn still sulking in summer. It was an Indian summer. She had slept deeply but now she felt the familiar unease move across her skin as she remembered where she was and why she was here. She sat up and turned her phone over. There were several texts from Jackson.

*Hey Masters, how are things going? Is reception patchy? Haven't heard from you much. Let me know x*

She wanted to write back: *Not patchy, just didn't want to be harassed about writing something. And I need some space. How many times have I waited for your replies? Why does your interest in me always increase when I pull away?*

But she got up and went into the kitchen.

The house was quiet; her dad must've still been asleep. She was desperate for caffeine. She made herself a cup of strong instant coffee in a mug she had to scramble around in the piles of dishes to find. She picked out the least dirty one, but still washed it three times. She winced as she drank it, looking around her. She was hungry and would have liked a slice of toast with some kind of spread, but she was scared to go through the pantry or look too closely in the fridge. She knew at some point she should go through them, that she should at the very least clean the kitchen. She tried not to examine the slick of grime around the sink, the floor that needed to be mopped, the countertops cluttered with stuff. Papers and bills and pens and beer coasters and fishing hooks and golf balls and cat food. Her dad didn't even own a cat.

Then she saw the teacup resting on the drying board, the same cup her dad had used when she was a child. There was something so heartbreaking about this that she felt winded with emotion. She dumped the coffee down the sink. She needed to get out of here.

She pulled on a fresh white T-shirt, her favorite leggings, and runners, and joined the track that edged the lake. The smell of mud and mangroves, an earthy rot, greeted her. The track was narrow—forged through the bush by many feet. It was scrub-lined and followed the curve of the water. A boy riding a bike with his father passed her, the boy calling out a hello and the man nodding in greeting. People were more friendly here than Sydney. She'd forgotten.

The track was a familiar path through the bush. The sun flickered though the she-oaks. It brushed her face, her bare arms with its warmth. When was the last time she'd been outside, in the morning, walking in nature? She'd once felt like this was home—she was raised on this water, among these trees, but her environment was the inner city now, the shaded streets and a desk under fluorescent lights. The pathetic pot plants on her tiny balcony. She had forgotten this feeling. Alone in nature, without the armor of her suit.

She came to a place where the bush cleared and the lake opened up. The reflected sunlight was dazzling. She took her phone out of her pocket . . . an instinct to get a photo . . . but Paige's last photo flashed before her mind's eye, followed by an image of sodden flowers, mossy rocks, hollow underwater eyes. She shivered and slipped her phone back into her pocket.

She kept walking, her breath quickening. She turned the conversation with Shep over in her mind. Did they really think Andy or some stalker had done something to Paige? Jane thought about the stories she'd written about women being killed at the hands of men. She knew statistically, horrifically, that this was the most likely scenario. While she hadn't known Andy well by any means, he seemed like a lovely guy who was clearly deeply in love with Paige. But that had been their wedding. Jane knew things changed. Dreams died. People wanted other things. Her mother had wanted other things. She tried to push the thought away.

Maybe what had happened to Paige had just been a tragic accident. Jane had covered so many deaths in water. Competent swimmers who got into trouble, parents who went into the surf to save drowning children only to drown themselves, their children unharmed. She'd seen the bloated shape a body took after too long in the sea.

She knew Jackson would push for some kind of coverage of Paige's funeral. He was always on the lookout for clickbait, and this, with its mixture of beauty and tragedy, was perfect fodder. And he knew she had an inside connection with the family. Discomfort made her quicken her pace. She enjoyed the burn in her muscles. She should probably keep her access to the local police quiet and not tell Jackson. She wasn't even sure why she'd contacted Shep when she didn't really want to cover the story. Maybe she'd actually wanted to be reassured, to get this uncomfortable feeling that there was more to Paige's death out of her head, but Shep had done nothing to reassure her.

*She was wearing the same flowers in her hair, a flower crown . . . in that last photo . . . a bit odd . . .*

She willed herself not to think about what that might mean. Her mind went instead to the tiny bit of tension between her and Shep. Had she been imagining it? She thought about how he'd already separated, his two small children. She wasn't even married yet. There was sometimes a different timeline for marriage and kids in small towns, she knew this. That was what she'd needed to escape as well. Yes, the nature was pretty, but her life in Sydney was where she belonged.

She stopped and took out her phone.

*Sorry, yes, reception patchy. Very sad. Will call soon when I get a moment x*

Jane walked on a little. Tried to get her bearings. How far around was she? She hadn't seen another human for a good forty-five minutes, since the boy and his father. She slowed her pace. She had gone farther than she'd intended. There, set into the straight silver white trunks, was the steeple of the Whites' house. It had seemed like it was much farther around the lake in their youth. She could just make out the top-most window through the trees. Jane had a sudden sense that she was being watched. She felt something crawl up her arm. She brushed at her skin but there was nothing there. She swung around. The track was empty. No breeze moved in the leaves and the lake was still.

A movement down on the bank caught her eye. Her heart, already fast in her chest from the walking, notched up a beat. A man. It looked like Andy. *No, it couldn't be.* He'd taken off, hadn't he? A stick cracked under her foot and she froze. His back was to her, and he threw something far out into the lake. It made a small splash. She watched the ripples peel off around it. *God. What was that? A phone? Some evidence?* She pressed her palm to her chest to try to quiet her heart. She thought about that shadow in the corner of Paige's photograph. Had he been there? Had he taken the final photo of her? Did he harm her and run? Did the police even know he was back?

No, she was being ridiculous. Was it even him? Yes, the broad shoulders . . . Then he turned—in profile she recognized the cheek-bones, the jaw. It was him. Why would he throw incriminating evidence into the lake so close to the Whites' house? It was probably a stone. A stick. But some part of her wanted to dive into the water and swim out to the place she'd seen it go under. No, surely what she was witnessing was his lonely, angry grief. She thought of all those death knocks. This wasn't a grief she could bear witness to, but something wouldn't let her leave. This was the man police were talking about as a potential suspect. He stood there for a while, his body impassive, still. Then he turned toward the house and she followed the track to edge closer. There was a rustle in the scrub and he turned around, a haze of trees between them.

"Is someone there?" He sounded scared. *Maybe it was a phone.* She froze, blood rushing in her ears. He took a step toward her, and she thought, *Shit, I either run or I declare myself.*

She stepped into the clearing. Thank god she was dressed in exercise wear.

"Sorry, hi, I'm Jane. Janie?" *He'd know me as that.* "Hi, I was just walking around the lake and I . . . I found myself here." An unexpected waver in her voice.

"Oh," he said, his shoulders dropping in relief. "You're a . . ."

"Friend of Paige." It sounded so strange. Talking about her as though she was still alive. Standing there after practically stalking him.

He nodded. His hands went into the pockets of his tracksuit pants. He was wearing a threadbare gray T-shirt and bare feet. He had obviously just gotten up and walked along the track from the house. She hadn't seen him since the wedding, but he'd made cameos in Paige's socials, an appropriate match for her with his tanned skin and even features.

"Her best friend, from childhood," he said. Pain crossed his face.

Jane swallowed. She wasn't about to disavow him of this belief.

"We'd known each other since we were in kindergarten." That was the truth.

He looked out to the lake. "I was just . . . this is about the time she used to come back every morning from kayaking."

He crumpled then, folded in on himself, and Jane found herself moving toward this almost-stranger. She put her arm around his broad back. It shook with silent sadness, and she thought about how in this moment, it seemed impossible that this man could have harmed his wife. She thought about how many times she had comforted people in this way. But this wasn't a story she could distance herself from, try to leave behind when she shut down her computer. She was part of this story, bound up in it in ways people like Andy had no idea.

As she crouched there with him at the edge of the lake, his grief rippling outward like a fracture on the surface of the water, she felt foreboding move through her. What was she doing hanging around? Realistically the funeral wouldn't be anytime soon now that the police were investigating and the body was with the coroner. She should walk back along the track to her dad's, clean his kitchen, do a grocery shop for him, call Jackson and tell him she'd be home tomorrow.

She was just straightening, disentangling herself from Andy, when she heard the screen door of the house bang. Mrs. White came out onto the veranda. Her face fell when she saw Andy hobbled like an old man. She was still in her robe, face bare, but she came down onto the grass in her slippers and took hold of one of Andy's elbows and together, wordless, they guided him inside the house.

Mrs. White still looked different from how a mourning mother should have looked. There was something too buoyant about her and her pink robe. But she put the kettle on and told them to sit at the kitchen counter. Andy had his head in his hands. No one spoke but the silence wasn't uncomfortable. It was tempered by the sounds of the kettle boiling and eggs being cracked over a bowl. Butter frying. Such small, comforting things. Jane thought about her father's kitchen.

Mrs. White set the table that overlooked the lake. She poured tea from the same china pot she'd used since Paige and Jane had first tried a cup of tea in this kitchen together, with too much sugar. Jane remembered all the times she had sat at this table and eaten the Whites' food when she'd felt adrift, grief-stricken, alone. And in this strangely familiar silence with the uncluttered space, a peace rose inside her, a feeling she hadn't felt in a long time.

# CHAPTER 16

# Paige

There is a lot of noise online. It's a white static roar. But silent. A silent yelling into the void. All those messages were questions wanting an answer that I could never give. I could hear them when I shut my eyes at night.

Only one broke through.

The strangeness of this other life I seemed to be living online. My own but not quite my own. Me but not quite me. When I looked at pictures of myself, my life, sometimes I didn't even recognize who I was. All the pretty pictures. My mirror world.

I wonder if that happens to movie stars and very famous people. Do their personalities fracture at some point so that there's a vast difference between the public and the private? Or do they buy into the smooth gloss of their own stories? Does it feel like make-believe and make-believe and make-believe? But if you play for too long, it becomes real. It becomes what you are. All those perfect pictures solidify into your own self-concept. It actually makes me feel sick now.

At first, he was just another name in the hidden requests in my DMs. I don't even know why I bothered looking there, because clearly they're censored for a reason. Men writing lurid things, fake companies wanting collaborations, women soliciting for sex. It felt like chaos going in there. A dark underworld that was always humming just below the surface. But there was a part of me that was drawn to the dark, to the broken things, the broken people. I think I'm like my dad in that way. And Buckley was beautiful. He looked a dead ringer for the tragic singer Jeff Buckley, whose CD I'd fished out of a box in my parents' garage and whom I'd been obsessed with for a time. His real name was Pete, but I christened him Buckley and he didn't seem to mind.

He had written me a poem. It wasn't actually that creepy . . . well, it kind of was, but it was so incredibly tender that I found my whole body responding—it gave me tingles. So, naturally, I looked at his profile and found that he was, indeed, a poet. He looked a lot younger than me, so in a way I guess that made me think that nothing would happen. He was studying poetry as a postgrad in Sydney. That impressed me, I've got to say. University was something other girls with better grades got into.

But as I got older, I started to wonder if I actually was smart. I'd always read books, they just weren't serious literature. At school my grades were average but I never, ever put effort in. But on this one occasion I wrote a poem. It wasn't a conscious thing, really. It arrived one day fully formed in my mind while I was on the beach at dusk with Viv, and I put it below an image of that sunset. It didn't get many likes.

He wrote to say that it was a really good poem and how much he liked it and sorry if he sounded like a weirdo, it just really resonated with him. I guess looking back it was my ego. Now, here, in this stripped-away place with no one but my own relentless company, I can see ego for what it is. Self-worth in relation to other people, to my place in the world. In a void there is no ego because I exist without the world's judgment. There would have been a time when I longed for a place without judgment. How freeing does that sound? To be without ego? But it doesn't feel like freedom.

It's the loneliness. It's that hollowness you get in your gut as you wake, when your body knows something bad has happened but your mind hasn't yet caught up. It's the glimpse you get—maybe passing a cemetery, maybe when you hear on the news about people in a shopping center gunned down doing their groceries on a Monday—that this life is fleeting. We are all telling ourselves a story that it won't end. It's the slap of realization that it will. It's our mirror world that we choose to look away from. Because what is reflected back to us is that in death, we will be alone.

And Buckley caught me when I was feeling lonely. Maybe what happened to Andy and me is what happens in bands when the lead singer gets all the glory even though it's a team effort. I could feel him pulling away for months, and I tried to pull him back. I remember a conversation we had one night after we'd put Viv to bed early. I'd wanted to make love. It was our way of connecting again. He was a gentle lover but there was a fierceness there too that my body responded to.

"What's happening to us?" I asked when I lay down and he didn't move toward me, and all I could think about was how he always used to hug me as soon as we got into bed. It was instinctual—that moving toward each other, as simple as the progression of a morning toward light. Our love had always felt simple, a given. When I listened to friends talk about fights they'd had with their husbands, I'd think smugly that it all just seemed too hard for them. That love was meant to be easy, supportive, natural. That Andy and I had what so many others seemed not to be able to find.

He was lying on his side, his back to me. He sighed. It was a tired sigh and it gave me shivers, because I could see that he'd almost given up.

"Do you really want to talk about this now? I'm exhausted."

I felt something inside me shrink. Some new vulnerability. I didn't answer, hoped he would go on, that he'd tell me why he didn't seem to like me anymore. But he switched off the light, still turned away from me, and I opened my mouth to say something into that heavy darkness, but didn't.

And now I wonder if everything might have been different if we had found a way to have that conversation.

# CHAPTER 17

# Audrey

Have you ever wondered how many people you've passed on the street, whom you've walked by in the supermarket, whom you could have shared a friendship, a whole life, a home with? How do people become intimate? How do people make friends? My brain used to have this question on a loop when I didn't have any. I didn't understand how to make that connection. How to break into a group, the things to say to sound normal.

That's why it felt like a miracle that I'd been drawn into the Whites' orbit. I was this lumbering outer planet, you know, the ones that are uninhabitable, full of dust storms, that are suddenly drawn close to the warm sun. It was the four of us—me, Janie, Paige, and Yas.

I remember the day I felt properly initiated into their group. We were at the Whites' house, upstairs in Paige's bedroom. The walls were white and there were polished floorboards and creamy rugs. There were fresh flowers in vases. It was like some kind of catalog. A domestic wonderland, so clean, so pure. Out the window, the lake looked as though angels would sing you a pathway to heaven in the late afternoons.

I wondered if Janie ever felt less than, like I did. Both our houses were hobbled by a kind of shabbiness that I always felt reflected in my own body. Our bedrooms were poky, with old carpet on the floors, patchy paint on the walls, a hole in the plaster board where I stuck my index finger each night with a kind of anticipatory horror. For what I wasn't sure. A spider bite? A place beyond the small confines of my life that led to another world? As I said, I read way too many fantasy novels.

I asked Janie once about whether she felt intimidated by the White sisters' perfection and she said that she didn't even know why Paige and Yas were friends with her.

We were sitting on my bed eating cherry candy. "Guess what Mrs. Hall said to me in English today?" Janie asked.

"That you are a brilliant writer and she loved your creative writing piece?"

"Ha. No. That it must be hard to always be in the shadow of the White sisters."

"Well, that's a supremely shitty thing to say."

"I know! I think she was trying to be understanding. She looked sympathetic when she said it, like maybe she was telling me to broaden my horizons."

"You're defending her."

"Yeah, but she's right. I guess I had this naive notion that . . . I don't know, in the eyes of my English teacher my love of words somehow eclipsed things like class and beauty."

"Guess not. Well, now you know, this is the real world, baby, and we're trailer trash."

Janie threw a handful of candy at me, and I opened my mouth but sadly none went in.

"With our cheap sugar thrills." I threw them back at her.

"And cheap paperbacks."

"No, seriously though. Speaking of trailer trash, Emmie Taylor said apparently there's this abandoned house and van by the lake. On our side of the lake. Some old couple lived there until they kicked it. The house is all locked up, but the van is open and still has all their stuff in there."

"Eww, sounds freaky." Janie braced her arms across her body.

"I think she was trying to scare me, but I want to go have a look."

"There'll probably already be weirdos hanging around there."

"Hey, I'm a weirdo."

"Not anymore. You're one of us now."

*One of us.* And I told her that she wasn't in their shadow. That she was smarter and kinder than they were, and that I liked her way better.

I think that was probably the moment we broke away from them. But secretly. Maybe no one ever really breaks away from people like the Whites. I think we both knew that they were our protection, hovering so close and yet never fully aligning with our real world. Pimples and battered books and scrounging spare change for the canteen, holes in bedroom walls. They were our buffer at school—being in the cool group. It's a hard thing to give up, that protection. And I soon came to see that Paige and Yas gave things to Janie, because they started to do it for me too.

"This is Dior eyeliner in 'Envy'—it'll bring out the green in your eyes. They're a kind of interesting hazel color, right?" Paige leaned in toward me, her Technicolor breath on my cheek as she traced the kohl over the soft skin of my lids. It felt intimate, like a lover. She smelled like rainbow dust and fruit chews, and I didn't have the heart to tell her that my eyes were just brown.

Yas took a bottle of foundation and painted it along my jawline with a brush. I felt like a blank canvas. A promise of something hovered between my belly and my heart, and when I looked in the mirror

I was transformed. My skin was poreless, pimples replaced by a pretty sheen. I touched my face and a smudge of warm beige came off on my finger.

"Ohh, time to raid the charity bin," said Paige.

I felt like a doll. One of the Barbies I had longed for and had gotten months, years after everyone else. I got the cheap version. The one whose hair was dull rather than flaxen silk. Her legs yellow plastic sticks rather than smooth and movable, a realistic skin brown.

The Whites kept a bin in their garage filled with donated second-hand clothing from the kind parishioners at the tree cathedral. When we lifted the lid it smelled like old sweat and mothballs but I didn't care. They produced a flowing black kimono with flowers and flecks of gold shot through it like a cherry-blossom night sky. Paige put it over her jean shorts and twirled and I wanted to be everything that she was in that moment. Then she gave it to me. The girl looking back at me in the dusty garage mirror was mysterious, unknown to me, and I loved her immediately. She smelled like incense and cigarette smoke, and someone else's sweat that wasn't my own.

That was the moment I bought into their dream.

# CHAPTER 18

# Jane

Jane woke early the next day. Everything was quiet except for the low drone of her father's snores at the other end of the house. Guilt snuck around her edges. She had returned yesterday, after eating breakfast at the Whites', to thankfully find the house empty. He must have been out fishing. But she hadn't been able to stay—it had felt like the walls were going to collapse in on her. She'd been so tempted to get in the car and drive to a motel. But she knew how much that would hurt him, so she drove to the beach, walked for a while and had a coffee, then picked up Thai takeout for an early dinner. They ate green chicken curry on the back porch, Jane slapping mosquitos from her ankles, her dad crushingly grateful, until she said she needed to make some calls for work and snuck off into her bedroom.

She didn't know how much longer she could stay here. The past was pressing in on her like the soggy, mold-bruised walls around her.

She felt suspended, lost, no longer Jane, but not Janie either. Could you ever leave behind the person you were, or did they remain trapped inside you like a sad old song?

Out the window the sun was rising behind a low bank of clouds. She wondered if Andy would be standing at the shore again this morning, waiting for a woman who would not come. Jane dressed quickly and snuck out just as the light was reaching the rotting slats of the back deck.

There was a dew-heavy coolness to the air, the only indication that it was autumn, and she breathed deeply as she walked. She felt the tight spiral of her thoughts loosen, lulled by the tread of feet on leaf litter, the twitter of tiny birds. She rounded the corner of the track and saw a shape move through the trees. A flash of white. A pale dress? Pale skin?

Her body reacted before her mind and she called Paige's name as she ran into the scrub. A jolt in her chest. Her breath came faster. No. Paige was dead. She was chasing ghosts. But this was around the time Paige had died. Right across the lake from here. Jane stopped, her pulse loud in her ears, her senses on high alert. The same feeling of being watched that she'd had at the Whites' house. The reeds in the shallows rustled and a bird called low and mournful over the water. Another movement in the undergrowth. Was she imagining things? The feeling was like walking through a cobweb. She brushed invisible strands of what, she didn't know, from her skin.

A dog appeared. *It was a dog.* She felt the spike in her adrenals ebb away as he inched closer to her.

"Hey, boy, who do you belong to?" She squatted and let him sniff her hand. She wanted to hug him she was so relieved. He was white with brown colorings, his rib cage protruding under his skin, but his eyes were friendly, sad. He didn't have a collar.

She walked on slowly, hoping he would follow her. She now had the patter of paws behind her. Somehow his presence made her feel safer, even though he had no allegiance to her. Maybe he was a stray.

She came to the steepled roof through the trees. She'd reached it faster than yesterday. She hesitated. She didn't really know why she was back here. The dog ran ahead of her into the clearing and barked twice. Yas came around the side of the house, a basket of eggs in her arms. Her hair was loosely plaited and she was dressed in a white smock and rubber boots. She could have been Paige.

"You're here again," she said, her voice emotionless.

Jane felt frustration buzz across her shoulders. "I . . . sorry, I started walking around the lake and . . ."

"It's okay, Mom gave you an open invitation." She shrugged and handed Jane an egg. It was still warm. "I think she wants lots of people in the house. People to cook for. So she can't tell one is missing."

Jane wasn't sure how to respond. She couldn't tell if Yas was being cruel or honest. Maybe it was both.

"Mom's lonely 'cause Dad's spending most of his time in town helping at the soup kitchen, even though it's his own family who actually needs him. He stayed there overnight. Mom wants everyone here, even the second strings, and Dad wants to be with homeless people. You know what he's like."

Jane thought back to their youth. Pastor White had always been involved in the community. He'd always been devoted to his church, his followers. They would be at the house for what he called "weeknight worship" and he would invite them home for lunch after church on Sundays. Paige had sometimes been a bit resentful of the second strings. "He's more devoted to his flock of sheep than to us," she'd once complained.

Jane knew she was the second string now. Maybe grief had made Yas even more brutal. "How are you doing?"

"How do you think I'm doing?"

Jane didn't respond. She thought about her own strange experience of finding out about Paige at work and it made her cringe to think about how she'd behaved.

At that moment the screen door banged, and a child with sandy hair came hurtling out of the house and down the stairs. Yas picked up the little boy and swung him onto her hip. Jane had only briefly seen the kids yesterday, getting into the car for a trip to the beach. Another child stood at the open door now. She was beautiful, not that the Whites seemed able to produce anything other than beauty. She must have only been two. It was Viv, Paige's daughter. She had the same white-blond hair—Paige's natural color as a child—and her fine features. Jane felt an intense sadness at what this little girl had lost. At what she wouldn't even properly understand was gone.

She followed Yas up the stairs and the girl ran inside. They removed their shoes and went into the house. The table overlooking the lake was set with breakfast just as it had been yesterday. Cutlery had been laid on linen napkins, cut flowers sat in a vase, and there was a plate of curled pink bacon, orange juice, a jar of muesli, and a jug of milk. Jane could smell toast, and coffee brewing.

"Oh Janie, you came." Mrs. White wiped her hands on a tea towel and drew her into a hug. A memory. As sharp and clear as her mother's perfume. *I'll be back for you, Janie. When I'm all set up in Sydney I'll come and get you and take you out of this sinking hole of a place.*

Jane bit the inside of her lip. "Are you sure? I was just out walking . . . and I thought . . . I don't want to—"

"Sit, sit. You're so welcome. I'm glad you're here." Mrs. White poured coffee from a French press. "Help yourself to toast and I'm just going to scramble the eggs Yas brought in from the chickens."

Mrs. White had always had something so serene about her, a certain way of talking and doing things that was considered, careful, precise. It had always felt like being looked after.

Andy came into the kitchen, this time looking like he'd been up for hours, fully dressed, wet hair combed. He scooped up Viv and put her in a baby seat at the table. "Hi, Janie."

"Hi." She gave an awkward little wave. It was strange that this whole family called her Janie. It was both unsettling and comforting, a bit like being back at this place.

"Did you go for a surf this morning?" Mrs. White asked Andy.

He nodded and bit into a slice of toast.

"I'll make extra eggs, you must be hungry."

"No, I just sat there in the water. Not much of a swell."

"That sounds good for the soul," she said, her voice chirpy as she whisked the eggs with an upbeat aggression. "You do whatever you need to. Viv slept in with me this morning, didn't you, darling?"

"Momma," Viv said softly.

Jane saw Andy's and Mrs. White's eyes meet.

He put down his toast. "That's the first word she's said since . . ."

There was so much pain in his face that Jane had to look away.

Mrs. White stopped whisking. "Honey, you remember what we talked about? That Mommy is in heaven with Jesus and the angels. She's here, my love, right with us."

"Momma," Viv said again, this time more forcefully, a piece of toast squished in her hand.

Jane put down her coffee cup. She wished there was something she could do to ease the tension that had descended over them all, as dense as Mrs. White's starched tablecloth.

"Mommy's not coming," said Andy. "Mommy's heart stopped beating. She's not here anymore."

"Andy!" Mrs. White rushed to Viv's side and picked her up from her high chair, smoothing her hair. "Don't speak like that!"

Andy's fist met the table. "I'm just telling my daughter the truth."

"She's two years old for goodness' sakes, she doesn't understand. She hasn't said a single word since Paige went to heaven."

"Well, there's no point pretending that her mother is frolicking with the angels when she's clearly not," he said, standing and taking Viv out of Mrs. White's arms. "It'll just confuse her."

Viv squirmed, her little body arching until Andy put her down. The child burst into tears.

Jane rose from the table, her voice softening, heightening. "Hey, hey, shall we go and see if we can find some ducks?"

She held out a piece of toast. Viv edged closer to her, and Jane felt the little girl's hand slip into hers. Her heart ached at this simple gesture of trust. *God, what am I doing?* she thought. *I know nothing about children.* She'd just needed to break the tension.

Andy and Mrs. White watched silently, chastised a little perhaps, as Jane walked slowly with Viv toward the door, the little girl gripping the toast in one fist, Jane's hand in the other. Jane looked back and Mrs. White shot her a conciliatory sort of smile. Andy had sat back down, his shoulders slumped.

The sun was more insistent now so she took Viv to stand under a shady spot at the lake's edge. As if by magic, ducks appeared and so did a smile. Viv broke off small pieces of toast and threw them into the shallows.

"Wow, the ducks know you," Jane said, crouching next to the little girl.

Viv fed the birds with a practiced confidence, one morsel for herself, one for the birds.

Jane was wondering if Viv was thinking about all the times she'd stood here with her mother and fed the ducks. How did you talk to a child about death anyway? And what did she understand beyond that her mother wasn't here anymore? Was it better to tell the truth so she might understand her absence, or speak comfortingly about the angels in heaven and Mommy looking over her? She was clearly traumatized if she hadn't spoken a word in days.

"Viv's doing strange things." Andy's voice behind startled her, and Jane stood so fast her head spun.

She pressed a hand to her chest. "Oh?"

"Thanks." He nodded toward his daughter. "You seem good with kids."

"Oh no, not really. I think she was just overwhelmed. Kids always like animals, don't they?"

"Yeah, she loves the ducks. Paige used to visit the ducks a lot with her."

"That's what I figured." They both looked at Viv, who was chewing on a crust. "Sorry, what were you saying? What kind of strange things?"

Andy's forehead creased. Squint lines were etched around his eyes as though he had spent a lot of time looking into the sun. Or maybe it was grief, exhaustion. "She's having night terrors. I mean, I think that's what they are. It doesn't help that her grandmother refuses to believe her daughter is dead."

"That must be hard."

"She's been basically mute since Paige died, and yet at night she wakes up and starts screaming and clawing the bedclothes, and I can tell she's not even awake. Her eyes are . . . weird . . . empty. I read about it, and you're not meant to wake them. Sometimes it goes on for, like, ten minutes. That doesn't sound like long, but . . ." He stroked his daughter's head. "Mrs. W said something about troubled spirits and is acting like she's possessed or speaking in tongues or something, and she prays over her. And Pastor White has apparently faith-healed people, so . . ."

"Oh god."

"You seem to be the only sane, normal person. Mrs. W is acting happy families, Yas is monosyllabic and consumed with her own kids and her baking business, as per usual, and Mr. W has taken off to help any family except his own. He's at the outreach center in the old hall where they hold services when it rains, but really it's for when he wants to preach to people and it's not a Sunday." Andy shook his head.

Jane thought back to Pastor White pressing people's hands between his, the warmth and intimacy with which he greeted them at the gathering at the house, the adoring way they had looked at him, knelt before him.

"I'm so sorry, Andy."

It seemed strange to call him by his name, too intimate, as though she'd reached out and touched the warm skin of his arm. She didn't really know this person at all, yet he felt known to her. *What is that?* she wondered. She could talk honestly with him. Was it because death made things very real very fast? Was it that it stripped away a layer of pretense that people could hide behind in ordinary life? Or was it something to do with being able to show yourself to a person? Did some people see you, really see you, as soon as you met them?

She thought of Jackson then. Of all the confusion, the pretense, the hiding her feelings to appear indifferent, strong. There was none of that here with Andy. It was like they'd known each other for a long time, even though they'd only properly met yesterday. Time was doing strange things, both concertinaing and stretching, like an accordion playing a sad song.

"That's why I took Viv up to my parents. I just knew things would be weird here, but then the local police there turned up and told me they were just concerned and wanted to know what my movements were, and that it would be great if I could go back home and make a voluntary statement. It made me feel like they'd chased me down, as though I'd kidnapped my own kid. But it was an instinct, you know, to go up north? I knew it'd be like this with Paige's family."

Jane wondered what the Whites had made of Andy disappearing. Was that why things felt a bit tense just now in the White house?

"Did the police understand why you left? You didn't get in trouble, did you?"

"I came back, obviously, and explained everything. They said they were just taking a statement, but they questioned me for ages. They said they might have more questions for me, but they let me go. I don't think this investigation is over yet, as much as Mrs. W thinks it is. Wants to pretend it is."

"I guess you're all just trying to muddle your way through this, doing your best." She found herself telling him about the death knocks, about all the ways she had seen people grieving. She didn't know why—maybe to try to reassure him that grief was unpredictable. That he wasn't failing his daughter.

"Do you think you could come back inside with us? It feels easier when you're there."

There was such vulnerability in his face that Jane felt something, some tiny seed plant itself deep inside her.

"Sure," she said, bending down and taking Viv's hand.

# CHAPTER 19

# Paige

They say men need their egos stroked. They say women need to do this in order to keep a man, to make him feel good about himself. I didn't do that enough for Andy because I thought we were above such things, that he wouldn't need such things. We never went back on the road as he'd suggested. Life just took over. We put Viv in a little daycare two days a week. It gave me time to get my errands done. I still wasn't treating my socials like a job but really, it was. I needed to go to the post office to pick up the things sent to me, plan my posts, my styling, source props, scout locations, and get the photographs taken. I also wanted to give Mom and Yas a break, because they were always at the house—Yas in the kitchen with her baking business and Mom being the homebody she is—and the care of the children always naturally fell to them.

Because I was busy, it took me a while to see the pattern. Andy was coming home later and later from the surf shop. He worked half the week as a barista in the cafe there and the other half selling surfboards. I used to forget which day was which, and that pissed him off, I think. But he didn't understand that the days bled into each other, as they do looking after a small child, when you're tired and trying to do your own stuff in thirty-minute spurts while your child naps or is engaged with their cousins without fighting.

He started coming home smelling of beer and coconut.

It was my turn to cook dinner, and we were in the kitchen. Through the open window I could hear the kids on the trampoline, my mother's singing as she tended the garden and kept an eye on them.

"Did you have a couple of beers at Soul Set tonight with the guys?" I tried to sound cool, appropriately indifferent, but my head had begun to throb.

"Yeah, it was Tam's birthday, so . . ."

"Who's Tam? From the shop? Have I met her?"

"I don't know, have you?" There was a cool tone to his voice. "Have you been in to visit me at work lately?"

"Um, I . . . don't know, have I? Maybe I've been too busy with Viv."

"She's in daycare. You could come in and grab a quick lunch with me."

"Okay, but it's only two days and you know that's when I get all my admin done. And you told me that you never know when you're going to get a break—that you don't have a lunch break some days."

"Well, I do now. And sometimes Tam and I go down to the beach to eat a sandwich."

I stared at him. "Okay, so what would you like me to do with that information, Andy? How would you like me to react? Am I meant to be happy that you're going on lunch dates, birthdays at the pub with this person?"

"You can take it how you want, Paige. I'm not attracted to her, if that's what you're asking."

My heart was actually hurting. I hadn't felt this way for a long time, and certainly Andy had never caused it. I felt burning behind my eyes, but I wouldn't let myself cry. I wanted to say, *Why are you being cruel?* But I dug my fingernails into my palm to stop the pain in my chest. Looking back, maybe it was my stubbornness that drove us apart. Maybe I should have shown my hurt, my pain, more. Been more vulnerable.

"I *am* asking that. It sounds a bit like you've given up on our relationship, Andy." My voice wobbled.

"Don't be ridiculous. If you'd actually seen Tam you'd know we're just friends. You're just acting like a jealous—"

"Like a jealous what? Bitch? There are so many things wrong with what you just said. So what? Am I meant to not feel threatened because you tell me this Tam isn't pretty or something? Is that it?"

"Pretty much. That's how it works."

"Oh yeah, nothing to do with whether you're having some kind of emotional connection with this person."

"I'm not having an emotional connection with Tam. She's like one of the guys."

"Well, don't tell me you're suddenly spending lots of time with this woman and expect me not to care."

"Do you though? I don't think you really do. It's all about Paige White, Paige White, Paige White." His voice made a whiny sound as he repeated my name.

"What the hell are you talking about? You do know it's you who sounds like a jealous bitch now."

We stared at each other. It felt like something broke, some easy cord that had always connected us. I could feel the loose threads of it between us and I wanted to grasp on to them, bind them together, and pull him back toward me, but instead I said, "Are you going to tell me to fuck off again?"

He got up and walked away, as though I wasn't even worth the dignity of a response. Mom and the kids came inside in a happy rabble.

Living in the house with my family meant we could easily avoid each other, talk around each other, hide behind the relationships we had with others. Pretend like nothing had changed, when everything was changing.

That was when I started checking his phone when he took a shower. That's when I got into his emails on the iPad that the kids used. I had always been better at technology than him. And I was right.

Of course I was right.

# CHAPTER 20

# Audrey

Emmie Taylor called us "loons" but she gave us the address. It was a flimsy 1950s house painted pastel blue on the "wrong" side of the lake, so not far from me and Janie's. The windows were laced with cobwebs, as though generations of spiders had lived and toiled there. A for-sale sign at the road said SOLD, but there was no one inside. We peeked past the webs through the windows at the empty rooms that had once held whole lives inside their walls. The carpet was half ripped up, peeled back to reveal stained floorboards, as though someone had started to renovate but then thought better of it.

There was an air of abandonment that made us quiet, and we didn't dare go into the house, even in the bright morning light, even with the high trill of cicadas, and kookaburras laughing in the trees. We followed a well-trodden path through overgrown grass around the side of the house. The caravan sat just shy of the shoreline. Where the house was spooky and isolated, the van looked sweet and welcoming. Maybe it was the rounded corners or the peach strip that ran down its flank. Maybe it was the lace curtains in the windows.

I reached out to turn the handle of the door, but Janie stopped me.

"I don't know. It feels kind of wrong. Maybe they . . . I don't know . . . died here."

I remembered my newfound hubris, my strength. "They probably died in the house. Let's just take a look. Might be locked anyway. Come on, remember, we're the trailer-trash girls? We can do this."

Janie held on to my arm as I turned the handle, and it gave. "It's open." I felt a childlike excitement bubble in my belly. It was like something out of *The Secret Seven* or *The Famous Five* books I'd devoured as a child. I took my body spray out of my bag as though it was mace, ready for what, I wasn't sure.

But the van smelled comforting, like tea leaves, the soap my gran used, and old but cozy blankets. It was perfect. Like a doll's house, everything in miniature, and I loved it immediately. It reminded me of being in a cubby house, of those childhood years that were so close and yet felt so far away now. Before our bodies started doing things we didn't understand, couldn't control.

The floor, the slide-in tabletop, and a curtain separating the van into two were all the same peach shade as the outside. Everything else was a plasticky fake timber. It thrilled me.

Janie opened the small timber cupboard above the tiny sink.

"Look at all these tins." She opened one and held it to my nose. "It's tea. Lots of tins of tea leaves." Herbal teas, flavored black teas. Teas that smelled like roses. Teas that smelled like foreign places we'd never been.

"Look, there's a kettle. Let's make some," I said.

She looked dubious but we found a brown teapot with a colorful knitted cozy and various floral cups with saucers. It was like playing dress-up out of an old magic box. Someone had clearly loved this van. The air of abandonment that the house held was not here at all.

"Oh, no water," I said, trying the tap. "Next time we'll bring our own water. And bread. Look, there's a toaster." It was one of those old ones where the sides opened outward, like a spaceship.

"It's not hooked up to electricity," said Janie, but I tried the toaster and it buzzed to life. We shared a conspiratorial look, as though tea and toast were fated acts of rebellion.

We moved past the little table and the banquette with the adorable striped cushions, to the filmy curtain that hid the rear end of the van. Sliding back the curtain felt like reading the opening line of a book, like falling down a rabbit hole. There was a small double mattress covered in a peach and white quilt, sun-faded pillows, and a colorful woolen blanket. Above the bed a shelf had been installed and it was filled with old paperbacks. We took a few down. We studied the covers, with their curly fonts and bare-shouldered women held in the arms of muscular, long-haired men.

"Ohhh, listen to this. 'Darce held his nose to Jamie's lustrous hair and breathed her in. She smelled like roses awakening on the morning dew.'" I pressed my hand to my chest and swooned a bit.

"Oh dear, we're going to read them all, aren't we," said Janie. She took out a sheet of folded paper that had been used as a bookmark. "Ed and Daisy," she said. "Maybe that was their names."

It was a bill addressed to Mr. Edward and Mrs. Daisy Wright. "This must have been their property. Look at the address."

"So why did they have the van if they had a whole house?"

"Maybe they came here for tea," I said.

"Obviously."

"And romance. These are her novels. Maybe this was her little reading nook."

"Maybe it was their sex van," said Janie, putting the novel down fast. "Ewwwww."

"Old people have sex."

"I think Daisy was probably having sex with 'Darce,' not Ed."

"Well, can you blame her though?"

We both studied Darce on the cover. He was dressed in a white cape and had long, light brown hair softly brushing his shoulders and chiseled cheekbones and abs. He looked like a sexy Greek god.

"Do you think they died within days of each other?" Janie asked.

"Who? Darce and Jamie?"

She grabbed the book out of my hands. "No! Ed and Daisy."

"Yes, I think they made love here every week for the whole of their marriage and when Daisy died of a heart attack—"

"From reading erotica."

"Shhh, you're ruining it," I said. "From fate taking her at the age of eighty-nine while she sat in her TV chair watching *Days of Our Lives* . . . Ed was so heartsick that he came here to the caravan every afternoon as the sun was setting over the lake and lay on the place in the mattress where he could still feel the shape of Daisy's body. He made her favorite tea—Russian Caravan—and then on the final afternoon with the sun streaming in, he closed his eyes and went to sleep forever."

"Oh my god, I'm crying."

I elbowed her. "You are not."

"Yes, I am." And she was. She had tears in her eyes, and I hugged her fiercely because she was so kind and had a heart like my own. That was how we started reading old romance novels and concocting the whole life story of Edward and Daisy Wright. We didn't know it then, but we were writing our first novel. Speaking it. Feeling it out. Finding the truth in these characters that seemed so real to us. Their faces merging with those of Darce and Jamie so that in the end, I couldn't separate our fictional creations from those of Rose Montgomery, the author.

We brought our own bottled water and boiled it and drank cup after cup of tea until our bellies were distended, because we could. We were drunk on stories and strong brew from chipped teacups.

It was our own secret garden. It felt, I realized, like poking my finger through that hole in my bedroom wall. A dreamscape hideaway, away from all the hard things and the disappointments we were both going through. A cocoon of hope. A kind of heaven when the sun streamed through and lit up all the dust motes so that it felt like we were in our own snow globe.

# CHAPTER 21

The lake became like a companion. I didn't know you could be so lonely that a body of water could become a friend. But it was endlessly shifting—the light on the water, the sounds of the birds, the occasional human that drifted across its thin, reflective skin. I also had only a thin, reflective skin keeping the depths at bay. I didn't used to be so solitary. I wouldn't have pictured that this was the way my life would pan out, in this log cabin on the edge of the world. That I would subsist on crackers and wine and the scent of gum leaves and lake brine.

I imagined at this age I'd be nourishing my body, taking the time to make healthy meals, not just fueling it. But I suppose I didn't think I'd be alone. But do any of us really know what life has in store for us? Life is a gamble. A folly of hope.

I don't mean to sound morose. There were moments of joy. The snap of the mosquito zapper heralding the end of the day, the breeze turning cool against my legs. I'd douse myself with citronella so I could stay outside for just a little bit longer. With the birds restless in the treetops, and the lake turning silver, then gold, purple, and then black. And the mornings, so still, no breeze, the girl in the kayak reminding me that I was not just the sum of my thoughts. I was bodily.

I had always been a reader and when I ran out of my own paperbacks, I started reading the books in the bookshelf. I was drawn to one with a green spine, newish. It was about the healing powers of nature. It talked about things that I already knew—how it reduced stress and anxiety and the like, but something I hadn't heard of before was the awe. How nature could help connect a person to something greater than the self.

It talked about how a group of volunteers were instructed to walk for fifteen minutes in nature each week. One group were given an intervention suggesting they cultivate a sense of awe during their walks. The other group just walked. Both groups were instructed to take selfies at the beginning, middle, and end of these forest walks. When scientists analyzed the group actively seeking awe against the other group, the walkers in the awe group made themselves increasingly smaller and smaller in the photos they took. The landscapes took over. Swallowed them whole. I imagined only a tiny corner of an eye, an errant finger blurred over the lens. The rest green, blue. Endless sky.

I think that's what I was feeling. The slow and blissful erasure of self. The thing I longed for most of all. That's when I started swimming. And when I started swimming, that's when I got close enough to see who the girl in the kayak was.

# CHAPTER 22

# Jane

The text message woke her from a dream. She sat up in bed and pressed her palms to her eyes. Her sheets were damp with sweat. She could still feel the leaf litter beneath her bare feet. They were at the tree cathedral, all of them. They were running from someone, though it was a feeling rather than an exact person.

She oriented herself, placed her feet on the carpet. She was in her childhood bedroom. She'd slept late. Paige was dead. She was at The Lakes. It was a constant reorientation, as though sleep had upended her, like a bottle shaken, hard. She could feel the pressure building behind her eyes. She focused on her phone, blinked. The message was from Jackson.

*We need to talk about the funeral. Do you know when it will be? Are you up to covering it for us? This story still has legs. Getting lots of clicks mainly on the strength of the pics. Also had a tip-off from police.*

And there it was. She'd just been waiting, expecting, dreading this. Paige's funeral. It was likely to be delayed because her body would have been sent to the nearest large town for the coroner to do an autopsy. Jackson knew that.

Jane had an image of Paige's body laid out on a steel slab. Who would have viewed her body? Would Andy have the mental fortitude? Or would it be Pastor White, who so naturally presided over births and deaths, christenings, and funerals? She rubbed her arms and pulled a sweater over her head. The mornings were getting colder.

She still hadn't called Jackson, just brief texts back and forth to say she was okay, that it was busy catching up with everyone. She didn't know what she was playing at, being so evasive. He had gone back into work mode. *He's appealing to the journalist in me. He's reeling me back in. I need to be professional about this,* she thought.

He was her boss, first and foremost. He was her hookup, her sometimes-lover when it was convenient for him. Right now, it was business mode. No more pleading, no more intimacy. He had his editor hat on now. She knew she had a job to do. She might be on a kind of unacknowledged bereavement leave but everyone knew you didn't just take your journalist hat off when it was convenient. *Are you up to covering it for us?* The royal *we*. He aligned himself with the company when he needed to use its gravitas, its power. She could feel him slipping away from her.

And then the bait—*a tip-off from police.* What was it? Did he know the inside information Shep had shared with her? She knew she had to call him. Not only for their relationship but, maybe even more crucially, for the security of her job. *Snap out of it, Jane.*

As her finger hovered over the call button, shame squeezed through her—she was sitting in her childhood bedroom in this run-down house, having slept in and done nothing these past few days except walk and eat. Yesterday she had stayed at the Whites' until the afternoon, not wanting to abandon Andy after their conversation. She'd eaten eggs from the chickens and nectarines from the garden. The children came and went from the table like little birds scavenging crumbs. Mrs. White had put on more coffee, and she and Andy had taken their mugs onto the veranda and watched the sun rise into the sky while the kids played in the garden, going between the swing and the trampoline. She and Andy had talked about simple things at first—the unseasonal heat wave, the tides and the surf, the children.

"I don't know how I'm going to do it without Paige. I guess I didn't get it . . . until . . . Now I realize how much she did . . . for Viv, for our family."

Jane didn't want to lessen his grief by saying that he was lucky to have the Whites, Viv's cousins as a ready-made family. She just stayed quiet and listened. Jane realized that all those years of listening to people talk about their tragedies had made her understand that sometimes all that was needed was a safe silence to talk into.

They must have sat there for several hours, because Mrs. White was calling the kids to come inside for lunch. Another lovely meal had been laid on a starched white tablecloth. Homemade soup, and bread that Yas had baked, with soft yellow butter.

After eating, it felt like she should go. As she said as much and rose to leave, Mrs. White asked her to go through Paige's wardrobe and take some of her clothes. Jane said she didn't think she could. She knew she shouldn't be entrusted with such an intimate task, but Mrs. White was so insistent. *Paige has so many beautiful dresses*, she'd said, refusing to use the past tense. *Clothing companies sent her samples to model.* The pride in Mrs. White's voice made Jane's chest ache. She said okay.

When she held the fabric of a long floral dress to her nose, it smelled like the perfume Paige used to wear. Jane realized this dress was like one of the old ones she used to pair with cowboy boots when they were sixteen. She remembered the faded floral fabric. It had been their uniform. Well, Paige's uniform—that they'd all copied. She hesitated above the bin bag for charity. Mrs. White came into the room and told Janie she must take the dress. She put it carefully into a paper bag.

Jane walked back around the lake to her dad's carrying the dress, but when she got there, she got into her car and drove to the beach. She couldn't keep this dress. She took it out of the bag and considered throwing it in the ocean, but then stuffed it under the passenger seat instead. She had walked up and down the shoreline all afternoon. Achieving nothing. Doing nothing.

*Janie kind of behavior.*

She had driven back to the house. Her dad had left a note under her bedroom door to say he'd gone to golf and that he would pick up sausages for dinner. Her heart squeezed, shame and sadness all mushed up together like a soft, processed meat. She'd loved sausages as a kid. Like every kid. What would Jackson think of her dad? Of this place? It was so far from her life in Sydney. But why was that life feeling like it was floating away, so flimsy, so lonely?

She looked down at her phone now and pressed Jackson's number. He didn't pick up and relief rushed through her. She felt like she should be showered and dressed and caffeinated before she spoke to Jackson anyway.

She took a quick shower, trying to ignore the luminous orange mold, her guilt like a slippery, dank organism. She dressed in the work clothes she'd arrived in. It felt uncomfortable to be in these formal clothes, at odds with her surroundings. *Why am I doing this?* she thought.

She made herself a strong coffee and went out onto the deck. He picked up on the sixth ring, just as she was about to hang up.

"Babe."

She felt her shoulders unbunch. She'd gotten Lover Jackson, not Boss Jackson, on the line.

There was a rustling sound. "Sorry, I'm just picking up breakfast on my way into the office." If she'd called ten minutes later she'd have gotten "Masters" instead of "babe." She heard him talking to someone, the phone moving.

"Okay, hi, hi . . . so . . . she's alive."

Shock zipped up her spine. "What?"

"Oh sorry, I didn't mean . . . did you think I meant Paige? No, I mean Jane Masters is alive."

Jane shook her head. What was happening to her? Of course Paige wasn't alive. She felt like she was going insane. "Sorry, it's been full-on being back. I've been busy." A lie.

"No, no, I get it. And I'm sorry to jump straight into work stuff . . ."

She knew this wasn't true. This was his manipulation, his way of taking back the power, but she made conciliatory noises.

"I don't want to pressure you. I know the toll it took writing the online story about Paige. I just wanted to see how you felt about things now."

*I feel numb*, she wanted to say. *I don't know who I am. I'm no longer Jane but I can't be Janie.*

She realized in this moment, in the silence that opened up between them, the crucial mistake she'd made, mixing work with pleasure. If she didn't do this, would he withdraw from her entirely? She'd told herself she had earned her place at the paper, but had she? Or was it just because she was sleeping with her boss?

No, she couldn't risk losing her job. She was no one without it.

"I'll do it. I'll do whatever you need. I'll cover the funeral." Her voice sounded distant, not her own. She knew the funeral date hadn't even been set. They wouldn't lock in a date until Paige's body had been returned to the family. She had time. That's all she had, but it was something.

"Great, great, great. Love it."

"What was the tip-off? From the cops?" She could feel herself slipping into work mode too.

"Paige had a stalker. That's why police are treating her death as suspicious."

"I actually already knew that." The words came out of her mouth before she could stop them. *You don't need his approval. You don't need to prove anything to him.* "I have a contact up here." Her hand balled into a fist on her knee as she spoke. *Damn it, shut up.*

There was a pause and Jane pressed the phone to her ear. She hated the way her heart was pounding waiting for his response.

"I knew you'd be on it. You're a superstar. You're *my* superstar."

# CHAPTER 23

# Paige

After I found the first one, I read all the emails. There was a new one almost every night. She was obsessed with him. They had surfing in common.

I had tried so hard to be that kind of woman. We lived in the surfing heartland. I knew that Andy would have loved to share that love of the ocean, being out the back, sinking your legs into the sea, letting the salt scour off your day. But I just couldn't do it. The salt stung my eyes, and the sun burned my pale skin. I got rashes from the chafing.

But now that I'm here, suspended . . . wherever I am, what silly, silly things I used to worry about. I wish I could go back to that girl and say fuck that. Worrying about your skin being perfect for photos. Trying to be beautiful all the time. For who? Because what does it matter? One day you're going to be in a place so silent, so lonely, that you'll start talking to yourself, that all you'll have left to keep yourself sane is thinking back over every tiny piece of your life to try to work out how you got here.

But I probably wouldn't have listened to myself. I wore hats and sunscreen to maintain my edgy pallor. And I know he found me beautiful. Ironically, he didn't want the little blond girl next door, no, he wanted me with my blue-black hair and red lips and porcelain skin. He wanted striking, mysterious. But, it turns out, not too striking or too mysterious. It turns out, he also wanted to be adored by a blond too. She wasn't traditionally pretty, this girl, but she had a strong body, tanned toned legs, loose waves in her hair. I knew because I visited him at the shop right after he'd told me that he spent his lunches with her. Of course I did.

I dressed in an expensive dress that I'd been gifted. It was low around the bustline, but I looked appropriately relaxed, taking care to fit into his world. I wanted to look as though I'd just dusted the sand from my feet. The surf shop was one of the nicer shops in the retail strip near the beach. There was a pharmacy, a real estate agent, and a small supermarket. The trendy hole-in-the-wall cafe was part of the surf shop and filled with a steady stream of people drinking fresh juices and espressos under the faded lemon retro umbrellas.

I bypassed the cafe and went into the shop. I saw her immediately, because she saw me. And I knew in that moment that she knew who I was, and that she had a thing for my husband.

I'm not proud of what I did next. I walked straight up to her and told her that her hair was pretty. I reached out and touched it. Maybe to see whether it was soft, or salt-encrusted. Maybe to see if she'd flinch. She didn't. I asked to see the new-season bikinis.

Her eyes flicked to Andy, who was over by the surfboards talking to a guy. I smiled. It was the moment I might have gotten her on side, right then. I might have confided something, said something self-depreciating like, *I can't wear those G-string bikini bottoms that everyone's wearing.* Make her not want to steal my husband. But I didn't say that. I chose a black floral bikini that was a scrap of material. My ass looking good in a G-string bottom was all I had at that point.

She had surfing. They had an immediate language that I was not part of. The terminology could have been a love letter. *Air and aerial and amped and ankle-slappers.* I had once shared a language with him. *Aperture, rule of odds, depth of field, the golden hour.* Once we'd had photography. He taught me that an SLR still took better photos than even the best new iPhone because you had control. He taught me about how to frame an image, about how an odd number is infinitely more interesting to the human eye than an even. That when presented with an even number of elements, the eye tends to gravitate toward the empty space between them. But that an odd number of things is perceived as a pattern rather than something incomplete.

I took the bikini into the change room, stripped off, and put it on. I stared at myself in the mirror for a few seconds and nearly lost my nerve. But then I thought about her eyes flicking to him as soon as I walked into the shop. I opened the door and she was standing right there. Her mouth sort of dropped open when she saw me.

"What do you think?" I asked, my hands on my hips.

She blinked for a moment and nodded a little too enthusiastically as though to cover her . . . what, embarrassment? I didn't rub her face in it for long, just thanked her and went back in to change.

I took the bikini up to the counter and he turned and saw me. His face lit up and for a second I thought I was imagining the whole thing. That's the thing Andy didn't know. It was the way he looked at me that made me feel beautiful, not any of the other things. That love had translated down the camera. I longed to get it back. That golden hour of our lives. The place I am suspended now.

He kissed me on the cheek. He didn't look at her once as he scanned my swimwear, applied his discount, and led me outside to a seat under the palms. That was what I didn't understand about it all. He was proud of me. I could feel it. We had a nice lunch. We even had an espresso after, with a scoop of ice cream because it was so hot. We talked about Viv, about the unit by the beach that we dreamed of renting. It was like it used to be.

I'm not sure why I didn't tell him I knew then. Why I didn't try to salvage things at that point. Maybe it was about control. If I told him I wouldn't be able to see what she was writing to him. What he was writing back to her. About me. About his life.

*It's actually really hard. She's so obsessed with this thing . . . She's changed. She didn't used to be like this. She thinks life is taking photos of her pretty head. I don't want my daughter to grow up thinking this shit is normal, you know?*

What's normal is not saying those things in an email to a little fucking retail worker who is in love with you. Maybe I was just biding my time. I could have pressed "reply all" at any point.

*Hi Andy and Tam*

*I don't think life is about taking pretty pictures of my head. I think life is about having the ability to feed my child and I do this by making content people happen to like looking at. People pay me and I can therefore stay home and look after my daughter, and just take some pictures, which I'd do anyway. And why am I even having to justify myself to you? To you both. Who are either of you to tell me what I can or can't do with my body?*

But I didn't write that. Maybe it also took away the guilt. If Andy got to have his Surf Girl, then I got to have my Poet Boy. It felt like I deserved him after reading their emails. It was a fair exchange. Besides, Poet Boy and I were exclusively communicating online. I didn't see him in person. All we did was write each other cryptic poems about our lives. He could have been a mirage. He was an enigma. I liked that. That was the attraction, of course.

# CHAPTER 24

# Audrey

It started with a note in my pencil case. It was a unicorn pencil case that shimmered when you moved it. I was always on the lookout for magical charms, good omens, things to protect and heal and illuminate. And Paige had that effect on people. She was like a lucky charm. Something to keep and conceal. When she shone her light on you, it felt like planets and moons aligning.

*Want to come to mine this afternoon to do our project? P*

I'd never been to the Whites' without Janie. I couldn't help but feel the ripple of importance that she had invited me, alone. There was a small part of me that thought, *I should tell Janie about this,* but it seemed silly.

*Sounds fun.* I slipped the note into her pencil case, which was black with purple love hearts.

Paige and I could have our own friendship, I reasoned. No one had ownership over anyone else. We were all friends, and we had a task to complete for school. That's what I told myself, but still, I didn't mention it to Janie when I waved goodbye to her outside math class and met Paige at the school gate.

Anyway, we didn't go to the Whites' right away. We walked home via the gas station to get smokes. I snuck them out from behind the counter while Paige was telling Mom about the art assignment we'd been paired together for. We had to make a sculpture or art piece out of found objects inspired by the natural world. I could see by the look on her face that this had sparked something in Paige. She told Mom we were going to walk back to her house by way of the lake and beachcomb for treasure.

From the way Mom was looking at Paige now, you'd never know that she'd looked at her and Yas disparagingly the first time she'd seen them walking barefoot across the hot concrete. That she'd warned me against them after the party where I took the fall. I knew she was just trying to protect me from being hurt again, but I think in a strange way she was proud of me for making friends so quickly, so easily. I knew she worried about me after the last school. All those times she went in to speak to my teachers, which only seemed to make it worse.

I heard her talking to Dad once when they didn't know I was listening. The walls in our old house were paper-thin. It was as though we'd gone from living in a house made of Popsicle sticks to a house made of Popsicle sticks that had been chucked in the bin and then fished out.

"The teacher apologized but said—wait for it—that some kids have a ready-made target on their backs, the ones who are a bit different. And sadly, Audrey seems to be just that kind of kid."

"Lazy teaching, that's what that is," said Dad. I could hear the clunk and clatter as he washed up dishes in the sink.

"Lack of care more like it. I mean, she may as well have said, 'Well, your kid's a weirdo so there's not much we can do.'"

There was silence and I snuck closer and peeked into the kitchen.

Mom had her face in her hands and her body shook. Dad dried his hands on the tea towel and came and rested them on her shoulders, kneading her muscles until Mom wiped under her eyes with the damp towel.

"So Audrey's a bit different from the other kids . . . so what? She's a fighter. She got that from her dad. She's stronger than you think, Char. You try to protect her, to shield her too much. Everyone gets bullied. It's life. Life is hard. It's an important lesson to learn as a kid."

And she did try to shield me, to protect me. Can you protect a person too much? I don't know, but I always knew Mom was on my side. What I wasn't sure of was if she was more upset about how resigned and useless the teacher was, or that I'd been labeled like that. *Weird. Different.* Even though I knew she was my mom and that she would love me all the same, it still kind of felt like I was letting her down. People liked her in a way they didn't seem to like me. She was an enigma to me. I had come from her and yet I didn't have that special quality that seemed to draw others to her. She said that she could see past the airs and graces people put on, the exterior cloak they wore for the world, and she could see the heartache and the vulnerability that they carried. I always thought that was a gift. I don't think I had as much empathy as her, or maybe I'd been hurt more than she had. But she taught me to always treat people kindly because you never knew what they were going through. You never knew their real story.

So, if Mom liked Paige, that was a good sign, and I took it. I was hungry for connection, for love, for acceptance. Dad was working on a car in the garage and he waved an oily rag at us as we passed, and Paige whispered and giggled and said I had a hot dad. I was used to that. I think people were surprised that two supremely beautiful people made me, but I was proud of them.

We left the gas station and headed across the hot, sticky tarmac of the only road out of town, toward the lake. We peeled off our shoes and socks at the lake's edge and sifted the cool wet sand between our toes as we smoked. There was the smell of the reeds at low tide and the hum of cicadas in the trees, smoke drifting lazily from our cigarettes.

"Let's make a talisman for the project." Paige had collected driftwood, shells, a feather in her palm.

I'd heard of talismans before in fantasy books—they were a charm to avert evil and bring good fortune, often a trinket or a jewel inscribed with a symbol. I was surprised someone like Paige knew about them.

"You mean, like a sacred object of some kind?"

Paige nodded. "All religions have them. Dad's talked about them in ancient Christianity, but they're also used in the Islamic faith. They're an object people wear that protects and heals them."

"They're usually a necklace or a ring . . . at least in the books I've read."

Paige traced a circle in the sand with a stick. "Well, Miss Walton just said we needed to make a sculpture or an art object. We could really make . . . anything."

"We could stick shells and sand and feathers on canvas," I said.

"We could use clay from the lake to sculpt something."

"Or take photographs of sand castles . . . or a video of them slowly falling apart." Her eyes looked lit from within.

"Or make something with feathers and wildflowers."

It felt like a creative seam had opened between us. It was a place free of judgment, where anything felt possible. A place of magic and mystery. Or maybe that's just what it felt like being in Paige's orbit.

"Something protecting and healing, like female energy."

A shiver ran through me when she said that. I looked at her sitting on that beach, her hair stark, beautiful against the pale sand, the light sky, and I thought, *No, of course, you would never have felt anything but protection from those around you, from the world.*

*A talisman can also harm*, I thought. But I didn't say it out loud.

# CHAPTER 25

# Jane

The afternoon sun was hot and bright and the bar looked like it belonged somewhere off the coast of Mexico. It was squat and concrete and rested casually like an elbow out the car door of the beach. The road was unpaved, and sand and dust plumed from passing vehicles heading up to the lighthouse. Once-red umbrellas had faded to a burnt orange and there was a halfhearted attempt at festivity in the colored bulbs that hung limply from the balcony. As though completing the theme, Shep already had a Corona with a wedge of lemon sticking out the top waiting for her.

She waved but felt a rush of shame as she approached him. How was she actually here in her thin-strapped summer dress? She was here to find out more about what had happened to Paige, yes. But for who? For herself or for her editor? And what of Shep, her "contact," who couldn't hide his enthusiasm when she'd suggested meeting for a drink? He was newly divorced. *Bad idea, Janie,* she thought. She corrected herself. *Jane.* It was harder to keep them separate the longer she was in this place. This beach, its insistent sun, had soaked up so many hours of her childhood, her adolescence. She could see too, the way her pale office skin was slowly coloring, browning effortlessly, as it used to. She told herself to buy sunscreen.

"Hey." She greeted him with a kiss, and sat down on a stool looking into the shock of light bouncing off the surf. This place might have been run-down, but that was the beauty of The Lakes. It was as though nothing had changed since she was a kid. It was just the ocean, unadulterated. She thought about beaches in Sydney with their metered parking lots and gleaming surf clubs and cafe strips. Here it was still unpaved roads, and cafes and bars with no hint of pretension or irony, just like it had been when they were young.

"Tough life, hey." Shep clinked his beer against hers and they took a moment to stare out at the water.

"This place seems like it's been here forever, but I don't remember it," she said.

"The building used to be a private hall. I heard some kind of hippy cult operated out of here back in the day, hence all the rainbow paintings and murals on the walls inside, and then they got cleared out. I don't think it was still going when we were kids, but do you remember there used to be that funny little setup here? An honor system selling shells and necklaces and things. And people just used to nick them without paying."

"Oh yeah, I remember. So random. I'd forgotten that used to be here."

"Anyway, the place got turned into a bar. Sometimes I like to have a cold beer here after work or if I have the day off."

"Got the day off today?"

"Yeah. What about you? Have you taken bereavement leave, or are you expected to be back in the office soon?"

Jane rotated her coaster. There was a picture of a skull on it. The

Day of the Dead. She'd been right about the Mexican vibe. "To be honest, I'm not sure what I'm doing." There was something about Shep—she couldn't seem to keep up any kind of veneer around him. It was the intensity of his gaze, his undiluted attention.

"Well, yeah, your world's kind of been turned upside down, so it's understandable." He took a swig of his beer. "I know all about how that feels."

She waited a beat. "With your—"

"Separation. Yeah, it's still pretty fresh. I'm lucky I've got work to throw myself into. Even though work may have been part of the reason for our problems."

"It's hard, working long hours. I'm lucky, my . . . well, I'm not sure—boyfriend, I guess you'd call him—is also in the game, so he gets it. But the long hours, the unpredictability of the job, it takes its toll."

"Damn right. Mentally too. Sometimes . . ." He shook his head. "Sometimes it's hard to explain what it's like to hear the things we hear . . . what other humans do to each other."

"You see the absolute worst. At least with journalism it's the worst but also the best. You see both. You see the good stuff, the inspiring stuff, the 'truth is stranger than fiction' stuff as well."

"God, look at us. We're barely halfway through our beers and we're already talking about humanity's flaws."

"Ah, humanity sucks. And it's also beautiful. Depending on which story I'm covering."

"Depending on which case I'm covering. Speaking of . . ." Shep shifted on his stool.

Jane felt the familiar slide in her gut. "Have you got something else on Paige's case?" Their eyes met. She saw hesitancy in his. "What is it?"

"Janie, are you sure you want to know?"

She swallowed. She wasn't Janie, she was a journalist. Needing to know was in her DNA. He knew that, but she could see he was trying to protect the person who had been Paige's friend. It moved something in her. She nodded softly.

"So, you know the flower crown I told you they found? Well, it wasn't around her head, it was around her neck. It was made of wire and . . . there were signs of a struggle, bruising, though it's looking more like she died from drowning rather than asphyxiation."

"Oh my god." She felt a thin membrane of horror stretch inside her. "What? Was she . . . ?"

"It's still with pathology but crime scene suggests that . . . And all of this is obviously very much between you and me, but it's looking more and more like it might have been intentional . . . Suspicious circumstances."

Jane shut her eyes. The light felt blinding now, the sun too hot. She could feel moisture being pushed out of her pores, beading on her skin.

"Hey, you okay?" Shep reached out and put his hand on her shoulder. It was cool, heavy, comforting.

"Sorry, it's just a shock. That someone would do something like that to Paige."

"We can . . . just talk about the weather? Have you been for a swim yet?"

She grimaced and shook her head. "I don't think either of us is the small-talk type, do you?"

He smiled ruefully, took a sip of beer. "Nope. Absolutely not."

"So, are there any leads? The stalker? Have they talked to Paige's family? Are they telling them there's going to be a possible murder investigation?"

He shot her a sidelong glance. "You don't sound like a journalist at all."

"Sorry."

"We're investigating . . . Haven't made much progress with the stalker. Her family will likely be interviewed again. Sorry if I'm making it sound like a case."

Jane thought of poor Mrs. White and her dreamy idea of Paige in her happy, heavenly place. God, how would Andy react? A sliver of something sharp, uncomfortable, lodged inside her. That morning that she saw him throw something into the water. What had that been? Should she mention it to Shep? No, of course not. Was Andy a suspect, even though he'd returned pretty quickly from up north and answered all their questions?

"Like I said, all of this needs to stay between you and me, obviously. The family haven't been told anything yet. They won't be until pathology can confirm it."

Jane made the gesture of running a zipper across her lips. But her journalist brain was churning, clocking over, analyzing. She was thinking about what Jackson would make of this news.

*You're a superstar. My superstar.*

She was treading on dangerous ground. It was unethical to be using this datelike scenario with Shep to get leads, but the truth of it was, that was how it worked. That was how the world worked. Favors and who you knew still counted for something. That was how journalists did their job. Was it her place to cover Paige's death when it felt so wrong to do so? Or was she just trying to please and placate the man who felt just out of her reach?

The crush of shame was back. No, this wasn't about her. This was about Paige. *Who were you now, Paige White?* Beyond the pretty pictures. Maybe there was nothing beyond the surface. She'd always been charismatic, a born leader like her father, but Jane hadn't really known Paige since she was a teenager.

Jane had her own faults. She was consumed by work, consumed by whatever it was she had with Jackson. But she told herself that at least she was consumed by something that felt bigger than herself. She had no interest in making herself into anything for consumption, as Paige had. She thought of herself as more outward-looking. Other people, world events, interested her. She felt that this was a big divide in a human's lived experience. There were people who didn't know what was happening outside their own narrow lives, their own narrow interests and needs. They didn't see themselves in a continuation with a wider world. Had Paige become one of these people? Given how she'd grown up, Jane couldn't blame her if she had.

Perhaps that's what happened when you grew up praised and adored for the way you looked. She remembered that first sting of jealousy she'd felt toward Paige. She'd turned thirteen before Jane, and Yas was already fourteen. It was as though a self-consciousness had descended on them like a too-warm blanket. Jane found it stifling. The acute self-awareness, the feeling of her body changing, of having no control. Before it, they had been free of their bodies, running with strong legs through shallow tides, sunburn on faces upturned to the sky. But with adolescence there was another layer that began to present itself. Who was beautiful? Who wasn't? It didn't really matter to Jane. That kind of thing didn't feature in her goals. But she recognized very quickly that with beauty came power.

Jane realized too that she wasn't ugly, and that was something to be thankful for, because she saw the way people were singled out for their physical differences, much earlier than thirteen, but at that age more intensely so. She thanked god that she had brown hair and brown eyes and brown skin in the summertime. She could blend suitably. She was a medium-bodied girl. She was safe.

Beauty could be a snare. She knew that. It could trap you, and it didn't matter how hard you pulled, something had to break to be free of it. An image came to her of Paige underwater, snared by some malevolent force, something deep and dark and unknown, and Jane felt dread trawl through her.

"Did you want to get something to eat?" Shep asked, breaking into her thoughts, drawing her back to the surface. "They do tacos."

She looked at him with his wild mane and welcoming eyes. He had almost certainly broken police protocol in telling her all that about Paige. He was so trusting, perhaps thinking that their childhood connection protected him. His loneliness and pain had weakened him. She could see it seeping out of him. *You and I aren't that different,* she thought.

"Sure," she said. "I love tacos."

They ate spicy fish tacos with their fingers as the sun rolled into the sea. They had made a silent pact somewhere along the line not to talk about Paige and the case anymore. Shep told her about his kids, the funny things they did, how much he missed them when his ex had them. But also how much of a relief it was to have time to himself without them as well. He was the kind of man, she realized, who would never bad-mouth his ex-wife. She wanted to ask him what had gone wrong. Why hadn't the marriage worked? But he had an air of bafflement about him, as though he'd been blindsided by her leaving. It was clear by the way he talked that it was her decision.

"What about you? You mentioned someone back in Sydney?" His voice rose a little. She could tell he was uncomfortable asking it, but he wanted to know. She felt sorry for him in that moment, and she realized this was the reason she couldn't see him as a romantic prospect. There was something about him, some tenderness, some homeliness, that reminded her of her dad.

"Jackson, yeah. He's . . . he's also the deputy editor of the paper. So as you can imagine, that can be challenging at times."

Jane had almost referred to him as her "partner." He wasn't her partner. She had referred to him as that once and he'd said, "God, I hate that word. It's so middle-class." She'd felt the heat rise into her face until she'd had to turn away, wounded, smarting as though he'd slapped her.

She looked at Shep's face now to see if he was disappointed, but he was a cop. He was good at keeping a poker face. She realized she didn't want him to get his hopes up. *I can't be the kind of woman you want*, she thought. *I can't be trapped here in this small-town life.*

*I would just do to you what my mother did to my father.*

# CHAPTER 26

# Paige

Maybe on a subconscious level, after I'd been to the shop to see the girl, I let myself get closer to Buckley. He had various names: the Poet, Buckley. His handle was @poetboy. He was new to Instagram. He asked me questions about growing his audience. He was someone who respected me rather than put me down for my success. I felt like he could see the full spectrum of who I was, who I was becoming, not just the wife, not just the mother. He wasn't threatened by me. I could tell he was a little in awe of me. And I returned the feeling.

He sent me snippets of his essays. He was studying poetry and philosophy. He seemed older, wiser than me, even though he was still in college. Or maybe that was just because he lived in his head.

*Have you ever woken from a dream you perceived as real? Descartes asserts that we cannot trust what is real, what is not real. Our perception of the world, of our senses, cannot be trusted. Maybe everything is an illusion.*

I'd never been to university. I had never read the musings of French philosophers, so to me he was on a pedestal from the start. He made me think. He made me think back to when I believed I'd get out of The Lakes, when I thought my world would be bigger. When I wanted to be a stylist or a makeup artist in New York. Why didn't I leave this place? What had I done with my life? I'd worked in a dress shop for a while after school, then at the hairdresser, where I learned how to section hair with a fine comb and fold foil into neat squares. I could trim hair into a blunt line. I did some makeup for friends' weddings. I was biding my time, but for what, I didn't know. I got another job at a nicer dress shop up the highway where they called me a "house model." I spent my weekends as the hostess at the door of the nightclub near work. It was never that I was lazy. I had lots of boyfriends who smoked too much pot or hit the booze. Then I met Andy the year I turned thirty, and then, and then, and then. That was the way life went, wasn't it? If you let it, it just happened without you seeming to do anything much. But not deciding was actually deciding. And then there was motherhood.

But that's the thing, it did feel like I got out of this place—virtually. My world was big online. It felt real. It all felt so real. But maybe Descartes would say otherwise.

When Buckley suggested we make a joint account @poet&paige— a place where I could post my writing anonymously—it felt like a beautiful secret. We hardly had any followers, and I loved that. I started scribbling things down first thing in the morning. I found that if I got out into nature and started writing, that's when the good stuff would flow. I was up early anyway. Viv tended to climb out of her cot and come into our bed at about 5 a.m. and I never really went back to sleep after that.

I just dozed in that half-dream state that Descartes spoke about. The borders between the two worlds—dream and reality, hazy. Sometimes we'd be back in the caravan traveling north toward those tall trees. Sometimes I'd be telling Andy that I knew everything, that I had read his emails. That he shouldn't be so trusting with his passwords, that he shouldn't be so trusting of me. I slipped in and out of consciousness and listened to the sounds of Andy and Viv breathing. I longed for proper, deep sleep. That's the strange thing about being so tired—sometimes you're too tired to sleep. So that's when I started just getting up. Finding some space for myself to be alone in nature. I took Mom and Dad's old kayak out from under the house and washed it down with the hose. I started slowly. But I remember that feeling of pushing the kayak onto the deep morning green of the lake. It felt like floating in the sky.

I couldn't paddle far at first—my arms got too tired, but the body is amazing. My muscles grew and soon I could see smooth shapes moving under my skin after a shower. Soon I could paddle all the way to the other side of the lake, where I would sit cross-legged on the fine white sand with my eyes closed for ten minutes every morning, the trees a cathedral above my head.

I would return and make myself a cup of tea and write my morning pages while the house slowly woke. Buckley taught me all about morning pages. Apparently if you write as soon as you get up, before you've engaged with other humans, and especially after communing with nature, your subconscious sort of bubbles up and that's where you find magic. He taught me about haikus—my favorite type of poem because it took its form from natural observations. He made me fall in love with those mornings. He made me fall in love with writing.

I had been taught reverence, that there was mystery in the world. I wasn't awed by the concept of the god that my father preached every Sunday, the Bible verses and the worship songs I'd been reared on, but I felt connected to the trees, the lake, the breeze. I didn't know why it had taken me so long to realize that words were the things that connected me to the mystery. Sometimes when poems came to me, they felt like sacred things too, as though I was touching something above and beyond what we see in front of us. And when my words touched another person, I knew it was true, because there is something we all share that's hard to articulate, but it's there. That's what my father always said.

*Reverence*
*A mirror world waits*
*Morning sun over the lake*
*Break the glass like bread*

Andy had Surf Girl, but I had Poet Boy. There was a strange symmetry in that. Maybe it was simply different parts in us that were unmet. Maybe we were changing, growing, but apart instead of closer. Or maybe it was just the sleep deprivation of parenthood. The idea that one person can meet all your emotional needs is such a naive one, but it's one our culture seems to peddle.

After I visited the shop that day for lunch, they talked about it with each other.

*Her: I'm so sorry I was really effing awkward yesterday at the shop. You and Paige seem really happy together. I feel like we should stop emailing. I know we're just friends but seeing Paige IRL I felt all this guilt. Then I started googling emotional affairs.*

*Him: Hey, you're just being a supportive friend. We can talk. I really appreciate that. And it's not like we're doing anything wrong. We're mates, right? Am I not allowed to have mates who are girls? She knows we have lunch together sometimes. I've been really open about that. Even Paige wouldn't stop me from having girls as friends. She's not controlling like that.*

*Her: Yeah, but maybe that's why she came in yesterday. I feel like she was sending me a message to stay away from you.*

*Him: Paige always gets what she wants. What about what I want?*
I wrote a haiku into the notes on my phone:

> *heart fragile as leaf*
> *a new green leaf on a bough*
> *twisted from a tree*
> *violently*

I broke the rules for that one. Poet Boy agreed the last line was crucial and that in literature, rules were made to be broken. We talked cryptically, skirting over things, like light playing on water. I told myself it wasn't the same as Andy and Surf Girl because we weren't sharing our innermost feelings. I didn't tell him, for example, that my husband was having an emotional affair. I just showed him a leaf twisted from a tree violently. And he understood.

At home, Andy and I pretended like everything was normal. It was during the day, when he was away, that we would exist in our mirror worlds. It was easy to hide from what was really happening beneath the busy surface of the routine of such a large family. I guess that's why it always seemed easier to stay at the lake house instead of moving out. Maybe if we'd actually taken out the lease on that little place by the beach, like we talked about that day that I met him for lunch, everything would have been different.

That's what you're left with in the end—all the "what ifs" and the loose threads of your life that you never followed. Decisions you never made, but in doing nothing, you made them all the same. Some would call it sifting through life's regrets, but they are unfulfilled promises in a way, paths you never took. I wonder what Descartes would have said about that.

They say it takes a village to raise a child and our village was ready-made, with Mom and Dad to help with the kids and Yas always there. In summer, Andy would barbecue outside with the lake darkening, the mosquitos circling, the slap of the screen door as kids came and went between the pantry and the trampoline. I think the smell of charred onions and citronella candles will always be the smell of home.

While Andy cooked, Yas and I would chop salads, drinking the cheap wine Dad stockpiled in the garage.

"You looked very glamorous on the clifftop today. Very wind-swept."

I elbowed her. "Shut up. I thought you hardly went on social media?"

"Occasionally, when I'm really bored, I look you up." She elbowed me back. "I do run my business from it, you know."

"Yeah but you don't seem . . ."

"What? Sucked in by it? Obsessed with it?"

I felt myself redden. "Yeah. You're not on it constantly."

Yas shrugged. "I just put up my cakes and sometimes someone will say something nice about them or whatever."

"How do you do that?"

"Do what?"

"Not care? Just have a more . . . healthy balance?"

Yas passed me a carrot dipped in homemade hummus. "Does this need more lemon juice?"

I took a bite and chewed, shook my head. She had the same ability as our mother to effortlessly make food taste delicious.

"Um, I guess because I don't put pictures of myself or the kids on there."

I felt my shoulders stiffen. She must have sensed that what she said had hit a nerve.

"I don't know. It's just not . . . it doesn't feel personal. And anyway, who's gonna say bad things about cakes, right?"

I laughed, trying to hide the discomfort I was feeling.

"How much did you get paid for that pic on the clifftop anyway? Just curious," she asked.

"Enough to make it worthwhile getting changed in the car, freezing my tits off, and to pay the photographer."

"I noticed the shots are a bit different. Andy's not doing them at all now?"

I shrugged. "He hasn't for a while. He's too busy with the shop and everything."

"Who are you using?"

"Myself when I can. My phone set on a timer. Also a few photography students from the technical school who want experience, like for that most recent one."

"Is Andy weird about that?"

"I don't really fucking care if he is."

Yas stopped chopping. "Hey, what's going on with you two? Trouble in paradise?" She thought we had the perfect relationship by virtue of Andy even being there, but she had a warped view of perfection. Her husband, Matt—she called him Matthew in the early days but then he became M, as though she couldn't even be bothered to say his full name—was fly-in, fly-out and only home once in a blue moon. Personally, I would have found that preferable at that point.

"Ask Andy."

We looked over and Andy had one of her kids on his back and was loading sausages onto the kids' plates. Her kids looked to Andy as a father figure. He liked that. He liked to be wanted, to be needed. That was my crucial mistake, I think.

I looked at Yas and her eyes had softened. Andy did that to women. He was a woman's man. Emotionally intelligent, kind. No one could hate him. I decided in that moment that I wouldn't confide in Yas. That's the thing about secrets. I wanted them for myself, twirling them around myself like a sticky net.

She raised a brow. "Are you guys not—"

"Having sex? Ha ha . . . well, more than you."

Yas put up her hand. "Well, that's not saying much. You know, there is one part of social media that I'm obsessed with—in a good way. There's a fly-in, fly-out wives' group on Facebook helping women deal with it."

"Do you really need a Facebook page?" I asked.

"It's called Wine and Orgasms."

"And people say social media's harmful."

"Honestly, those women keep me sane. It's a great, weird little community. I've never met them and yet feel like I know them, which is more than can be said of my husband."

*I know the feeling*, I thought.

CHAPTER 27

# Audrey

Paige and I spent two hot afternoons cloaked in the cool air-conditioning of the library, researching good omens and symbols, goddesses and ancient rites. The library was a soulless cement block on the edge of town, but it felt like a castle in a fairy-tale forest to me.

"Here, look . . ." Paige had an old book open in her lap. We were in our uniforms, sitting on cushions right at the back. There was no one around. It felt like we were a million miles from The Lakes. We could have been in Mesopotamia.

"The ancient Egyptians used talismans during rituals and secret occult practices. Blacksmiths would craft precious charms for people to wear on their person. Priests, shamans, and diviners carried talismans to ward off evil."

"Do you actually believe in evil, you know, the devil and all that?" I asked, and Paige looked up. "I mean, an actual deity responsible for evil?"

I'd learned in the short time of knowing Paige that she didn't shy away from controversy, from confrontation. It was actually what she sought, what she thrived on. That's the thing you learn when you're always on the outside looking in—to read people fast. You think it might keep you safe.

Paige put down the book. "I've tried believing in all of it. It's how I was raised, you know?" She shrugged. "I didn't know anything different until a few years ago when I started to . . . I don't know, ask questions, I guess. Maybe that's why I'm sitting here reading about ancient Egyptian religious practices instead of at the beach with my friends."

It felt as though she'd pushed my chest with the flat of her palm. She may as well have said, "why I'm sitting here with a freak."

She must have read my face, because she added, "I mean, my other friends. I'm trying to figure it all out, I guess."

"I don't," I said, emboldened by her innocent cruelty. "I don't think there's a devil, or a god. I think they're just the way humans have interpreted the best and worst of their natures. I think people are capable of great selfishness, evil you might call it, and I think it scares us. It's easier to disembody it . . . think of it as some half-man, half-goat with horns. God and the devil are symbols, not actual entities."

"Yeah, I know what you mean, but Dad has told me some pretty mind-blowing things. He's actually done exorcisms and stuff, and he's saved people's lives because God told him they were in danger and he went to them, stuff like that."

"Really? How has God told him?"

"He said he gets these visions. It's like a feeling about a person. They'll just jump into his mind for no reason, and he knows he has to check in with them. He's actually saved people from taking their own lives because of it."

"Do you really believe that it's God, though? Maybe it's actually his humanity. Maybe he's a really empathetic person and he's reading their expressions, their gestures, and he knows they're sad."

"Yeah, but how do you explain the timing? That he has a vision of them just when they're in crisis?"

"Maybe there's magic in the world, forces working that we don't entirely understand. Maybe it's energy."

"Energy, God . . . it's one and the same. What do you think prayer is? He also says prayer works. He's seen so many miracles because of it."

"Or again, could that be the energy of a hundred people all sending positive energy toward a person?"

Paige shrugged and I sensed she wasn't willing to question her father too much. She looked down at her book again and I knew the conversation was over.

"Here, listen. 'There are three types of talismans. Muslims, Christians, and Jews used these symbols in three ways—carried on the body, hung above a bed, or as medicinal properties infused into baths or food.' Oh my god, I have the best idea for our art piece."

"What?" My skin tingled.

"We could make our talisman out of some medicinal property, from a plant or flower."

Paige's eyes shone. She was so different in that moment from the girl I had viewed with trepidation and awe from afar only a couple of months ago, and I wondered, not for the first time, how often we ever got to see the full spectrum of a person, what they showed, what they hid, whether there was ever some essential truth to a person. Whether there was a touchstone of goodness or evil, or whether it was all an elaborate and shifting illusion.

"What kind of plant or flower?" I asked.

"Well, to continue the religious theme, what about angel's trumpets? They're a type of flower."

"What are their medicinal properties?"

"Death," she said.

The hairs on my arms stood up.

Paige laughed. "But this is art, right? It's meant to push boundaries. They look like beautiful bells, and yet they're really poisonous. We have them in our garden, white ones. Mom warned us since we were tiny never to touch them, never to eat them."

She must have seen the hesitation on my face because she kicked my foot with hers. "Am I freaking you out now, cool city girl? You're meant to be the one who's seen everything. Don't tell me you're shocked."

I shook my head. "No, it's a cool idea." I was already scanning the shelves for a dictionary of plants. I found a book and read the definition out loud.

"Angel's trumpet has been shown to cause a handful of symptoms related to changes in perception, including confusion, delirium, wandering thoughts and ideas, and auditory and visual hallucinations. They may cause sensory sensations that appear real but are not."

We picked them from her garden, licking our pinky fingers as a dare and laughing, wondering if we were hallucinating. We hung them on wire, bound them with dried reeds, decorated them with the feathers of cormorants and crakes, and the wildflowers that edged the lake. We explained to the class that we'd made dream catchers, imbued with good omens and charms and the medicinal properties of the flowers, which were traditionally used in folk medicine to treat common ailments such as asthma, sleep disturbance, and depression. We got the top mark in art.

We left out the bit about how they could also harm. We left out the hallucinations, and the death.

# CHAPTER 28

# Jane

The days were getting hotter when they should have been cooling and crisping. The cicadas remained steadfastly shrill in the still lake air. It felt like she was trapped under a glass jar that was fogging up, making it hard to see out. Trapped under her peach duvet, skin slick as she woke. Her father's windows beaded with moisture in the mornings, the outside cool clinging to the panes. She swiped a finger down the glass and it came away wet. It was as though the house were sweating. She felt mired in the same soupy stagnation. An image came into her mind—a body submerged, pale and swollen, green lake water.

*I can't leave.*

She couldn't return to Sydney. She didn't have the strength to face Jackson and his subtle manipulations, his story expectations. Besides, Easter was coming, and the staff at the paper would be picked to a skeleton. The city, her real life, the copy and coffee and deadlines, seemed strange and unreal to her now. It was as though she'd slipped back in time—the lake threw up hot light and everywhere there were reflections, refractions of the person she had tried to leave behind.

It felt like there was only one way to exorcise Janie.

Her dad left for golf early. She watched his truck drive away. She went to the local supermarket and bought trash bags, two buckets, a mop, and enough cleaning products to service a hotel. It felt good. What was the saying? *Cleanliness is next to godliness.*

She moved through the house systematically, filling trash bags with broken crockery that had been wrapped in newspaper but never discarded, plastic bags stuffed inside other plastic bags, balls of rubber bands, glass jars in every imaginable size, bags of clothing, old shoes, a pile of ancient instruction manuals for things that had already stopped working, broken umbrellas.

She pulled on rubber gloves and washed the dishes. She scrubbed the grime from the kitchen sink and the tiles, and wiped the counters of what looked like months of dried food. She vacuumed and mopped the floor that was exposed.

She opened all the windows in the living room and let the hot breeze usher through the house. She stood in front of the pile of newspapers. There was a small part of her that wondered if he would be upset—she knew that some of her articles were probably in there—but she had to be brutal. There was so much stuff, surely he wouldn't even notice. She filled black trash bags with faded newspapers that dated back to the 1980s. She opened boxes packed with electrical hardware. Power strips and cables and old telephones, each one attached to a memory. She found the white phone she used to talk to Paige on as a teenager and put it to her ear. But instead of Paige's voice, she heard another voice.

*I'm sorry, Janie. I can't stay here. It's suffocating me. He's suffocating me.*

Jane swallowed back the stale taste of dust and memories. She stuffed the phone into the trash bag. She stood and took it all out to her car, her arms aching with the effort. The bags were straining, stacked full of her father's things. They filled the trunk and the interior of the car.

*He's turned our home into a rubbish dump.*

She went back into the house and grabbed her car keys. She would drive to the dump before he got back.

*No one can be expected to live like this.*

She was starting the engine when her dad's truck pulled into the drive. She clocked his look of horror as he noticed the bags piled up in her car, and froze. She felt like a child who'd been discovered stealing money from her parent's wallet.

He got out of the truck in slow motion, as though walking underwater, like a person who'd gone into shock. *How can I do this to him?* she thought. *After everything he's been through.* His eyes looked hollow, confused.

*It's not you I'm leaving, it's him.*

He stood, his arms slack by his sides. He looked resigned, and that broke her. Her hand touched the button to lower the car window, to explain, to plead with him to understand that she was trying to help him, but her body wouldn't respond. She knew if she pressed that button, she would be carting all the bags back inside. Their eyes met and she slowly shook her head.

*You could have helped me. You could have sided with me instead of him sometimes. He has a problem, Janie. We both know it.*

He turned and walked inside the house. She didn't try to wipe away the tears.

She drove north along the lake, her chest aching. *Why am I doing this to him?* she thought. *What am I trying to achieve?*

*She made him worse when she left us.*

*She made me worse.*

*She broke something inside me.*

Jane couldn't breathe. She pulled over into the shade of a bank of she-oaks. The lake sparkled like cut glass through the trees. It felt like she was coated in shame, in dust, in dirt, in memories. The blast of the air-conditioning did nothing to ease it. She got out of the car. It was so hot. She ripped off her T-shirt. She was in a sports bra and cutoff shorts. The breeze lifted the sticky hair from the nape of her neck. It smelled like salt and mangroves. It smelled like relief.

*What are you doing, Janie? Jane. JANE. Get back in the car.*

She took off her sneakers. The sand slid between her toes. Then she was wading into the water, up to her knees, up to her thighs, and she dove. A long, cool stroke of respite. She didn't know how she had resisted its pull for so long. All those hours she had spent in this lake, swimming, playing, duck-diving, with Paige, with Yas. Whole summers spent between their favorite spots—jumping from the rope swing, and into the cool pull of the deep channel. Squinting into the prisms of light bouncing off the surface.

She dove down. Her hands touched the soft bottom and she lifted her face toward the light and opened her eyes. Dark hair tangled in her fingers, a white petal floated across her vision. She was suspended in the deep green. Something snagged around her ankle. She shook her limbs, panic building, but the sensation clung on, like seaweed and salt dried to skin. Her lungs ached, black spots appeared in her vision. A face. No, a skull picked clean of flesh. Hollow bone. She brushed at her ankle but found nothing there. She burst to the surface.

Shep's words were in her mind.

*It was around her neck. It was made of wire and . . . there were signs of a struggle.*

Jane's feet found traction and her lungs found air, but it didn't feel like enough. She was breathless as she scanned the shoreline. Water and bush and sky. Trees as far as she could see. Nature, so beautiful one moment, could turn to something frightening, something unknowable the next. She tuned in, waiting to feel that strange sensation of being watched again, but she was completely alone. Had Paige thought she was alone that morning? Why had she kept going out on the lake by herself when someone had been stalking her? It didn't make sense. Why hadn't Andy stopped her? Who had been there with her, taking that final photo so early in the morning? It must have been the man who'd been terrorizing her and then disappeared. It couldn't have been anyone else, surely. Jane shuddered, cold now, despite the sun on her shoulders.

She got out of the water. She was shivering as she walked to the car. She peeled off her wet shorts and found Paige's dress balled up under her front seat where she'd stuffed it a few days ago. The crushed silk looked like, felt like, guilt. She pulled the dress over her head. A figure was moving on the path up ahead and she got into the car, the warmth of the cabin like a hug. She was about to start the engine when she saw that the figure was Andy. A dog, her dog, the one she'd found, rushed up to the open car window. Andy waved, she cringed. She was sitting in a car full of rubbish bags wearing his late wife's dress. He would think she was psychotic. Her foot rested on the pedal. She was tempted to speed off and pretend she hadn't seen him, but she knew that would be cowardly, and she already felt like a coward for what she'd done to her dad.

She got out of the car, pushing her wet hair off her face.

"Janie, hi. Hot, isn't it? The water nice?"

Jane stood by the car. She didn't know where to put her arms, how to greet Andy. A kiss? How did you greet the mourning husband of your dead friend when you were wearing her dress? To her horror, she felt tears in her eyes. She brushed them away.

"I'm so sorry. I'm wearing Paige's dress. You probably think that is so weird and it *is* weird. It's just that it was in my car, from when Mrs. White gave it to me when we were cleaning out her stuff. And this car is full of my father's stuff . . . and I was on the way to the dump and I just . . . I don't know, I was so hot and I just jumped in the water and my shorts were wet and then the dress . . ."

Andy's face was strained. How had she been so fucking thought-less? Some of their best memories were probably tied to this dress. Maybe he'd taken her to dinner in it, and now it was stuck to her still-damp body. She watched him swallow something back, probably his own emotion, and she wished she had just driven away.

*You are a coward.*

He reached out and pulled her into a hug. The cicada drone went up a notch and the dog licked the salt from her leg. They stood there for what seemed like a long time, the strange intimacy she'd felt with this man the last time she'd seen him still there. And even though hav-ing her damp body pressed against his was probably even more inap-propriate than what she'd just admitted, it felt like everything, all the turmoil inside her stilled.

"I don't know what I'm doing either," he said so quietly into her ear that she wondered if she'd imagined it.

When they parted, she found it difficult to look at him.

"Do you want to sit down for a bit? The dog probably wants a swim here too," he said.

"You've adopted him?"

"Mrs. White fed him and so that was the end of it. He's part of the family now. He's been a good distraction for the kids. For Viv."

Jane thought of that plaintive little voice calling for a momma who would never come again. She scratched the dog's soft ears.

Andy led them to a place where a paperbark tree had fallen into the shallows. The roots were exposed but the tree was not entirely dead. Jane wondered if it was being kept alive by the mangroves and mud crabs, the rich ecosystem of the lake. She tried not to think of what that same system did to a dead body.

They sat on the trunk, dangling their legs in the warm shallows. Andy bent down and scooped water into his palm, wet the back of his neck. Jane felt a confusing mixture of emotions run through her watching the droplets roll down his skin.

As though reading her thoughts, he said, "Grief makes us do funny things, hey."

She didn't trust herself to even speak right now. She picked at the soft flesh of the bark with her fingernail. She watched a column of ants cross the tree's pale trunk. This place was peeling her back. She didn't even know what was underneath. Or maybe she did, and that was the problem.

"Paige's body hasn't been released for burial yet, so we're planning on having a memorial service, the day after tomorrow, at the tree cathedral at dawn," he said.

She waited a beat to see if he would say more, but he didn't. God, maybe he didn't know about the police's suspicions. She couldn't be the one to tell him. And Jackson . . . he would want her to cover this memorial. *You said you'd cover it.*

She wanted to put her head in her hands but instead she nodded. "Let me know if I can help in any way."

"Mrs. W said you might like to say something. A eulogy. Seeing as you're Paige's oldest friend."

The smell of soft crab carcasses, sunbaked reeds, rotting leaf litter rose around her. "Oh, I . . . um." It felt like her professional and personal lives were colliding, like the opposing forces of a riptide, pulling her too far out.

"Mrs. W mentioned you lived with them for a while, when you were younger. I didn't realize."

His words echoed over the still water. She squinted into the white-hot glare coming off the surface. The reason that house felt so familiar to her, sitting eating breakfast at that table, so natural. "My mother left."

*Why are you telling him this?*

"Left?"

"She left us." Jane swallowed, trying to stem the words coming out of her mouth, but it was like something had released inside her now that she'd entered the lake, swum beneath its surface. "That's why my car is full of trash bags. I'm trying . . . I'm trying to . . . to help my dad."

Andy looked down into the water and she realized she wasn't making any sense.

Jane continued. "She left because he has a hoarding problem. His house is . . . it's got a lot worse since she left, obviously."

"So, she left you with the problem."

Jane laughed through her nose. "It took me a long time to see it like that. I thought she was ashamed of me too. She said she'd come back for me, but she didn't."

"That's when you moved in with the Whites?"

"It was so long ago. I can't really remember exactly what happened, but I think I used to sleep over there a lot and there was a period where I was . . . there all the time. I was embarrassed by my dad, I guess. That he'd caused my mom to leave us."

"Do you have a relationship with her now?"

Jane bit her thumb. "No, not really. I mean, she's in Sydney, and she's very keen to catch up these days, now that I'm a journalist and have my own life and a very clean and minimalist apartment."

"She sounds—

"Superficial? Flaky? Selfish? Narcissistic?"

"I was going to say 'like she's making an effort now.'"

"No, she's always got an ulterior motive. Sorry, I've made this about me when we were talking about a eulogy for Paige. I'm so sorry, I'm behaving exactly like my mother."

"Hey, it's okay." He reached for her, and their fingers touched on the tree branch. The intimacy of it made everything still. But it seemed to be the same brand of comfort as their hug. She told herself that's all it was. They were both stripped raw by grief, by shock.

He drew his hand away and rubbed at his jaw. "Well, I was raised by parents who campaign for drugs to be legalized, and smoke and sell weed for a living up the coast, so your mom and dad sound pretty normal and conventional by comparison."

"Wow, how was that growing up?"

"Let's just say that I became the parent pretty young. They were always telling me to chill. I spent a lot of time at the beach, in the surf. But I wanted to do more than do drugs and sit around pretending to be an artist. I taught myself photography, and as soon as I could, I left. I spent years traveling around the country, living by the beach, picking up work where I could, taking pictures. I was heading south to Sydney when I met Paige here."

"Your wedding was beautiful."

He looked out onto the water. His eyes were slits. She couldn't read the expression on his face.

"So, you were heading to your parents' place after Paige died?"

He pulled one of his legs up, rested an arm on his knee. "Yeah. I reckon in times of shock we crave home, no matter what kind of home it is . . . or was."

"Yeah, like I never thought I'd come back here."

"I've always felt, I don't know, at home here. I think that's why I was attracted to the Whites. I know they've been acting a bit weird these last few days, but I guess that's understandable given the circumstances, and deep down they're so normal. So stable and nice. It's something I never had. Paige took it for granted, you know? Her loving, caring, secure family. I think I married her family as much as I married her."

It was a strange admission, but it was a day for strange admissions. Andy threw a stick and the dog bounded out into the lake, ripples reaching the shoreline.

"The Whites seem to attract strays," Jane said, and she suspected they both knew she wasn't just talking about the dog.

# CHAPTER 29

# Paige

There's a filter you can use, and it's called Goddess. It makes you so beautiful. It makes your skin as smooth and bright as morning sand. You can do this for any part of your body. You can use technology to pretend you're perfect. You can start to believe that this illusion is real.

I don't know what made me so obsessed with beauty. Now, being stuck in a place of endless light, of ceaseless beauty, it feels claustrophobic. What I'd do to be able to escape this tiny, bright caravan. I'd open the door and breathe sweet, cool air. I'd rip down the makeshift movie screen, the sheet strung between the trees outside. I'd make the images of other people's lives going on and on stop. Or, what I'd give to be able to pull down shutters, for everything to darken for just a few hours, so that I could rest. So that I could lose consciousness for a while. For this strange illusion to stop.

But I know I have to stay awake. And I can't take down the movie screen. Because I'm waiting for the next picture of her to appear. Image after image of beauty. Were they people I followed? Is that what I'm seeing? I don't know anymore. It's all a blur. All I'm looking for is my Viv. Everything has narrowed down to this. This and the memories, all the memories except the memory of how I got here.

It feels like days, months, since I saw a new picture of her. How long have I been here in this place? Am I going to have to wait and watch my little girl grow up this way? In single perfect images coming through haphazardly over time infinite? And then when they finally arrive in the feed, they're images that don't reflect any of her real life. Our real life. Her bossy face when she fed the ducks and they squabbled over the scraps, the way her laughter bubbled up from her belly, the tantrums and the tears and then the hugs that followed. None of those things, the real things, are here in this half-world. Just occasional empty pictures of her smiling face. Are they even real, these pictures? Or is it all just my subconscious? A strange dream played out in front of me. I am in a construct of my own making, I realize that. This is the irony set out for me, to sit within and contemplate ad infinitum. This is the way I chose to live my life. And here, I am also consumed by it.

That, and the perpetual worry. I'm a mom who does not know where her child is. I always knew where Viv was. My subconscious knew, even if my rational mind was otherwise occupied. Napping in her cot, behind me on the play mat. In the next room with her cousins. Outside on the trampoline, with Mom in the garden watching on, with Andy at the shops. At daycare. With her grandparents, with Yas. I always, always knew exactly where she was from the moment she was placed beside me in the Perspex bassinet at the hospital. An invisible chain linked us (and oh how I resented it sometimes over the years) but now that it's broken, I'm broken. Now I don't know. This is my hell.

What's happened to her? Where is she right now? Is someone

holding her hand? Giving her the oat biscuits she loved as a treat? Cutting her grapes in half? Washing her face with the washer in a way that avoids getting soap in her eyes? Watching her around water? I always thought when I died she'd be a woman, able to look after herself. Or that I wouldn't worry about those I left behind because my consciousness would be gone. I was wrong.

I was wrong about so many things. I was wrong about beauty. I used to spend a long time getting my hair and makeup just right. I learned from makeup tutorials how to contour my face to hollow the cheekbones. How to do a perfect winged eyeliner. I would rim my eyes in white pencil for the illusion of illumination from within. I dyed my hair and eyelashes black every month to keep that fresh blue tint that offset my skin. Then there was more to be done. I would spend hours getting the right camera angle, chin down, gaze fixed but soft. I'd read once that Marilyn Monroe looked down the lens of the camera and imagined seducing a lover. I would go through hundreds of photographs that the photography students would send me until I found just the right one. Another thing I had learned—take endless photos. Take and take and take and take and then there would be one or two gems. That kind of feels like a metaphor for life now. I guess I was vain. Vanity, vainglory, is one of the deadly sins. I guess I enjoyed the seduction. I enjoyed the power. But it was also more than that. It felt like a kind of protection. I thought my beauty was my protection.

My protection instincts kicked in with Andy's girl. That's what I tell myself, anyway. And it's not what you think. I drew her close. I wasn't above subterfuge.

I started going into the surf shop a few times a week for lunch with Andy. I'd purposely leave my face natural, pull my hair back. I'd wear a T-shirt and loose pants with sandals. She was wary of me at first. I'd been a bitch that first time with the bikini. But I'd ask her if she wanted me to bring her back a juice or a coffee. She'd always say no with scared eyes, even though I tried to make my voice, my face, friendly. Eventually she said "yes" and then we'd chat for a while about something inane, like the weather, or I'd ask to see what kind of shorts they were selling. Or flip-flops. Clothing items I knew she'd wear.

Then one day I invited her to come and have her lunch break with me and Andy. She looked around, as though I was asking someone else.

"Oh . . . I wouldn't want to . . . intrude."

Part of me wanted to laugh right to her face. *You don't want to intrude on our lunch and yet you're happy to email my husband every second night.*

"You won't be intruding," I said. I didn't give her the chance to say no. I hooked my arm through hers and pulled her out to the cafe.

I picked up the menu. "What's your favorite here? You must've tried everything."

"Um, the burgers are pretty nice."

I hadn't eaten a burger since I had morning sickness with Viv and that sort of food was the only thing I craved or could stomach. "Yum. Okay, I'll get the haloumi one."

Andy came over and hovered awkwardly, like a waiter. I had to check myself from calling her Surf Girl. "Tam is joining us for lunch."

He looked confused. Poor Andy. Sometimes I think men only understand such a small part of the way women communicate. Even the emotionally intelligent ones like Andy. They see the surface layer. The pretty reflection, the thin, shiny veneer smeared on skin. They can't see the murky depths, the hidden flaws. They can't read the other, more subtle cues. The way we can deliver slights with silence. The way we can punish with what we withhold. The way we can make other women uncomfortable with a single word, a look. It's learned very early. It's a kind of social survival mechanism.

"Oh, all good, I'll just grab a coffee," he said, nodding toward the takeout counter.

I stood and took his hand, pulled him down into the chair between us. I think this quality is the thing—not my beauty—that made me successful in life. I'm stubborn. I have a will to survive. I was not going to lose Andy to this girl.

"Andy loves burgers, don't you, babe? Let's get him the beef. Or do you want lamb? Tam, what would you recommend for him?"

I used her name a lot. She flushed a deep shade of pink. "Oh, they're all good. They come with fries."

I wanted to laugh darkly. God, she was so ordinary. *Is that really what you want, Andy?* I thought. A burger-with-fries kind of girl?

Instead, I smiled. "I guess you guys need lots of carbs after surfing. How's the surf at the moment anyway?"

Tam's and Andy's eyes met. This was the essence of their connection, after all.

"Yeah, pretty decent," Andy said. He wasn't going to give me anything. Maybe he knew me well enough to get an inkling of what I was doing.

Tam stood. "So, haloumi and the beef?"

Andy nodded, his expression resigned.

"I'll go order at the counter. Can't be away from the shop too long."

I noticed she didn't say "we." "What are you getting, Tam?" I asked.

My eyes were urging her to say it. *Beef.* I knew that was what she actually wanted. But instead she said "haloumi" and I knew I had achieved what I needed—for her to align herself with me rather than him. I watched her walk away.

Andy was looking at his hands clasped together in front of him.

"What are you doing, Paige?" He didn't look at me.

I wrestled with a knot of emotion that had formed in my chest. *What am I doing? What am I fucking doing? You have the audacity to ask me that? I'm trying to save our marriage. I'm trying to make you and this woman realize that what you're doing is wrong. That I am a person. That for all my faults, I don't deserve to lose the man I love in this banal, halfhearted way.*

But I didn't say any of it. I looked him in the eyes and said, "I'm having a burger, Andy."

When he didn't respond, I went on. "Do you remember how much I craved them when I was pregnant with Viv? You drove god knows where . . . the McDonald's up the highway in the middle of the night to get me one."

It was me trying to pull him back onto common ground. Our daughter. This was the man who had sat behind my shoulders as she came out of my body. Who had mopped up the blood with a towel. Who had looked at his daughter with an expression that I'd never seen on another human's face before.

I guess that's the thing. People are complex. They can be two things at once. They can harm and they can heal. And maybe we're all capable of both.

# CHAPTER 30

The water felt like it was cracking through me—like a shard of ice against teeth. Like a glacier forging through rock. Cold. But it shifted a part of me that had been frozen, bound. Everything left me in that moment of submersion. All the pain, all the darkness. My tight-spun thoughts loosened. It was like a baptism. It was, I know now, awe. I could have swum in the middle of the day when the lake warmed like a bath, tiny fish wallowing in its shallows, the soft tickle of reeds around my shins. When everything went silent under an insistent sun. But instead, I chose the morning, the glancing cold, the rousing of the day when everything felt reborn. I felt the pull of a new dawn. I had never been a big swimmer. But those days in the cabin I was not like myself. The habits I'd lived with for most of my life seemed to drop away.

Maybe everyone reinvents themselves at least once in life—leaves their past behind and allows themselves to start again. Or, at the very least, maybe everyone has experienced a point in their life when they've wanted to. But how many actually do? How many take a flight to another country where no one knows their name? Leave their job and find a quiet cabin by a lake and go there to simply exist? Or perhaps it's just really lonely, broken people who feel the need to reinvent themselves.

But maybe we are all reinventing ourselves all the time. What is the self after all but a construct of the stories we tell others, the stories we tell our own minds. I've always thought a singular sense of self to be naive. I think one person can be capable of being and doing many different things. I think we can even surprise ourselves.

That's how it felt when I found myself so deep in the lake that I couldn't touch the bottom. I imagined eels squirming below my beating feet and panic knotted my muscles, but I screwed my eyes shut and kicked out farther. Then the numb relief came. My trajectory through the liquid resistance became smoother each day. I could feel the weight of the past lifting off me. It felt strangely effortless, as though nature were whittling my body and my mind at the same time.

I didn't see her in her kayak every morning. Maybe she wasn't there every morning, or maybe our paths didn't always cross. I had never been one to rely on clocks. Or maybe I had in the real world, but on the lake, time was measured by the slow slide of tides and the shadows moving from one end of the veranda to the other. My iPhone was rarely charged. The birds woke me. A skein of wild geese. The crickets and frogs lulled me to sleep. If I make it sound idyllic that's because it was. Or maybe I'd decided that was the story I would tell myself.

I'm not sure if she saw me swimming. I felt like a stealth shape. And no one comes out onto a large, empty body of water in the very early morning to interact with other humans. It felt like a sacred time, the shroud of mist, the sun crouched low in prayer. The wind whispering through the leaves. Awe warding off all evil, keeping the world safe.

# CHAPTER 31

# Audrey

I f Janie was jealous of Paige and me and our talismans, she didn't
show it. She and I still spent our Sundays at the caravan, tearing
through the bodice-rippers and drinking tea. Sunday was "family
time" at the White household, where I would imagine them playing
board games and eating roast lamb with rosemary and then Pastor
White leading church on the lake. It meant there was no friendship
competition on Sundays.

Paige was still inviting me back to her house after school, though,
where Mrs. White would bake us cookies like something out of an
American sitcom, and then Paige and I would sneak off into the bush
to talk about stuff that scared us and smoke and drink tiny sips of Pastor White's sherry out of a school drink bottle. Paige would tell her
mom we were going fishing, and she'd halfheartedly put a piece of
bread on a hook and chuck it into the water.

Once, when we were feeling a little tipsy, the line went taut in

Paige's hands and we both jumped up, our cool, alcohol- and cigarette-fueled indifference abandoned. We jumped up and down in anticipation as we reeled in the line, but by the time it was spooled around our ankles the fish was gone.

It felt like I was leading two lives. I was greedy. I didn't want to tell Paige about the caravan because it felt like it was Janie and my dollhouse dream, our sacred place, and I didn't want to tell Janie about my afternoons at the Whites' because there was a daring, a kind of intrigue with darkness that Paige and I shared, something that Janie didn't have.

But Paige had a knack for not being left out of secrets. She asked me once what I thought of Janie's place, with its heaving piles of stuff lining the walls, and I accidentally said we didn't hang there much. She already knew we didn't go back to my tiny room behind the gas station because I'd told her I didn't like it there and that I'd rather go to her house after school. Maybe she knew by the way I tried to change the topic, by the nervous flutter of my hands.

She must have, because she followed us one Sunday morning.

She knocked on the little lace-curtained window and Janie and I nearly had a heart attack. No one ever went there. We peeked out and then let her in, exchanging wary glances. It felt like we'd been found out.

Paige played it cool, naturally.

"Ohh, what do we have here?" She stepped inside, taking up all the air, all the space. Her eyes widened as she ran her fingertips along the table, clocking our tea party for two, our novels lying down, spines splayed.

I told her Janie and my made-up story about Ed and Daisy, the old lovers we believed had died here (I embellished that bit to appeal to her sense of the macabre). It caused a tiny ripple in her lips, and I could tell she was a little creeped-out, and satisfaction curled through me like smoke from her cigarettes. She didn't say anything for a long time, just touched the surfaces as though stroking a pet. I could tell she was stung that we'd had this without her. That we'd hidden it from her. That it had been mine and Janie's.

Maybe that's why she decided to say what she said.

I made tea but Paige didn't want any. She took out a pack of cigarettes and found a teacup to use as an ashtray. That was the thing about Paige, there was something about her that made you want to make her happy. That afternoon we lay on the lumpy mattress head to foot chain-smoking, tapping the ashes into the teacup resting on Paige's stomach, reading out the saucy bits from the novels.

"'He caressed her creamy thighs until her lips parted.' Which lips are we talking about here?" asked Paige, and we all giggled. "Hey, speaking of inappropriate things . . ."

Paige closed the book and rolled onto her stomach. Her mascara had smudged under her eyes, and I noted that I should smudge mine like that too. "I heard my parents talking about the early Christmas party at the pub last weekend. They didn't know I was listening. Apparently all anyone was talking about was your mom." She pointed at Janie. "And your dad." She pointed at me.

The way she pointed her blue-varnished fingernail at us made it feel like we were in trouble.

"Apparently, they danced together at the end of the night, and it was like something out of *Dirty Dancing*. Or . . ." She flipped to the cover of her book. *"The White Knight's Jousting Stick."*

"That's not really what it's called," I said, laughing, trying to make light of what she'd just said, slapping the book away. But inside I was churning. I glanced at the title. *Illicit Affairs.*

Janie and I shared a look. Her eyes were huge. I wished it was just the two of us right then, how it used to be. I regretted drawing Paige close, wished I'd invited Janie back to the Whites' house all those times after school to fish and smoke in the bush.

"What do you mean? *My* mom?" asked Janie. She looked about twelve. I wanted to hug her.

Janie's mother was almost never home. I'd only met her a few times when we'd gone to Janie's place after school. She was always working late at the real estate agency. She had this sort of wispy Marilyn Monroe hair and painted lips. She was beautiful in that heartbreakingly flimsy kind of way. There was something vulnerable about her. It was probably what made her able to sell houses.

Paige smiled like a little cat who's just been fed. The rumors were, Paige explained, as she took her time to paint the picture for us, that it had been a 102-degree day and things had gotten a little wild in the pub's courtyard. The heat hung on like a distant uncle's unwelcome hug, she said, snickering, and someone had made a fruit punch that no one realized was full of booze. And the food was late coming out and the DJ was playing love songs. And the "couple"—she made air quotes with her fingers—in the corner had been chatting all night, probably on account of their daughters being friends, and then that last dance, well . . . Paige fanned herself with a book.

Janie and I looked at each other and laughed nervously.

While most of me didn't believe Paige, another part of me was trying to work out if Janie's mom and my dad had ever actually met before. Had Janie's mom bought gas when my dad was there and chatted by the hot pies or the toilet paper rolls? I hoped to god he didn't have grease on his face like a massive cliché, or wasn't wearing one of his lame seventies rock T-shirts that I knew my mom found attractive in that weird way children don't want to know about. Maybe they passed each other in the strip of shops where the agency she worked at was located. It seemed ironic that that's where Janie's parents had met. She told me that back in the day, her mom was on reception and her dad was a real estate agent. Funny, I couldn't imagine him in a suit. Her mom worked her way up to the position of being an agent herself, and her dad hurt his back and went on some sort of compensation and retreated into himself, into his house. I guess people change.

I wished Paige wasn't there lying between us chugging out smoke. We'd be able to breathe, to talk properly. I wanted to tell Janie that there'd been voices—raised and hushed, raised and hushed—all week, followed by silences so thick I could part the air with my fingertips, like a curtain. That Mom had been going on long walks and not coming home for ages. That when I'd confronted her, she'd said she and Dad were just having a disagreement over something with the business, but not to worry. Whenever a parent tells you not to worry, that's when you know you actually should.

Janie might have told me there was another rumor—that Tim Hartwood had told her he'd seen her mom "canoodling" with someone who wasn't her dad on the path to the beach.

I thought Paige just said it to wound us, to separate us. Maybe she was just saying what everyone else was thinking. It felt like we were the last to know, though of course, we couldn't have been. We just lay there under the blanket of smoke that I was sure Daisy wouldn't have approved of, and it felt like slow suffocation. Perhaps if we'd been able to talk properly there wouldn't have been as much blame. Now that Paige was here, it was as though our bond had been, not broken, but diluted. That's the thing about threes. There is always someone, if only ever so slightly, ever so minutely, on the outer. At that moment I felt the shift, and it was me.

Power shifts so subtly between humans. We use it to hurt, to heal, to get what we want, even if we're not aware consciously that we're doing it. Or maybe we are.

# CHAPTER 32

# Paige

An image of a cup of coffee scrolls past the window outside. It's creamy, with a flower pattern in the milk. The cup and saucer are aqua. I remember how crema used to taste. It reminds me of the little things we used to do—text each other a picture of a really good coffee. Or share something weird or funny Viv had done. Or send a link to a new show we could watch together. He hated my reality TV, I disliked his bushman documentaries. We both liked true crime. Or sometimes we'd just send heart emojis, stuff like that, for no reason at all. I tried to reinstate these little things because I couldn't pinpoint exactly when they'd fallen away. But I could feel him pulling away from me, shutting down, and when someone closes off to you emotionally, it's very hard to get through to them to fix it. I tried.

But it's so hard to send a heart emoji to someone when there's an unspoken gulf between you. There are only so many hearts you can send out into the world unanswered before the lack of answer becomes the response.

Maybe that's all love is—these tiny intimacies, the fragile everyday threads that bind us together. Now that I'm not in the physical world anymore, I've realized that life was simply each small everyday thing strung together—the sound of bird call out your window; the smell of freshly ground coffee; the relief of hot tears on your cheeks; the warmth of sun on your skin in winter; the taste of ripe fruit; hugs from your daughter fresh from a bath; waking up feeling better after illness; a conversation with a friend; the first sip of a cold glass of wine; a summer thunderstorm; eating a meal at the table with your family. I don't miss the likes or the adoring comments from strangers. These are not the things I miss. I don't know why when I was alive the small things weren't enough to make me happy.

Maybe I shouldn't have been so passive with Andy. Maybe I should have pulled him up on his "friendship" with Tam, but I knew after that first fight that he would just accuse me of being jealous and it would go around and around in circles, with him getting more and more defensive and angry, and me getting more and more distressed and accusatory. It felt like a kind of gaslighting that was so exhausting I couldn't even go there. If I'd said I'd been reading his emails, I would be the untrustworthy one because the truth was they *were* just friends. And I honestly did believe that he hadn't slept with her. So why did it feel so hurtful? Why couldn't we fix it?

Andy's withdrawal sent me further down the online rabbit hole. I started posting every day instead of every second day, so the algorithm began to favor me. I got bumped up in people's feeds. I got more likes. More comments. It seems to be the rule of life: the more you have, the more you get, whether it be wealth or adoration. More sponsors contacted me and sent me their products. I used Mom's walk-in wardrobe to store all the beauty products, the clothes. All I had to do was pick and choose what to feature—items that resonated with my "brand," my "aesthetic." No one ever seemed to want anything back.

When you're not getting love or affirmation in the real world, but it's abundant in your online world, that's where your energy is drawn. Buckley wrote me beautiful things but there were others too, real connections. The good thing about social media is that sometimes it does actually connect you in an authentic way. I found a girl, Jess, who lived forty minutes south, who had trained herself to be a makeup artist purely by following YouTube tutorials. She made her own videos, and they were good. She was really talented. I sent her a message saying I liked her work and she offered to do my makeup. She kind of became my assistant. I never thought I'd be someone who had an assistant, but she blow-dried my hair, applied blush in feathery strokes, and talked about her cats while I answered emails from sponsors and uploaded content. I paid her in product. But it was a weird thing. I remember the very first time she saw the table full of shiny pots of lip gloss, rainbow palettes of eyeshadow and a whole desert of foundation shades. Her eyes lit up and she squealed and pressed her hands to her face in disbelief. She was so grateful. I remembered feeling the same way the first few times these gifts arrived on my doorstep. But somewhere along the line, it was as though the gifts started to lose their meaning, their specialness. Maybe because there was just so much of it. I saw how Jess started taking it for granted, and realized that had happened to me too.

I was able to streamline my creative process by outsourcing, and it made me feel powerful, successful, that I could employ other creatives, that I was a business owner as well as a wife and mother. The photography students weren't always amazing, but I liked giving them a start and they were happy with a small fee and a tag on the post.

Mom would often make them lunch and listen to their life story. And if Yas was baking, she'd send them home with cake.

One or two really had a good eye for landscape. That had been Andy's aesthetic from the start; it felt "on brand"—I said that phrase without irony and I was unflinchingly faithful to it. I always took photographs outside with a natural element. Viv and me in matching white dresses, her tiny rubber boots, hand in mine, collecting fresh eggs from our chickens. The two of us dots in the distance on the beach at dusk; gathering wildflowers in baskets in the forest; a simple picnic of fruit, cheese and bread on a gingham rug. And if we were ever inside, there would be flowers or greenery in the distance. I guess the nature made me feel like it was all of a grander design than just photos of me. But maybe that was one of my mistakes.

Jess and the others wanted the exposure and the tag on my post, but they were also doing it for love. I really believe that I was successful because at the start I loved making beautiful things and sharing them with people. There was a purity to it. It was undiluted. I can't pinpoint exactly when this changed.

It began to consume me in a way it hadn't quite before. I had a perfectionist streak, and it felt under scrutiny so I needed every single picture to be perfect. I needed to look tiny, tinier than before. I needed all the photos in my grid to be color-coordinated. I opened my content to all the platforms. I began to make video content with filters. I went to sleep thinking about all the influencers who had bigger followings than me, and wondered how they'd managed it when I was working from early morning to late in the evening. The last thing I'd do every night was to scroll my feed and feel needles of disappointment prick my skin. The funny thing is that I knew rationally I should be grateful for everything I had, proud of everything I'd created, but somehow it never seemed to be enough. All the algorithm showed me was what I didn't have, what I hadn't achieved yet.

It consumed me in a way that seemed inevitable in the end. I say that Buckley was my emotional affair, my crutch when Andy pulled away, but he was nothing compared to my relationship with the grid. I think that's why when everything changed, I took it harder than I might have otherwise, because that world had become more real to me than my real world.

# CHAPTER 33

# Jane

They sat on the paperbark log in the lake until the water turned pewter, the sky turned velvet, and the dog fell asleep.

Jane wasn't sure how they'd talked for so many hours. She'd shared snippets of memories about growing up with Paige, and her life in Sydney, her job, and he'd told her about his love of surfing and photography, how he wanted more than working in a surf shop.

They didn't talk much about Paige's death. He didn't probe into her mother leaving. It was as if they both sensed that these were pressure points, bruises that didn't need to be pressed when life already felt tender. It was easy between them. The water around their ankles was as tepid as bathwater. It made Jane realize she'd become used to always having an agenda with people, with Jackson. It all felt like work. This felt different.

The wind had picked up over the water, the sun had lost its sting and sunk. Her body was stiff when she stood up. They laughed that they felt old. The dog roused. They walked the darkening track back to her car, through the long shadows of the trees. The cicadas droned on, but softer now.

"You didn't make it to the dump," said Andy as they reached her car.

"It was a fool's errand, really."

"What are you going to do?"

She touched her fingers to the window, to the black plastic bags squashed against it. It felt impossible to get rid of all this stuff and impossible to return it. She felt suspended, at a loss.

"Come back to the Whites' tonight. There's always room. We'll walk back and you can leave the car. You can decide what to do tomorrow."

Jane felt relief flood her. She wanted so much to follow Andy and his calming, centering presence. To be absolved of responsibility for her dad. But she couldn't just leave her father not knowing where she was. She thought about all the times she'd punished him in exactly this way after her mom had left.

But she couldn't go back there either to that stifling, sinking house.

"Thanks," she said simply, and Andy nodded. She took her phone out of her bag.

*I'm sorry about your stuff. I'm just trying to help in the only way I know how. Staying at a friend's tonight. Be home tomorrow.*

She didn't expect a reply. He checked his phone haphazardly, but he'd check it when she didn't arrive home and now at least he wouldn't worry. She slipped her phone into her bag and slung it over her shoulder. Maybe that's what had made the day so peaceful too—she couldn't think of the last time she'd spent a whole afternoon immersed in nature, not checking her phone, her feeds, the news.

They followed the path around the lake. A gibbous moon was rising. Jane wasn't sure what she was doing, what it meant, but she surrendered to the moment. Birds calling over the water, the soft lap of the tideline, the steady rhythm of her own breath. The Whites' home was lit up against the dark trees. There was soft music playing and the smell of burning wood coming from the fire pit. A voice carried over the lake.

"Are they having a party or something?" Jane asked.

"I don't think so."

As they got closer, she saw there were about ten people gathered around the fire and that Pastor White was standing before them, talking, his arms outstretched. Men and women sat on logs, their faces upturned in the firelight.

"It looks like Mr. W's back," said Andy.

"What are they doing?" Jane asked, watching Pastor White bow and raise his head, the congregation mimicking. The effect was like a slow, unified nodding. A single voice in song cut through the darkness.

"Looks like weeknight worship."

She couldn't remember this from her childhood. Jane rubbed at her bare arms. They were just praying and singing, she told herself. But there was something unsettling about it. She could almost feel Jackson peering over her shoulder, urging her to take a photo of this strange ritual. If he knew what an "in" she had with Paige's family . . . Her words to him over the phone came back to her. *I'll do whatever you need.*

"Come on, let's go around the back of the house," said Andy.

They slipped in the open door and found the kids watching TV in the lounge, their hair damp from baths, in their pjs. Jane felt a familiar pang of something between gratitude and envy, and she realized what Andy had meant about choosing Paige's family as well as Paige. *Perhaps I did that too,* she thought. She chastised herself for even thinking about taking a photo earlier, of betraying them when they had opened their home to her yet again.

Viv saw her dad and ran to him. He picked her up and kissed her hair. Mrs. White came into the lounge, greeting them both warmly.

"Thanks for looking after Viv all day. I had a longer walk around the lake than expected."

Mrs. White squeezed Andy's arm. "Nature is food for the soul. Speaking of food, isn't it wonderful—Pastor's back and he's brought some new people into the fold. They're from the outreach center. We'll do a light supper afterwards. I've made some food . . . I hope it's enough."

"What does Pastor White do at the outreach center?" Jane asked.

"It's an extension of our tree cathedral, our calling to look after the disadvantaged, the lost. Stephen is their shepherd, guiding them toward the light."

Jane wasn't sure how to respond. "That's very kind," she said.

Mrs. White made a dismissive gesture with her hand. "Oh, it's what we do. I love having people in the house and you're more than welcome, Janie, you know that. Paige's bed is . . ."

*Empty*, Jane thought.

Mrs. White shook her head.

"The trundle is still under Paigie's bed if you need it."

Jane felt tears gather behind her eyes. This woman might have her head in the clouds, talking about shepherds and healing light, but her heart had always been in the right place. "Thank you."

"Maybe you two could do story time and put these kids to bed. Yas is taking a bath after bathing all the children. She's been baking all day."

Andy switched off the TV and the kids moaned collectively, but Yas's kids raced upstairs and brought back their favorite books. Andy read *The Tiger Who Came to Tea* and *We're Going on a Bear Hunt* with voices and gestures and the kids were soon jumping on the couch asking him to read the books again. He rolled his eyes at Jane but did as he was told, and she thought, *No, this is not a man who could have harmed his wife.*

On the second reading, Viv climbed into her lap and rested her head against Jane's chest, then looked up with big blue eyes.

"Momma?"

Her body jolted at the words. "Oh no, honey . . . you'll always have a mommy. You know yours loved you very much."

"No momma."

Jane closed her eyes for a beat. Her throat ached. She looked at Andy but he was involved in telling the story, Yas's kids hanging off him. Jane felt the enormous responsibility of her response weigh on her.

"She didn't leave you on purpose, sweetheart. I knew your mommy since she was a little girl and she loved you and your dad more than anything."

"Momma sad."

The hairs on the back of Jane's neck stood up. "What do you mean, honey?"

"Momma sad at Dadda."

Jane shuddered and her grip tightened on Viv. She adjusted the little girl so she could look into her eyes, her voice a whisper. "Was Mommy upset with Daddy?"

Viv looked into her lap. "Dadda no feed duckies."

Jane's shoulders dropped. Kids said random things. Maybe Andy and Paige fought sometimes. It wouldn't have been unusual, most couples did. And little kids saw everything as more dramatic than it was, didn't they? She knew she probably shouldn't read too much into anything Viv was saying, she was so little, her language skills were limited, and she was traumatized. But Jane couldn't shake the discomfort that had snuck inside her.

Andy was suddenly next to them. "Come on, Vivi, it's time for bed." He nudged Jane. "We can have some wine on the veranda after I've put her to bed."

Jane spoke too brightly. "Okay, sure, sounds nice."

As she watched Andy take the kids upstairs to bed, she couldn't help the thought that had slipped into her mind: *Has anyone asked the two-year-old what happened the day Paige died?*

"Janie, would you mind helping me?" Mrs. White was standing at the door with oven mitts on her hands.

Jane got to her feet. "Oh, sure."

The kitchen smelled like sponge cake and frying onions.

"I've made a big casserole and we have Yas's leftovers from her baking for dessert. Can you help me take the food out to the outside table, please?"

Jane picked up a stack of plates and followed Mrs. White outside.

The worship by the fire pit had concluded and people were mingling. They were a mixed bunch. Some seemed like they might have been homeless or sleeping rough. Pastor White ushered a man with threadbare clothing toward the table of food. A middle-aged woman embraced Pastor White. Another approached him and he placed his hand on both of their heads and they kneeled before him. Were they *weeping*? This was a new level of religious fervor. Or was it?

A memory came to Jane of another gathering by the lake. Was it here or at the tree cathedral? How old were they? Just children. There had been a fire just like tonight. The feeling from that night was what lingered. The dark water, flickering firelight. There was a man who had frightened her and Paige and Yas. Speaking nonsense, raging. Pastor White had calmed him, saying words Jane hadn't understood, and taken him out into the water. They had all gathered around in the shallows, their faces shadowed, the only light coming from the fire, Pastor White easing the man's writhing body into the water.

Jane felt a chill move through her. Had these gatherings at the house been taken into account by investigators when considering potential suspects? Did anyone know who these people actually were? But she looked around and everyone seemed like they were having a good time. Mrs. White called her over and Jane stood behind a table piling food onto people's plates. They were all so grateful and friendly. Andy came out after a while and poured drinks. It felt surprisingly good to be helping people in this simple way, even though she was confused about exactly what it was they were doing.

Pastor White saw her and drew her into a hug and he was just Mr. White again, Paige's dad. Jane felt tears building behind her eyes, thinking of how she should be with her own dad, not someone else's. She did feel so welcome in this house. As with Viv's strange comment, she was probably reading into things—having her skeptical journalist hat on, rather than the empathetic one the Whites seemed to wear so easily.

"That felt a bit like *The Tiger Who Came to Tea*," said Andy as they stood beside the table picked clean of food.

"You made a very good tiger drinking all Daddy's beer."

"I do my best." Andy looked sheepish and Jane laughed.

"I can see you take story time very seriously."

"Paige used to tell me I should make a YouTube channel. Do all the voices. You know, like that guy all the moms love."

"Oh yeah, I think I know who you mean. Children's entertainer turned sex symbol. Yeah, I can see it."

Andy laughed and she wondered if his cheeks had warmed as much as hers. "Well, Paige was always wanting to put everything online for the world to see."

Was she imagining the thin strand of resentment in his voice?

Andy went into the house and returned with two glasses of red wine. "Come on, let's get out of here."

She hesitated, only for a second, her gut doing strange things, before following him down to the water. The moon was high in the sky and provided enough light for them to find their way along the track.

Andy stopped at a log and they both paused in front of it, laughed, and sat down.

"It's been a day of sitting on logs," Jane said, enjoying the wine, the soft night, his body close. "Hmm, I needed this."

"Me too. I wish there were more days like this. Sad and hard, but bearable, you know?"

She could just make out the whites of his eyes in the dark. She felt something stir inside her.

*No,* she thought, *you can't be having these feelings. You're tired. You're stressed. Andy is grieving his wife.*

A light breeze combed through the tops of the trees, over the water.

"Are you cold?" he asked.

"No. I'm fine," she said, but she didn't feel fine. She felt confused, emotional. She wanted to ask him about Paige, about their relationship. Whether she'd been okay before she died. Whether they'd been okay. But she didn't know how to start, or whether she should ask. But they'd been so honest with each other today; they seemed to have a clear line of communication running between them. Maybe she just had to say something.

"Andy, Viv sort of . . . I'm not sure exactly, but it seemed like she asked me if I was her new mother tonight . . ."

"Oh no, I'm so sorry. Ah, that's . . ."

"Heartbreaking . . . I know. It's okay, really. It's just, well . . . she also seemed upset. She said Mommy was sad with Daddy, and I guess I wanted to—"

"She said that? She's hardly said a word since Paige . . ." He sighed deeply and ran his palms down his face. "Oh god."

"Sorry. I shouldn't have mentioned it . . . Are you okay?"

He was silent for a long while and then she realized he was crying. She moved closer, feeling the tension in his body, like the coil of a spring.

"Oh, I'm so sorry," she said, putting her arm around his back.

They stayed like that for a while, the night sounds, the lake, growing louder. Eventually his body stilled, and he wiped the sleeve of his T-shirt across his eyes. "I'm so sorry. I've just been, I don't know, trying to hold it all together for Viv, trying to get my head around the fact that she's gone . . . Confused."

"It's okay, there's no map of how to navigate this time. It's so hard what you're going through, Andy."

He turned to her, and their faces were very close. She could feel his breath on her cheek. He took her hand in his. It was warm. There was something about his grip that made her go very still.

"Thank you," he said and leaned toward her until his forehead touched hers.

Everything went quiet, slowed. It felt like the tide pulling out. As though all the breath and all the blood in her body had stopped moving. Her veins closed, her heart went still. The only sensation was his hand in hers and his breath on her skin. Then he did what she knew he would. He kissed her. Everything rushed back in and all the stillness between them, all the calm, ruptured, and his hands were at her neck. She gripped him. The kiss was urgent. It felt like jumping into deep water. A sound came out of her that she barely recognized. She pulled away, mortified. She glanced behind them, suddenly aware of not being that far from the house.

"Oh god." He blinked and shook his head. "I'm so sorry, Janie."

She swallowed and pressed her fingers to her lips. "Ah, I'm . . . I'm not sure why that—"

"Too much sitting on logs," he said.

"Too much wine," she muttered.

They laughed awkwardly and avoided each other's eyes. She was about to stand up, break the tension, when he spoke.

"Paige and I were having lots of problems." His voice was pained. Jane said nothing.

"It felt like we were growing apart, you know? She had a lot of attention. She even had a stalker. I found it all really hard, you know?"

"Yeah, of course. That can't have been easy on you both." She tried to choose her next words carefully, to not reveal what she already knew and so she didn't appear to be prying. "The stalker, do you know anything about him? Have you had a look on her feed? In her messages? Have the police asked?"

He nodded. "I obviously told them. One of her 'fans' tracking her down in real life. He came to the house apparently. But he seemed pretty harmless—or at least Paige said she wasn't that scared. It was me who was more upset. I know the police have access to her accounts, but I haven't looked since . . . I can't face it, Janie. I know the police think that maybe he did something to her and they're trying to find him. I just think, maybe she . . . she wasn't coping . . . maybe she did something . . . to herself."

There was a movement on the water, out deep, and they both turned.

"A fish," Jane said, but her breath was shallow. "What makes you say that?" Was it her place to tell him that the police thought otherwise? The image of him throwing something into the water returned to her. It wasn't her place to tell him.

"She was struggling, you know? The way they found her boat capsized."

"What do you think happened?"

"The truth is, I don't know. She was emotional that morning. Maybe because it was her birthday, everything was more intense. I only saw her briefly before she took the kayak out, but she wasn't acting like herself."

His words, their implication rang into the silence.

"Have you told the police that?"

"Yeah."

"But she wouldn't . . . she wouldn't leave Viv?"

Something passed over his face that she couldn't quite read. Was it a hardness? Anger? "What do you think, Janie? You knew her, maybe better than me. What was Paige capable of?"

Jane braced her arms around her body. *You know what Paige was capable of,* she thought. *No, that was so long ago.* She felt very suddenly like an impostor here. Kissing Andy. Acting like she belonged in this family. No one in this family knew what had really gone on between her and Paige all those years ago. They believed in the longevity of their friendship.

Should she tell Andy the truth? He'd been so honest with her.

"I . . . I'm not sure I'm qualified to answer that. Paige and I . . . we hadn't spoken for a long time." What she didn't say was, *after everything that happened.* Instead she said, "We'd both changed a lot, I think, since we were at high school."

Had Paige changed? Could a person change? Was Paige a good person? Was she, Jane, a good person? She'd just kissed a man who was not hers to kiss. She thought of Jackson and winced.

"That's okay," said Andy. "You were still her friend."

"And you were still her husband."

He took her hand in his and squeezed it.

No, it didn't matter what had happened in the past. Paige was gone. It didn't matter what mistakes she had made, she deserved the truth about her death to be uncovered, for a perpetrator, if there was one, to be caught.

Jane thought of that look of worry on Viv's little face tonight as she'd said the words, "Momma sad at Dadda." She thought of the sound of something heavy hitting the surface of the water as he threw it.

"Do you think I could log in to Paige's social media? Finding people, research, is what I do in my job. Just in case there's anything there about the stalker that could help us." She waited, her breath held.

"I don't know what you'll find, but sure. It's in both our names. The username is AndyPaige and the password is Vivbaby, all one word."

*God, what Jackson would give for this kind of access to Paige.* She let her breath slide out silently. She could never betray Andy after he'd been so trusting. Surely giving her the password demonstrated that he had nothing to hide. That he was innocent.

But Andy was wrong about Paige. He hadn't been there when they were sixteen, when Paige had held Jane's sobbing body night after night, crying for a mother who had gone. Paige might have been many things, but surely, she would not have left her daughter.

# CHAPTER 34

# Audrey

It was the flick of people's eyes. They couldn't, or wouldn't, look at me. That's how I could tell that everything had changed. I had a heightened sense of these things. It's because it had happened before. When the tide changes, you're looking for ripples, but this felt like a wave.

By the time I'd walked from the school gate to English class, my body felt numb with dread. Was I imagining that girl actually moving away from me as though I had cooties? Was that smirk on that boy's face meant for me?

It's a strange thing about girls—things are never straightforward. Because when I walked into the classroom, Paige was standing at the back with another girl and a boy I didn't know, and she looked over and she smiled at me. My hollow tummy filled up and I told myself I was an idiot. I was *imagining* things. Isn't it funny the stories we tell ourselves to soothe the sharp prick of our instinct?

I approached slowly but smiling.

"Hey Auds," she said. Another good sign.

Janie walked into the classroom behind me and I saw Paige's face light up. She squealed and ran to her, pulling her into a hug. Janie looked confused but then Paige whispered something into her ear, and she laughed. I felt both pairs of eyes on me. It felt like my heart severed in two. It felt like obliteration.

But against all my better judgment, I walked toward them. "Hey, guys, what's happening? What's with all the squealing?" I tried to keep my tone relaxed, cool, as though my heart weren't a tennis ball slamming into the net of my chest.

Janie looked awkward. Paige fixed me with an unfriendly glare. "Squealing? I'm not a pig."

"Oh no, I didn't mean . . ."

Paige threaded her arm through Janie's and together they turned away. Janie looked back, her expression pained, but she let herself be dragged. She sat down at a desk next to Paige.

I wasn't sure what to do. Try to sit next to them, or take the hint? I decided to act like I didn't care. I sat at the back of the class and tried not to cry. Mrs. Hall was talking about the novel we were studying and usually I'd be engaged, interested. But all I could think was that it was all my fault. I'd betrayed Janie by being exclusive with Paige, wanting her to myself all those afternoons. I didn't deserve Janie's loyalty because I hadn't given her mine. And Paige was such a cheap trade. I had a moment of shattering clarity. I knew what I needed to do. I went to the front of the class and told the teacher I was feeling sick. Then I walked out of the school.

It was hot, early December. The endless stretch of summer holidays was close. This should have comforted me, but instead all I could think was that I'd be spending them here, alone. I licked salt from my top lip as I approached the gas station. Heat shimmered over the asphalt and my school shoes stuck to it. The tinkle of the bell as I entered the store. Mom was behind the counter. She often did the weekday shifts. She was wearing one of her favorite dresses, and lipstick. That was the first clue that something was off. But I was so focused on my task. I had infiltrated Paige's group with cigarettes, and I would do the same again now. I just had to distract Mom while I reached under the counter.

"Honey?" Her face was creased with worry and I resented her for it, for being so in tune with me.

"I just wasn't feeling good, so I came home."

She came to press her hand to my forehead and I had to resist the urge to swipe it away.

"I actually feel okay now. Maybe I'll just have an acetaminophen and walk back."

"That's a long way to walk in this heat. Why didn't they call me?"

"It's fine, Mom. Can you just get me a painkiller?"

Her eyes fixed on mine. "What's going on?"

I hated how she could read me, see into me.

"Nothing."

She cocked her head. It was a thing she did when she knew I was hiding something.

"I need some cigarettes, okay?"

"What, Audrey? No."

"Do you want me to have friends or don't you?"

"Not the kind of friends who make you sneak them cigarettes."

"But you were so proud of me for finally fitting in . . . and that's the currency they trade in. Can't you remember being sixteen?" There was a meanness in my voice.

She sighed and pulled me into a hug, but I pushed her away. "You don't understand."

"Then help me understand. What's going on? I thought you were really happy with your new friends."

"That was last week."

"What about Janie? She's a true friend. She doesn't need cigarettes in exchange for friendship."

I shrugged, noting that she hadn't mentioned Paige. "I don't want to talk about it."

"Come on, I'll drive you back to school."

"I can't go back there."

"Sometimes we've just got to do what we don't actually feel like doing. That's the thing about life."

She held her hands out and looked around her, and perhaps for the first time ever I saw her objectively. I saw past her being my mother and saw that she was not the kind of woman who could have imagined herself working behind the counter at a gas station. She looked like she should be sketching, or arranging fresh flowers in a vase, things she did with care and grace. Dad was living his dream, fixing cars and bikes. But I saw the sacrifice that my mother had made in allowing him to do that. I wondered how many people actually got to be where they wanted to be in life, and what was the cost of that?

She must have sensed my overwhelm, my despair. "You know what, honey? Let's do something, just the two of us. No school today."

I felt a little buoy of hope. She saw it and grabbed my arm, a look in her eye.

"What about the shop? Is Dad around?"

My mother averted her eyes. "He's just in town or somewhere tracking down car parts." She walked to the door and turned the sign around to Closed. "There's another gas station up the road."

We drove north with the windows open, the radio loud and the hot wind in our faces. I didn't really know where we were going, and I don't think Mom did either, but that was the joy of it. All those times in the city when I'd get home from school feeling rejected and alone and there was nowhere to go but narrow streets—now it felt like we had somewhere to go. We stopped at a roadside kiosk at the tip of a headland and ordered fish and chips and bought sweating cans of Coke. We sat on the warm spongy grass overlooking the beach and licked the grease and salt from our fingers. We felt the sugar fizz in our veins.

We continued along the highway until the open road turned into the outskirts of suburbs, with hardware stores and shopping malls. This town had a mall—something The Lakes lacked and Mom steered toward the entrance. We didn't often go shopping together—she wasn't a mall kind of mom—but maybe she wanted me to feel better about myself. She could sense the cycle starting again. She let me choose a new novel from the bookshop—one that looked as dark and twisty as my insides felt. And she bought me a blue and white polka-dot dress from a cheap clothing store that made me look for a moment in the mirror as though it wasn't me.

On the drive back home, she didn't ask me to explain my despair, she didn't make me talk about it. Instead we just sat in companionable silence watching the hot road go past and the treetops shimmer in the heat. We reached the beach where we'd eaten lunch, and Mom flicked the indicator and the car crunched into the parking lot. She got out and stood with her eyes squinted against the late afternoon sun. She looked so beautiful and so strong in that moment.

"Come on. It's boiling."

We threw off our shoes and ran through the dunes toward the surf in our clothes, laughing because we never did things like this. I jumped in first. The water was so cold it stole my breath. Mom plunged in after.

Later, we sat on the sand and let the sun dry our hair to our backs.

"Don't let anyone make you feel bad about yourself, Audrey. Will you promise me that?"

I laughed under my breath. "No."

She laughed in return. "Seriously, what's wrong with these girls?

Why are they so fucking mean? Who the fuck do they think they are?"

My mother never swore. I wanted to ask her if she was okay, but I didn't know how to. I guess I was scared of what it would mean if she wasn't.

"Do you think maybe it's me, Mom?" My voice wavered.

"Oh, baby girl. You're too good for this world. You're yourself and that's all you ever need to be." There was a ferocity in her voice that I'd never heard before.

"I mean, I've tried so many times to fit in, and I never do." A tear slipped down my cheek.

"I see the way you and Janie talk. She's your people. Sometimes it takes a whole lifetime to find your people. And you know what? All you need is one person to see you and love you."

I knew by the look she gave me that she meant her as well, and I wanted to say that she didn't count. Mothers don't count, because everyone knows they're biased. But maybe Mom was right. I thought about the backward glance Janie gave me when Paige dragged her away. Maybe I should write Janie a letter, ask her to meet me at Ed and Daisy's so we could talk.

When we were home and showered, and drinking tea on the couch in front of a lame game show Mom sometimes watched because she was a trivia nut, we heard Dad come in. Or rather we smelled him. He always smelled like diesel fuel and grease. He didn't say anything about the shop being closed for the day. He just went and got a beer from the fridge and went outside and then we heard the growl of a motorcycle engine.

"Dad's been tinkering with his bike a lot lately," I said. That's what he called it, "tinkering."

I looked over and saw the muscles working in Mom's jaw. "Hmmm."

I wanted to ask if everything was okay. I thought Paige had proba-bly made up the rumors about my hot dad and the Christmas party because she was jealous of Ed and Daisy's, but I think something in me guessed from Mom's behavior that day that there might be more to the story, because she was acting like me—like we had nothing left to lose.

I found out the next day that there was something more to lose.

# CHAPTER 35

# Paige

I told myself I was making content to connect, to share. But what I came to realize was that I could never *not* be performing. I think I told myself it was because my livelihood depended on it, but it was more than that. I wanted so much to be liked. What is a "like" on socials though, really? I ask myself this a lot, as I watch the endless feed of people's lives play out without me, the world going on and on.

But for what? What am I watching? How did it all come down to a little love heart or a thumbs-up or a smiley face? How did this become the interface through which we perform and then see our lives reflected back? What would our great-grandparents say if we could tell them how things are now? Would they ask where this will all end?

It ended for me; of course it did. It's a rule of life that all things that go up must come down. Change is the only constant. It wasn't anything big at first, just a few comments here and there saying that my posts didn't feel very authentic. Then there were others, mostly from women, saying that I was setting up other women to fail. That my photos with my daughter were showing an unrealistic, unattainable, idealized version of motherhood. That parenting wasn't all collecting eggs for breakfast, picnicking under the almond trees for lunch, and walking on the beach at dusk.

When I read those words they reached me, because I knew this so keenly. Because underneath the pretty pictures I was feeling alone. Maybe that's why I was so compelled to create the pretty pictures in the first place. It all felt like an antidote to my real life. My whole life I'd felt pigeonholed, and this was me controlling the narrative. It was me finding the joy and beauty in the day and wanting to share that. Trying to connect. It was keeping me from the despair of feeling like I was a single parent. Of the loneliness of having the person you love pull away.

I understood at that moment that just wanting to create something beautiful was no longer enough. It was true, I felt like I was portraying who I wanted to be, not who I actually was. I was working angles, holding in my stomach, using filters. I might have told myself that I didn't need to be beautiful, but the truth was, I did. It was my currency. I'd known it since I was a small girl. But it didn't feel right anymore.

So, I pivoted.

I started analyzing what other people more popular than me, younger than me, were doing. I realized a movement had begun away from curated, perfect, color-coordinated photos to something more #authentic. To show something more real, more relatable. Messier. Maybe I could do away with the professional photo shoots and the matching dresses with Viv, the filters. Suddenly it all seemed so twee, so fake, and I felt a rush of shame, then something like relief that perhaps I could allow my followers to see a more raw me, a more true me. And that they would still, or maybe because of that, love me.

I started posting photos of nature without me in them. A shell in the sand. A feather. A sunset. The still lake as my kayak cut through it. They didn't get as many likes but I didn't care. Then I took a selfie of me and Viv when we'd just gotten out of the surf, the texture of my skin real, makeup-free, and not that flattering. I posted photos of the chaos of the kitchen table at the end of the day. For a while people responded to it, maybe recognizing something of themselves if they too were an overwhelmed mother of a small child.

I could see a distinct change in my feed from the day I pivoted. I began to share some of the poems I'd written and posted with Poet Boy on our account. Days when I felt sad, I wrote sad words and posted that. Days that I felt bloated, I said so. I was candid about how I'd "performed" my life up until that point. On a particularly hard day, I took one of my posts where I looked perfect and deconstructed it. Told of the toll and the effort that one picture had taken—the hair, the makeup, the professional photographer, the right angles, the fifty photos that didn't make the cut, and then the filters. I named it all. Then I talked about how insecure I had become. How hypercritical of my body, my face I was. How tired I was of it all.

The media picked it up.

I know some influencers are embroiled in controversies. They've said something #offensive and they have a big platform, or they've shown too much skin. Or conversely they've had a rant that #connects with people. Maybe they go viral because a news organization basically rips off one of their posts—maybe a nice relatable post about a postpartum body or something like that, and then online newspapers all over the world pick up the content.

That happened to my story too.

I got so many more followers. I got so many people praising me for being honest. For calling out the machine of social media, for the body honesty. But I got hate too. That's the thing people don't realize about being in the public eye—there's a cost. And at some point, you've got to ask if it's worth paying.

*False modesty is never a good look.*

*Eat something. You need a meal.*

*Congratulations. Now you have even more attention. Hypocrite.*

*This woman disgusts me. She's so ugly.*

*Everything that is wrong with the female gender right here.*

*I feel sorry for her kid. Whole life on the net before you know how to talk.*
Tragic.

*Oh boohoo, it must be so hard being so beautiful and white and privileged.*

*Go kill yourself darling and do the world a favor.*

*I bet this chick was the high school bully. Sorry hon, well now you know how*
*it feels.*

It was like a virus. A disease. It infected everything.

It didn't matter if I posted a #nofilter photo, or an honest, heartfelt comment, people didn't want to see my idealized life, but they didn't want the real me either. It forced me to realize that I was still always portraying an idealized version of myself for the world. Always performing, always doing tricks like a trained dog. It disgusted me. I disgusted me. And I'd brought this on my daughter too.

I deleted Instagram from my phone. Then I turned it off and hid it under my bed. For the first day it was like coming off crack cocaine. My whole body ached for a fix. Missed messaging Buckley. My hand reached constantly for the familiar shape of it. It had become an extension of my body, but mainly my mind. But gradually, after another twenty-four hours, my feet started to touch the earth. My senses awoke. I no longer reached for my phone as soon as I woke. I watched the play of light in the sheer curtains. I listened to the bird call as I rose and put slippers on, drank cold water. I had done these things every morning, but I'd been scrolling. I hadn't noticed any of it. My mind was not as full, not as fast. It felt free. I felt different.

"So, I've given it up." I was bathing Viv when Andy walked into the bathroom and stripped off his wet suit. He was naked, and the tan lines on his arms and legs made him look strange and beautiful.

"Given what up?"

"Social media. My phone's been under the bed for two days."

"Seriously?"

It hurt that he hadn't noticed, but we were in a holding pattern of inattention.

"Yeah."

"And? How does it feel?"

"It feels good." I started to spike up Viv's hair with frothy shampoo. I picked her up, wet and soapy so that she could see her crazy hair in the mirror, and we all laughed. It was such a tiny moment, inconsequential, but it was probably the first time in a long time that we'd all just been present.

Andy made her hair into a mohawk, and we laughed some more. "I respect what you've done, Paigie." He hadn't called me that for a long time.

I hadn't told him about the negativity that had preceded my leaving. He would have been all *I told you so,* and I couldn't handle him being right. I'd stopped checking his emails. It was something about letting the cards fall where they may. It was something about letting go of the control I was trying to have over everything, everyone. By extension, I also let Buckley go. He was a crutch. He wasn't real, just as the person I presented online wasn't real.

I did so well at the start. I wrote more. Viv and I did things without me thinking about how they could be turned into a photo opportunity. I helped around the house more and helped Yas with her baking. She taught me the importance of sifting flour and precise measurements, and how to manipulate fondant. It felt different doing things with my hands. My senses were keen, and time stretched and changed in ways I'd forgotten. Things became less urgent. Andy felt like he began to return to me. He wasn't competing with my phone for attention when he came home. He wasn't competing with a wordy boy who was a figment of my imagination.

We started to have sex again. Andy was a good lover. We'd always had chemistry. It felt strange that we hadn't for so long, but I guess the power balance had changed. It felt like something between us had mellowed.

At 3 a.m., lying in bed, sometimes it was hard, though. I thought about all the opportunities sitting in my inbox, in my messages, that I was just ignoring. Opportunities to go to places, meet people, make money. It felt like life was passing me by. FOMO. Such a cliché. It felt like an itch that I was resisting scratching, but it didn't mean it wasn't there. Then the sun would come up and I'd take the kayak out onto the water and I'd realize that none of it was real. That all I needed was my lake, and Viv and Andy and my family.

But of course, the world doesn't work like that either. Without @paige_white I was unemployed. Andy didn't say anything for a few weeks. I was a mother and an aunt and there were always things to be done around the house. Food to be made. Kids to be fed and entertained. Washing to be put on. I would find myself folding a crisp white shirt and placing it on top of a neat pile in the laundry basket in the sunshine and having the urge to take a photo. I started to feel that creativity knead at me, soften my resolve.

Then Andy said in bed one night, "So . . . are you going to get a job?"

I had to stop myself from laughing. "Well, I'm helping Yas with her cakes."

"But that's her thing, isn't it? Does she make any money?"

"Yes."

"So yeah, I've just been thinking about our apartment by the beach, getting some independence. We don't want to sponge off your parents forever."

*I had independence. I was completely independent. And you couldn't handle it.*

"What, you want me to apply to be a barista at the coffee shop?"

"Or what about the hippy candle shop? You like candles and incense and all that shit."

"Are you serious?"

"Well, I'm just saying it'd be good to, you know . . ."

"No. I don't know. Good to what?"

"Get some more money. We can't live with your parents forever."

"Oh my god, are you serious? You're telling me to go and work in a store when I had my own business?"

"Yeah, but you're so much happier now, being offline."

"Are you sure it's not you who's happier, Andy? With me making myself small?"

"What the hell are you talking about? I just wanted you to live in the real world, Paige. I just wanted you to engage with your daughter and with me. I wanted to live without everything being a freaking photo op."

"Well, Andy, maybe that's preferable to selling incense or making coffees for a living."

It was a low blow, but I couldn't help it.

His jaw jutted forward. "I'm not saying you have to apply for a job tomorrow. I'm just trying to work out what your plans are. *Our* plans."

I softened. It had been better between us. He was coming home straight after work most afternoons. The threat of Tam seemed distant now, almost silly. "What about a compromise? What if I worked on my business, but I only did it for half the week? Put in screen-time limits, things like that. And you could take the pics, get back some of your creative outlet . . . but we'd only do it, like, three days a week. Go back to basics. To what it was at the beginning."

"I don't know, Paigie, you're so all-or-nothing."

I grimaced. He had me there. "Yeah, I know, but I want to try to be more moderate. I was unhappy. We both were." My eyes filled with tears, and he touched my cheek. He drew me to him and we made slow, tender love. There was longing and hope in it. I realized I needed hope. I needed a bigger world than this small one that seemed to be getting more and more minuscule. I needed more than just being a mother, doing the domestics.

The next morning, after I got back from kayaking and Andy had gone to work, I reached under my bed and took out my phone. It felt like a dead thing, blank and dark. But I felt something, some need, some excitement, weighing it in my palms. I turned it on.

I would write a *fuck-you* post saying I was going to keep making beauty in the world. I was going to keep taking photos of myself looking beautiful if I felt like it, and I was going to do and say whatever the hell I wanted. People didn't have to look. They didn't have to follow. I was the orchestrator of my own life. I could curate it how I wanted. Everyone, including my own husband, was judging me. So fuck them all.

I opened the app and anticipation welled inside me.

But something had happened while I'd been away. Something I couldn't have anticipated. I guess I'd just imagined that because I wasn't on there, things had somehow suspended, but that was my first mistake. It never stops, it never goes quiet. It goes on and on and on. It goes on without you. And people were angry that I'd left with no explanation. There was speculation I was dead.

Buckley had gone quiet. He'd disappeared too.

# CHAPTER 36

# Jane

Jane looked up at the dark ceiling. Shadows moved against a sheen of moonlight. She could hear the wash of the shoreline through the open window. She could smell the brine. The lake smelled different here. How was she here, in Paige's childhood bedroom, lying in her bed? She pressed her fingers to her lips. How had she kissed Paige's husband? *It's an illusion that we have control of our own lives*, she thought. A week ago, she'd been on track in her life, obsessed with Jackson, committed to her job above all else. She'd been happy, hadn't she? Or at least she hadn't been bored. She'd been on track to something.

She could feel the shadows moving inside her now, the darkness edging in, like sharp branches sticking into her insides. How had she come back to this? She'd done so well, she'd forgotten. She'd got out, kept moving. It had suspended the darkness, the sharpness, somewhere that she no longer associated with herself, but now, here she was, full circle, doing things badly and letting the past creep in and corrupt her, just as Paige had corrupted her. Because that, if she was being real, being truthful, was what had happened, wasn't it? She let the memory stalk into her, spiky, scratching. She couldn't resist it anymore.

She saw herself—a young girl lying in Paige's bedroom on the trundle bed. The night after her mother left had been stormy, cold. She'd run all the way from her house around the lake, lightning scouring the surface of the water, her clothes clinging to her, heavy and cold like a shroud she couldn't shed. It looked like heaven, like hell, or somewhere in between, the sky and lake lit up like that. Pewter, silver, a black horizon, strobes of purple light. She couldn't tell where the water ended and the sky began.

Mrs. White had wrapped her in a fluffy towel and made pancakes for supper—"supper" was what she'd *actually* called it, and Janie had felt so coddled, so looked after. The whole family had prayed for Janie and her dad, and even for her mom, around the kitchen counter. It had felt surreal, dreamlike, with lightning igniting the sky and then plunging everything into darkness. Jane remembered wishing the Whites' belief would bring her mother back. She lay in the bed next to Paige, unable to sleep, the grumbling storm receding.

"You're a badass running all the way here in the storm. You're lucky you didn't get struck by lightning," said Paige, hoisted up on an elbow, peering down at her from under her dark bangs.

Jane wanted to say that it felt like she'd already been struck by lightning and that's why she hadn't been afraid. When the worst had already happened, when your mother had left you, her hair sticking to her face in the rain, her eyes streaked with apology and mascara as she got into the car and drove away from you . . . when your father tried to hug you but you'd screamed at him that he was a fucking freak and it was all his fault that Mom had left . . . when you'd lived that, you weren't scared of a storm. You almost wanted the lightning to strike you down. But how could Paige, with her perfect fricking family with their pancakes and prayers, understand such pain?

"Can you believe Audrey's dad? With his Bon Jovi hair and his motorbikes? Your mom didn't stand a chance," Paige said softly.

Jane had felt like a bar of soap had lodged in her throat. Her mouth was loamy and thick with it.

"I mean, I'm not saying he's sexy or anything like that, ewwww, it's just I don't think we can blame your mom, with everything going on with your dad and the house . . ." She trailed off. "She was like, the perfect target."

Jane rolled over and drew the blankets up over her ears. She didn't know how to reply. She didn't want Paige to say anything else. And she couldn't say what she really wanted to say, because who and what did she have apart from the Whites now? She was a girl without a mother. Mrs. White had told her that her mom would come back for her, but Mrs. White was thinking about how *she* would behave, not how Jane's mother would behave.

Jane couldn't help the sob that escaped her mouth. Then the tears came, hot and salty. Paige lay down beside her and wrapped her arms around her.

"We'll look after you, Janie. It's going to be all right. You can stay with us as long as you want. We'll be like sisters. You'll be the third White sister."

Jane wiped her face on the sheets. She knew she should feel comforted by that, so why didn't she feel safe?

Paige hugged her tighter. "I don't think we should talk to her at school anymore. If her Bon Jovi dad hadn't come to town, you'd still have a mom."

Jane remembered the feeling, the deepening of her grief. Audrey was the best friend she'd ever had. She thought of Ed and Daisy's by the lake. Their secret world. It all seemed childish now though. They'd been playing tea parties and reading romance novels while their parents had been doing god-knows-what with each other. It was horrendous. It was all so sordid. But what was the alternative? Awkward conversations with Audrey about their parents having sex? She knew Audrey loved her dad, just like Jane loved her mom. She hated her. But she loved her too.

Paige stroked her hair, telling her in her soothing, low voice that everything would be okay, that it would be fun being sisters, sharing a bedroom, borrowing each other's clothes, until Jane fell asleep.

Jane woke to the screech of birds across water. She could smell the salt from the lake seeping in through the open window, and the perfume Paige used to wear when she was sixteen seemed to linger in the air. Was it infused in the rug, the sheets, the walls? She shook her head, reorienting herself. No, she wasn't a girl anymore. She was a grown woman. She wasn't Janie, she was Jane. Paige was dead. She thought of Andy, and that kiss reached her mind like a soft blow. It hurt, but it hurt good. God, what on earth was she doing? She couldn't stay here. Not with Andy. Not with the memories seeping in.

She got up. She was still in her clothes from the day before. She couldn't bring herself to wear Paige's again. It was early, and the lake was shrouded in mist. She would leave a thank-you note on the kitchen counter. Or she'd text to thank the Whites for having her. She shouldn't really contact Andy again. She thought of little Viv and her questioning eyes, wondering if she was her new mommy. Her heart ached for that little girl. No, things were getting too weird. It felt like the past and the present were collapsing in on each other.

She tiptoed downstairs. The house was bathed in soft morning light. She felt that twinge inside her again. *Imagine growing up in a house like this, so filled with light and warmth? So free of clutter.* The kitchen counters were clear, ready to greet the new day with a clean slate. The floors were bare. She snuck out through the front door, closing it behind her with a click.

The mist hung low over the water. It had invaded the garden, shrouding the trees and grass in a humid blanket. She wondered if she was dreaming when she glimpsed it through the fog. A police car was parked at the end of the drive, just under the trees. Her heart accelerated. Why were the police here? Were they on guard or something, due to the stalker? Was Andy still a suspect?

She joined the track around the lake, hoping she hadn't been seen. When she was far enough away, she stopped, breathless, and took out her phone. She texted Shep.

*There's a police car outside the Whites'. Do you know what's going on?*

She watched as he wrote back almost immediately.

*They're taking Andy in for questioning.*

*What? Really???*

*New info. Someone has come forward.*

Her mind was racing. What did that mean? Why hadn't they told the family that they were treating Paige's death as suspicious? Did they suspect the family somehow? Were they playing their cards close to their chest? Had they bugged the house or something? Or was Andy just being taken in to tell him that police suspected Paige had succumbed to foul play? She needed to know more.

*Can we meet?* she wrote.

The dots arrived, disappeared. Arrived again.

*I shouldn't really give you any more info, Janie, sorry. It wouldn't really be appropriate at this stage of the investigation.*

Shit. He knew she was close to the Whites. She'd lost him. She took a deep breath. She felt her rational mind engage, the journalist in her rouse. She knew how to get people to talk, to get to the truth. Avoid yes/no questions. Appeal to the human, the person behind the job.

*Sorry, rude of me to text so early. I know you've put yourself out there. I don't want to put you in an awkward position. And this is Friend Janie, not Reporter Janie.*

*No worries, I just don't want to compromise the investigation. Shit is getting serious now. And yep, I'm an early riser too.*

*I'm at the lake. Early walk.*

*Nice, it's beautiful at this time of day.*

*It really is . . .*

The dots . . . She took a gamble.

*We should meet for a walk one morning.*

*I'd like that* ☺

*They don't think Andy did it do they? Surely not.*

*I guess they'll know more once they've interviewed him.*

Her pulse was racing. *No,* she thought. Andy could not have put wire around his wife's neck and strangled her.

*I've spent some time at the Whites' house cleaning out Paige's stuff and I really don't think he would have hurt Paige.*

More dots but no reply.

*I have good instincts, Shep.*

*I get it, but I think we both know at this stage in our careers that all the good instincts in the world can sometimes be wrong.*

She tore her eyes away from her phone and looked out onto the lake. The mist clung to the shoreline like low cloud. The tree cathedral on the other side was shrouded. *How do we really know what someone is capable of?* she thought. An uncomfortable feeling was growing in her gut.

*We don't. You know we don't,* her mind whispered.

Or it might have been the sound of the she-oaks that rimmed the shore.

Were these strange feelings she was having for Andy clouding her judgment? No, she had to go with her gut. She had to warn him. God, why did she feel this way? It was just one kiss, wasn't it? They had swapped phone numbers last night before they parted on the landing.

*In case you can't sleep,* he'd said, going into the bedroom he'd shared with Paige, she to sleep down the hall in Paige's girlhood bedroom. Was she reading into the smile he gave her just before he closed the door? She had lain in bed and touched herself, thinking of those lips on her body as she'd slept in his wife's childhood bed. Guilt and desire had coalesced inside her. God, things were getting messed up.

She had to tell him about the police.

*Andy, it's Janie. I got up early to walk around the lake. There's a police car at the end of the drive????*

It was still early. She waited.

*Hey. Really??*

Another, a moment later.

*I can see it. Where are you?*

*I'm just around the track, near where the old rowboats are.*

*Stay there. Coming.*

She walked into a thicket of she-oaks where three boats had been pulled to shore. Everything was so quiet, so still. It felt like she was the only person on the whole lake. She looked out past the bull-rushes. *Is this how Paige felt?* Jane sat down on an overturned hull. The paint was peeling away, stripped by the elements. She pulled it off to reveal raw timber beneath. That's what this felt like, a peeling back of everything she'd built up to protect herself over the years. But was it protection? A man who was unavailable to her, a job that kept her so busy and exhausted she didn't have time to think. Avoiding her father. What was she doing here waiting for a man she'd just tipped off about a possible police arrest? Could she trust him? Should she tell him everything she knew so that it wasn't a surprise when they interrogated him?

He was in bare feet, pushing his hair out of his eyes. God, he was beautiful.

"I snuck around the back. What are they doing just sitting there at the end of the drive like that?"

"I thought the same thing," she said.

He shook his head, rubbed his palms down his face. "God knows."

"Andy, sit down. There's something I think you need to know."

His eyes locked on hers and he sat down next to her on the boat. "What? Janie, are you okay?"

She sighed. "I have a friend in the local police. He's been giving me some info . . . I guess on account that we used to be friends, that he knows I'm Paige's childhood friend and desperate to know what happened."

"What kind of info?"

"I just spoke to him then. He said the police are here to take you in for questioning."

"Argh. Not again. I told them everything last time."

"There's something else, some new info, and Andy, there's something else you need to know. The way Paige died, they're treating it as a possible homicide."

"What do you mean?" His face was blank.

She wasn't sure how much she could, should, tell him. She didn't even know if she was operating on up-to-date information. It was just what Shep had told her a couple of days ago. "I'm just worried, why they're questioning you . . . I . . . I don't know why, how this has happened . . . so fast . . . but I care about you?" She felt her face flush. She realized she'd asked it as a question. It was a question. How had this happened, and did he feel it? "And I don't want Viv to . . . lose her dad too."

"Hey, hey, hey, don't, Janie. Don't go there. It's fine. I'll just tell them the truth. There's nothing to worry about. I don't think it was homicide. I'll tell them that. I'll tell them what she was going through. And I would never hurt Paige. You know that, right?"

There were tears in his eyes. She couldn't help herself, she reached for him, gathered him to her. They held each other like that for what seemed like a long time. Then he raised his head and his lips brushed hers very lightly. *I'm dreaming,* she thought. It's all the mist. I'm still asleep in Paige's bedroom. The police car, this kiss, it's not happening. But his hand was behind her head, drawing her mouth into a deeper kiss. She felt her eyes roll back and her body move forward. His arms wrapped around her. His body was so much more powerful than hers, honed in the ocean, in rips and currents, and for a moment, she thought about how Paige had died early in the morning on this lake, how the police were sitting in wait for this man.

A tiny part of her asked, *Is he being honest? Am I?*

She pulled back and their eyes met. She swallowed. "Andy, I . . ."

He shook his head. "I know, the police . . . We shouldn't . . ."

But he brushed his thumb over her lips with such tenderness, and there was a look of such pain in his eyes that she knew she had already given in. She pulled him toward her and they lay down on the sand between the hulls of the boats. The air was thick with moisture and the sand was littered with dried reeds, seagrass, and the slight smell of rotting vegetation, but she didn't care. His hands moved down her body, over her breasts, her stomach. She pulled him to her face. She kissed him hard, met his emotion.

*This is wrong,* her mind said, *you are not the kind of person who is capable of this,* but she couldn't stop her body. She didn't want him to stop. The need in her was too great. The anticipation of him was like nothing she'd ever felt before. Jackson came into her mind fleetingly, and his intensity, his intellectualism, his pale office skin revolted her. She wanted this man with his nature-honed body. His raw emotions.

There was a rising need in the space between their bodies, an unspoken connection, something that seemed to be a natural extension of everything they'd shared on that tree trunk over the water. Grief and pain, but also an exquisite tenderness. It didn't feel within their control. She was about to give herself over to whatever it was, when he gently put his palm to her chest, creating a physical barrier between them.

"I'm sorry," he whispered.

The mist was lifting off the lake, dispersing.

As they lay there trying to catch their breath, she wondered, *Can you see me from your watery grave? With your husband, near where you died?*

# CHAPTER 37

*I was lying to myself. I knew who she was, the girl on the lake. Of course I did. Her whole life was cataloged online. As if we wanted to know about what she ate (a lot of salads, a lot of eggs from her chickens), what she drank (plant milk in her coffee), the kind of vitamins she took (fish oil and probiotics), her morning skin routine (various organic products she'd been sent to talk all about). But really we did want to know, because we all watched her, didn't we? We liked to judge her for her earnestness in living this beautiful life, but we couldn't stop looking, could we? Was it just because she was beautiful? It's easy to hate the beautiful. They're easy targets. Yet some part of us wants to be like them. It's confusing. Isn't that the appeal of these grids of photos we're all looking at? Isn't that the deal we make with the devil inside us? The voyeur? Because no one is watching how many times we view things, because there's no repercussion for what we say on there. Maybe, shamefully, our true selves live there in the ether.*

*But seeing her out there each morning, so vulnerable, so alone against the line of trees, so tiny in such a vast body of water, without her products, her makeup, her oat milk, her humanity was more apparent. It made me see her slightly differently, I guess. And she had gone quiet online. I was checking.*

# CHAPTER 38

# Audrey

It wasn't even lunchtime before I heard it. There were two rumors apparently. The first was that I read bodice-rippers alone in a creepy old van where someone had died. The second was that my dad had broken up Janie's family and that he and Janie's mom had ridden away on his Harley-Davidson. Kind of cool, no? But what the hell? Dad didn't even own a Harley. That was his dream, but he couldn't afford the real deal. But there was no point defending myself. Because there was drama and romance in both these rumors; they spread like little spot fires around the school. And I knew who was behind them.

As I walked the hallways, my sneakers squeaking freakishly on the linoleum, I felt their eyes on me. It was happening all over again. And some part of me felt relieved, I think, that here I was on full display. They'd finally found out that I was an impostor. People like me weren't meant for popularity. Who I was fell too far out of the remit of "normal." I used words like *remit*, for starters. If my body had fit better, maybe I could have gotten away with my brain. But it didn't. I was not made to tread the middle ground in any way. I was excess. Excess brain, excess body. I don't know why the world couldn't accept that. I was too much. I had always known that and had lived trying always to make myself smaller. But something in me always broke out. I didn't mean it to. I wanted, god, how I wanted, to just shrink myself.

It was, I knew, survival of the fittest. We were learning about Darwin's evolutionary theory in science class. It was a jungle out there that I couldn't adapt to. I clung to the idea that there was something brave and idealistic about being yourself despite the overpowering influence of natural selection. I clung to the fact that the Harley story did make my dad out to be quite cool. *I'll tell him tonight,* I thought. *We'll laugh about it, and Mom will give him the side-eye and ask if he's been seducing hapless female townsfolk with his motorbikes. They'll put a vinyl on the old record player, Fleetwood Mac or the Beatles, and maybe Dad will make Mom a gin and tonic with lime in one of the vintage glasses she liked.*

I went into the playground as though I were going into a war zone. I hung my head but I was watching, wary. I didn't know where the snipers were. The three of them were sitting together in the prime spot in the shade under the tree. They were huddled together, as though they were whispering secrets. My heart felt like it scrunched right up into a tight ball. I knew I had to try to get Janie away from Paige and Yas. But I could see by the puffiness of her face that she'd been crying, and as I got closer I could see that the White sisters were sort of cradling her, supporting her. A seam of worry split me down the middle. She didn't actually believe it, did she? I knew I couldn't approach—I was scared of what Paige would say to me. Like a helpless gazelle—or maybe that's not quite the right animal; maybe like a hippo, caught in the line of sight of its predator, I slunk—no, lumbered off. But survival of the fittest isn't just about physical strength. I had mental acuity, I knew deep down this was my survival card. I went into the building and opened my locker. I wanted to get inside it and curl up and shut the world out. But, let's face it, if I lived in a body that could fit into my locker, I probably wouldn't be in this predicament to begin with. I just stood and stared at it, wishing I knew what to do and where I could go.

I couldn't leave school again. Couldn't expect Mom to take me on another shopping road-trip adventure. My hands found the worn covers of two of the romance novels I'd brought from Ed and Daisy's. I smoothed them and breathed in their tea-leafy scent. They were brown and spotted and gnarled and comforting, like old people, and I wondered whether I could just spend the rest of my life working at a nursing home with people who would be kind to me and see me as a young person with her whole life in front of her. Where I could borrow some of their shiny-eyed hope in me. Where I could get a tiny glimpse of the perspective they had, having lived an entire life. Then I thought how tragic that would be because I knew I was smart, that my brain could take me places, anywhere really. I guess part of me, the smart part, the self-preservation part, knew what they would tell me—that this was only high school, that I had a future beyond these people with their mean, narrow minds. That I could actually do anything with my life. And I wanted Janie to see that too. That for people like Paige and Yas, this was the pinnacle of their lives—being the queen bees, stepping on other people to keep themselves propped up. Small-town princesses who would never get out because they didn't realize they needed to.

I ripped a page out of one of my exercise books, scribbled a note to Janie, and hid it inside the novel:

*I'm sorry. I don't know what on earth is going on. Will you meet me at Ed and Daisy's after school?*

I knew the code for Janie's locker. I only ever needed to hear or see something once to remember it.

I don't know how, but I got through the rest of the day. People made revving noises like a motorbike when they passed me, either that or moaning as though they were having sex, which told me that was a part of the romance novel rumor I had evidently missed.

I went home and, honestly, no part of me thought that rumor about Dad was true. But then I smelled baking and I knew something was wrong. Mom was standing in the kitchen with a cake on a cooling rack, an oven mitt on one hand, a knife in the other. She baked when she was very upset. She and Dad would joke about it. It smelled like the coconut cake I loved. My heart sank.

She looked up. She smiled but her eyes were empty. I knew.

"Where's Dad?"

"Dad left for Sydney for a few days. Something with the business." She swallowed. "I made your cake." Her voice was as sweet as the smell infusing the air, but it was too sweet, cloying. I felt nauseous from it.

"There's a rumor at school."

The knife in her hand clattered to the countertop. "This goddamn town." She steadied herself against the bench, lifted her chin, and picked up the knife. She sliced two pieces of cake and put them on plates. "I added oranges this time. I'm not sure if it's worked."

I saw how strong she was being for me. How it was killing her. How unfair it was that he'd brought her here—it was his dream to have his own mechanic business in a small town, and now she was left here.

We sat down at the plastic table with our cake. It was like some flimsy card table people used for picnics, not a table to eat all your meals at.

"Is he coming back?"

She shook her head. "No, it doesn't work with the orange."

I didn't know if she was saying no to the cake or my question. Or maybe I did. She pushed the cake away and took mine before I'd even had a chance to taste it.

I ran from the house. The afternoon was hot, but I ran around the lake, the glare off the water mixing with my tears and blinding me. I ran all the way to Ed and Daisy's. Part of me feared that some school-kids might be there, but the truth was, people were spooked. It was kind of remote, kind of weird. A bit like me.

As I opened the door and went inside, I felt nothing but calm, held within this little peach-hued capsule. I filled the kettle and took down the little tin of Janie's favorite tea—strawberries and cream. I found her favorite green teacup with the matching saucer, and I sat down and waited while the tea brewed strong and fragrant, just like she liked it. I closed the curtains and didn't dare read a book.

# CHAPTER 39

# Paige

The first note arrived in my physical mailbox with @paige_white scrawled at the top. It was handwritten in loose script on the back of a postcard that read, "Idyllic Lakes District." The photo was of the tree cathedral and the lake beyond.

*your father was a cult leader*
*there's a reason he acts like a god*
*google solaris*
*and all will be told*

*Silly, silly, silly girl.* That's what went through my mind. People online are never who they say they are. I wasn't who I said I was. I was a sad girl trying to live a happy life. I was an ambitious woman who had married a man who couldn't deal with that ambition and so I was trying and failing to make myself smaller for him.

But are any of us really showing the world our true selves? Are any of us who we say, who we think we are? Maybe we're all capable of much more, or less, than we realize. More of the good, more of the bad. Maybe people can't be pigeonholed into good and bad. But it's safer to think that they can be. That's the way we make ourselves feel safer in the chaos. That's why we created heaven and hell, isn't it?

If you really think about it, yes, we're putting our "best" selves online, but really, isn't all of life in the presence of other people performing? Imagine if we could see through walls and into houses, into rooms. All the base activities taking place—the washing of dirt from our bodies, the shitting, the fornicating. These things are natural, but we hide them. We pretend they don't factor in our day-to-day. When we leave our houses, we do so with clean teeth, brushed hair, makeup on, politeness (mostly) in place. People are generally very civil in real life.

But the things people wrote to me online—the cruelty and brutality—no one had ever said to my face. Is that because of the way I looked? Did that and my privilege protect me before? Yes, it did. I knew other people had insults thrown at them on the street, in the playground, because they were thought of as different. There are so many ways to be different. I came to realize that people are more cruel than I'd imagined. I came to realize that they probably thought terrible things, but they just didn't say them to my face. I came to realize that the online world is just reflecting what people are really thinking, but now openly saying. It has removed the barriers.

For thousands of years humans have kept dirty secrets, thoughts, hidden, under wraps, even though every one of us knows that these things exist. That this is what it is to be human, to be weak. The temptation. Eve in the garden, the snake, the apple. We have created whole myths and belief systems to explain it, to simplify it, to blame the woman.

So, with the anonymity of the online world, the walls are dissolved, the rooms laid bare. Has the online world encouraged those base selves or simply exposed them? The dark web. What horror lies there?

What is that if not a portal into humanity's most base desires, the darkest parts?

Buckley and I had debated religious theory. He was studying religion as well as philosophy and I had been weaned on Christian doctrine, he said. He asked me if I believed I was a good person beyond the ethics I'd been raised with. I said how could I ever know this with any objectivity? I was deeply entangled with the ethics I'd been raised with. I guess because he seemed interested in good and bad, right and wrong, I assumed that he was good. I don't know why I made that assumption. Maybe my mistake was mistaking intelligence for virtue.

I wasn't too worried about the postcard. At first I assumed it'd been sent from some creep online who had somehow gotten hold of my home address and googled my father. I had a post office box for PRs to send goods through to, but sometimes people found me.

I showed Yas the postcard and she laughed. We googled the cult name, of course, but nothing really came up except a self-tanning brand.

"Fruit loop, obviously," she said. "They're out there. Just last week a guy emailed asking if I could make a dick cake for a stag party. I mean, WTF?"

I'd laughed. It had made me feel better, but something in me was a little unsettled. When you've seen messages from people telling you to kill yourself, some deep sense of perceived personal safety shifts, even if you try to laugh it off. All the rationale in the world doesn't stop the low gong of your instinct from sounding.

I'd looked closer at the postcard and realized it had no stamp.

The second postcard arrived the next day. The handwriting looked more freaky. The letters were bigger, as though written by a child. I felt my stomach turn and a sour taste filled my mouth as I read it.

*I can get you out.*

It was ironic, because it felt like the walls were closing in online. Everywhere I looked there was another image of myself, another version of me reflected back. Mother, whore, beauty, beast, abomination. I didn't know who I was, or who I was trying to be anymore. It felt like one of those funhouse games where the deeper you went the more lost you got. The images started to warp, elongate, bloat. I couldn't see who I was amid all the refraction.

It niggled at me. Some tiny part of me wondered if my father could have done something a bit cultish once while leading the church. I loved my father. I respected him above all people, but had he actually been a good father? All those times that he'd been off tending to his "flock" rather than his family. Times when I'd needed him and he wasn't there. Because there was always someone in need somewhere. Maybe he'd been a bit of a shit dad, actually. A feeling, old but familiar . . . *envy. Another of the deadly sins.* It occurred to me that maybe he'd given more to his followers than to us over the years. Could someone hold such sway over a group of people without having somewhat of a god complex? That was the bit that struck me. *There's a reason he acts like a god.*

*We all worship him.*

I thought about the power he had over people. The power people seemed to want to give him. That natural charisma. The way he preached, his eyes closed, swaying, as though taken by something none of us could see. He told me once it was the Divine Spirit. He'd probably say it was the same feeling I got when a poem came to me. Something outer, something other, something you surrendered yourself to.

I found something online. It took a while—I really had to look. It was an excerpt from an old local paper from the eighties, and there was mention of a cult in the lakes district that had been raided and shut down after a drug bust. I thought of all those times when Yas and I were young and drinking that Dad had lost his shit at us. I couldn't imagine him getting drunk, let alone doing drugs. Then I thought about all the times he had been there at the head of the dinner table and prayed for us, for whatever big or small problems we were going through in our lives. How much he seemed to care. But it spiked my suspicion that maybe there was something to the cult thing.

When the third postcard arrived, I had all but made up my mind. But maybe that was an excuse I was making because I really wanted to see him in person.

*I'm sure you've worked this out by now, but it's actually @poetboy. Did you like the cult shit? It was in the form of a poem so thought you might have guessed. I'm staying at the caravan park by the cathedral with friends. I lost my phone. Offline at the moment. You should try it. So free. Meet me at the altar tomorrow? That seems appropriately dramatic for us, doesn't it?*

It made sense. He had disappeared online. He knew what town I lived in, the lake, my poetic inspiration. All those haikus I'd written. He was smart, it was easy for him to find me. And maybe part of me wanted to be found. He was my dream boy. The person who had helped me skirt the pain of Andy's betrayal. But I knew he was my betrayal too.

And I was so curious. What did he look like in real life? Would we have the same chemistry we had online? Would he look like Jeff Buckley? The postcards had unsettled me, but then I saw them in light of him, and that he had seen them as art. That they were little poems. I thought it was actually quite clever. And I was relieved about the cult stuff. That it was all just a weird joke.

Of course I went to meet him.

# CHAPTER 40

# Jane

"I'm sorry, Janie, I shouldn't have . . . I'm a mess right now." Andy shook his head and pulled his knees to his chest. He looked out onto the water. "But I didn't harm Paige, I promise you. You believe me, don't you? Yes, we were having problems, but I loved her. We were trying to work things out."

The mist had burned away. The sun was rising higher in the sky. The lake was so still that every sound, every movement was amplified. A bird of prey skimmed the surface, a gleaming silver fish caught in its talons. Jane watched it disappear into the tree line.

She nodded, said she believed him. She did believe him. He was a good person, wasn't he? *He was.* She was sure of it. She had a good radar for these things, didn't she?

They sat there silently, chastened. She was shivering. She could still see the imprint of their bodies in the sand. She brushed the evidence lightly with her palm, as though this could erase what they'd just done.

"What are you going to do, Andy?"

He looked toward the path that led to the house, the waiting police car.

"What can I do?"

What was she going to say? *Run. Run away with me. Leave our complicated lives and start somewhere new.* Hadn't she done that before? Running away to Sydney? Yet here she was, drawn back to the place of her deepest shame. Her swallowed-down memories. And here she was again, feeling ashamed for what they'd just done.

*I can never get away from myself.*

"I'm going to give Viv a hug, and then go with them, answer their questions. I can't disappear again. They'll really arrest me then."

He drew her roughly to him, kissed her hair. "Thank you, Janie," he said, and then he was gone down the track without another word.

Jane sank to the sand. She rested her head against the cool wood of the boat. She wanted to crawl under the hull and stay there, cocooned. She couldn't go home to her dad; she didn't want to go back to the Whites, who were probably being told by police that Paige's death was now a murder investigation, and that Andy was being interviewed, was maybe a suspect. She thought of Jackson, how he would kill for this inside information. How much he would love her for it, but how much of a betrayal it would be to give it.

How had she ended up here again, right in the thick of things and yet strangely detached, on the outskirts?

She watched the bird of prey return from the tree line, soaring low over the water, searching for more fish. She let her mind drift, like a fishing line trawling, loose in water, snaring, dredging up memories from the deep.

Jane took out her phone and opened the app. All the many faces of this girl who had haunted her over the years. Always in Paige White's shadow. Always hoping she would keep her close, confer her charm and power, keep her safe. Her teacher's voice, the whispered gossip around town returned to her.

*It must be hard to always be in the shadow of the White sisters.*

*Aren't the Whites kind to take in poor Janie Masters after her mother abandoned her and her father, well, we know all about her father and that house . . . No wonder she ran off with the handsome mechanic.*

Had she even liked Paige White? Who had she been beyond her beauty, her power? Could anyone see her beyond those things? She'd had an aura, and everyone had wanted to be in it. But why? Why?

*I hated Paige White.*

## CHAPTER 41

# Audrey

The tea went cold. I made another pot. I waited in Ed and Daisy's until the low moon leaking light through the she-oaks scared me. I wondered what I was doing in this cold little caravan in the backyard of an abandoned house. And I could see suddenly, without Janie, how everyone at school thought it was creepy. That's the thing about entering the dreamscape, the magical place through the wall where you poke your finger: It changes the way the whole world looks. And just one other person can transform a sad old van into a treasure trove.

It occurred to me that maybe Janie wouldn't come. Maybe she hadn't got our secret code—the note hidden in the novel in her locker. But I didn't want to go home. I *couldn't* go home. I couldn't face that depressing little house filled with the smell of baking, mixed with the cloying fumes of gasoline, reminding me of Dad. Mom's suffocating hope. What was she hoping for? That he'd come home, and we'd all eat cake like some perfect family? The scary thing was that until now I had secretly thought I did have a perfect family. Not Paige White perfect, but I had a mom and dad who loved each other and made each other cocktails, and danced in the living room to scratchy old record albums and who could be real with me. Or so I'd thought. I couldn't face how stupid I'd been.

I must have fallen asleep. I peeled my cheek from the laminated peach tabletop. The teapot with its knitted hat looked absurd. Everything was gray. The dread that crept into my body sometimes, the feeling of freefalling into pain, the way it leached all color from the world, was here now.

But something had roused me. Two fast raps, then two slow. Janie and my special knock.

I opened the door, feeling like I was floating, the dread lifting like a cloud. Hope can make you float. Janie's face was red and puffy. I pulled her in and hugged her. She felt like a baby bird, her shoulders small and bony. I hated my father so much in that moment, for what he'd done to us, done to Janie. And the thoughts that had been circling inside my mind suddenly coalesced.

She slid into the banquette seating and wordlessly poured, then sipped her cold tea. I lit two candles so we weren't in complete darkness.

"I'm going away," I said.

She looked up and there was surprise in her eyes.

"I'm a burden to Mom, and I want her to be happy," I said. "After what that fucker did to her. She can start again. Find a man who isn't a narcissist. He was obsessed with Elvis. I don't know why that wasn't a dead giveaway."

"Paige says he looks like Bon Jovi," Janie said.

I shook my head. "Hmm, I hate how much he'd like that comparison."

Janie put her cup down in its saucer. "Did you know?"

"What?"

"That he and my mom were—"

"How can you ask me that?" I could feel tears building behind my eyes.

"Had he done this before, I mean? Had other affairs?"

"Of course not." But as I said it, it felt like something, some insect crawled over my chest, and I brushed at my collarbone. I wasn't sure. I wasn't sure of anything anymore.

"I can't stay with my dad in that house." Janie's voice was measured, but it sounded dead, resigned.

"Come with me then," I said, wanting to grab her arm but resisting. I could sense she needed time and space.

"With you where? We're only sixteen, Audrey."

She'd never called me that before. I was Auds. I could feel the little chink of light that had opened up inside me start to shrink.

"Where would we go?" she asked, her voice even flatter.

"To Sydney. I know Sydney. We can get jobs."

"What are you talking about? Do you know what happens to girls like us who go to Sydney on their own?"

I laughed under my breath. "Beautiful girls like you, maybe. Not girls like me."

She scrunched up her face. "I don't think that makes a—"

"Difference? Matters? Is that what you were going to say, Janie? Because I think we both know that's not true. It's all that matters in this freaking world." My voice cracked and I hated myself for it, but I went on. "If I looked how you look, how Paige and Yas look, I wouldn't have spent today with people harassing me in the corridors. I would be untouchable, like you."

"It's not about that, Audrey."

"Really? What world do you live in, Janie?"

"I'm not beautiful like they are," she said.

"Are you fucking kidding me?"

Janie shook her head, and I realized she really didn't think she was beautiful like the White sisters, even though they were all made of exactly the same stuff.

"I'm not like they are."

"Yeah, you're right, you're actually not. Your life is going to be bigger than this backwater town. You can have a big life because you're fucking smart and sensitive and real as well as beautiful. So come with me then. I've lost a dad, and you've lost a mom. Don't you see? That binds us."

"Great, we're bound by assholes," Janie muttered, but I could feel her softening, weighing up what I was saying.

I laughed and there was a hint of a smirk on her mouth.

"How long do you reckon it was going on between them?" she asked.

"I don't know. I don't know anything. My mom won't even tell me what's really going on. She keeps saying Dad is away doing stuff for his business. Maybe it is just a rumor, a coincidence that they left at the same time. Maybe they both just walked," I said.

"It's not a rumor. *My* mom wouldn't have just left. There had to be a reason, a good reason. She just got in her car and left. She said she was leaving Dad, but she was leaving me, really. At least you've still got your mom. I've got nothing now but a dad and a house full of crap."

"When we get jobs we're going to find a neat little apartment with no mess and no clutter," I said.

"What about school?"

"We really only have to do year twelve. We can do it at TAFE and then go to uni. Or you can do a three-year cadetship at a paper without uni."

She laughed. "You've got this all planned out, haven't you?"

I shrugged. She knew me. "Meet me here tomorrow at five p.m. I'll bring one of Dad's old dirt bikes. I know how to ride it."

"Are you serious?" I could tell by her face that she wasn't buying it. She wasn't buying any of it.

"I've known how to ride it since I was a kid," I said.

"Auds, we're still kids."

Maybe it was because she was calling me my proper name again, maybe because it was the way she said it, with a softness back in her voice. The chink of hope, of light, shone bright. "Well, I guess we're about to grow up."

# CHAPTER 42

# Paige

He was not waiting for me at the altar and so I followed the track into the bush. I'd never really spent time at the caravan park next to the tree cathedral. I mean, I knew it was there, but it was just a place for summer tourists. I think Yas and I bought an ice cream at the shop once after church and the park had a depressing air that didn't match the glossy posters of the beach and lake. It was busy in the summer months and deserted over winter. There was something a little spooky about it, I guess, because of all that shade. Not much sun got in through the tall palms. But there was a row of tiny cabins that sat right on the lake. The view from them must have been nice, and in the summertime you could see beach towels hanging off the wooden balcony rails like bright beacons.

Maybe I should have told someone where I was going. I nearly told Yas, but he felt like a secret. Just like that deeper part of me, the poetry, was a secret. We're all keeping aspects of ourselves hidden, and that was what I'd done with him. He was my guilty little secret. And I was pretty keen to see what he looked like, if I'm really honest. Was there some part of me that could see a future with this person, even though he was younger than me and an intellectual?

There was a man sitting in a chair on the veranda at the first cabin. He was looking out onto the lake. His face was in profile. He was probably in his late forties or early fifties. Salt-and-pepper hair, a strong jaw. He took a sip of a beer. This wasn't the right cabin. Would I have to go and door-knock each one? There were four. I started to feel my rational mind click in, tell me this was not the best idea. But I continued walking to check the next cabin. Someone called my name. A man's voice.

I turned, hoping I guess, to see Jeff Buckley loping toward me, haloed in afternoon light, walking softly through the leaf litter, barefoot. I'd formed an image in my mind—he wore faded black jeans and old band T-shirts under adorable cardigans in winter. His hair was to his shoulders.

But the voice had come from the man on the veranda. He hadn't said "Paige White," he'd said "at Paige underscore White," and that's when my stomach dropped. I fumbled for my phone in my pocket. I don't know why, I guess it felt safer to be holding it. *How funny. How ironic.*

I didn't say anything in response. I just stood there, and it felt like how in dreams your limbs stop working and you're trying to move but nothing is happening. You're in quicksand. He held up a hand, an appeasing gesture.

"It's me. It's 'at Poet Boy.' It's Buckley."

My brain felt like it spasmed then. This strange place opened up, this halfway place between my online and my real worlds and everything turned upside down. This was a fifty-something man, not my Buckley, the boy I thought was younger than me. But as my brain started to catch up, I saw it. I saw that this *was* Buckley, only older, much older. There was the same thick, wavy hair to the shoulders, the strong brow and deep-set eyes, the full lips. He had been handsome in his youth. He was still attractive. It was the poet as I'd seen him in all the images, but older. Then I realized. All I had been looking at were the tiny pictures he presented to me. How could I have been so stupid, to think he was who he made himself out to be? I knew that lesson better than anyone, and yet I'd fallen for it.

"I know what you're thinking. Hear me out. Please, Paige."

The way he said my name, with such intimacy. He had a beautiful voice, deep, highly educated, with a slightly English lilt. I railed, because what we'd shared *had* been intimate. Our words, our creativity, and through that, our hurts, our pains.

"What the hell is this?" The words flew out of my mouth.

"It's me. I'm still the person you spoke to online."

Thoughts were teeming through my head. I thought about why I'd done this. Was it to get back at Andy? Was it to feel desired? Was it to feel smart when all my life I'd been underestimated? Such a sadness moved through me. I didn't reply. What I wanted to say was, *Well, you're clearly not the person I spoke to online. You're fucking old,* but we were alone in a deserted caravan park on a vast lake, and no one knew I was there. Some deep survival part of my brain kicked in. He was being nice. I needed to keep it that way.

"The photos I used. They were me, just me twenty . . ." He rubbed at his jaw. "Thirty years ago. I studied philosophy and religion at uni. Everything I told you was true."

I wanted to say, *Is this some kind of sick joke?*

Instead I followed the ringing in my ears, the kick in my gut telling me to placate, play nice. I said, "I was just surprised. Of course, I can see it now. You still look like Jeff Buckley."

He smiled. He was still attractive; he had kind eyes, the lines around them etched in softly. They were the same eyes that had drawn me in online. I knew my civility was keeping me safe. I didn't know how this would play out, but of course, he knew me after six months of online conversations, he knew what to say to make me stay.

"I've got beers. We can sit overlooking the lake and I'll explain everything."

"Oh, I should . . . I need to get back." There was a slight waver in my voice that I hated.

"Please, Paige. Don't be afraid of me. I'm the same person you've been speaking to for months. I'm not here to hurt you, I promise. I just need to explain why I'm here. Like the postcards said, it has to do with your father. That's the why of all of it, really."

My whole body was buzzing. My mouth went dry. *Your father.* I'd written off the cult reference as an odd joke, but now was he telling me this was why he was here? I guess it was fear I was feeling, but it was also a warped curiosity. I was so torn. Should I run? Should I stay? I thought back to the postcard . . . *cult leader* . . . *solaris.* Was he saying that was true? There was that tiny part of me that needed to know; the fact I'd found that small mention of it online—that made me stay. Or maybe it was actually the part of me that doubted my father, that had always seen him as a man larger than life, magnetic but distant. It was both those things, I think, that made me follow him up the steps of the cabin.

I scanned the three other dwellings. They were close, tucked together like little green and brown ducks on the shore. One had a towel drying over the rail. Other people were around. It was coming up to Easter holidays, not the dead of winter. I worked to steady my mind, my breathing. The lake lulled me. The sun just above the tree line turning everything golden. I realized I could see the tip of my house, the chimney and sharp slope of the roof. It was comforting. I stood there, watching the lake, watching him out of the corner of my eye. He sat down. I stayed standing, shielding my eyes against the light.

"I just want you to know that Poet Boy wasn't a lie. Everything we said to each other, everything I wrote, that's who I am."

I felt my eyes prick with tears, because I realized in that moment that I had probably fallen in love with Poet Boy. It wasn't only the weird stuff about Dad that had drawn me here, but a deep caring for this person's spirit, the things we'd shared, and a need to see him, to touch him in person. Ironically, how much more I'd been able to show of myself online, with some anonymity, without the filter of my looks. How I'd found some deeper part of myself through the way I'd connected with this boy, this man. That here was a person who had seen that I could be smart, creative, powerful. That I was more than a mother, a wife, a pretty face, an influencer. That I could notice small things about the world and write them into a fabric to wrap around myself. It was this deep vulnerability more than this strange scenario that terrified me the most.

"Okay," I said, but I didn't move to sit down. "So, who are you? You're obviously not at university."

"No, but I do teach for the university online and through local libraries. I've been published. Small, independent, long-form-poetry publications. I'm literally Poet Boy, or man . . . a poet who drifts from town to town staying in camping areas, living out of my car, out of my tent. I've splurged with the cabin. God, I know how sad that sounds."

"It doesn't sound sad," I said, strangely touched by this admission.

"I guess creatives in this country have to make a choice. You can live very frugally as an artist, or you can get a menial job. I've chosen the former."

"That's brave."

He laughed softly, then looked out onto the lake. "So, this is your lake," he said, and I smiled. "I've read so many words dedicated to its beauty, and I've got to say, your words do it justice."

"You think so?" I could feel myself blushing. I could imagine him teaching poetry online out of the back of his car with his refined voice.

"Can I get you a beer? A cup of tea? Sorry, I—"

I shook my head. "No . . . thanks. I just . . . I want to know about the Solaris stuff. Why did you really write that?"

"Yes, sorry. You deserve to know why I'm here as an older—I'm sure you see me as old—man, why I did what I did." He ran his hand through his hair. "Where to start? I didn't mean for us to get as close as we did. I was trying to track down your father. He ignored my emails to the church. I wanted some closure on that part of my life. That was my motivation for getting in touch. And through him I found you. If you remember, I commented on something and then we started talking on DMs. My profile picture was me young, and I didn't correct you when you assumed I *was* young. Maybe some part of me . . . well, I was processing what my life might have been if I hadn't got involved with your father when I was young."

I felt frozen to the spot. A long-ago memory flashed through my mind. Looking up at my father, so tall, his hands raised in the air, the luminous white of his robes, the way people would reach out to touch the flowing fabric, the way being gathered into it would feel so safe.

"Solaris, it was a thing before you were born, way back when," he went on. "It was this shitty thing . . . a group that me and some mates got sucked into. Headed by the inimitable Stephen White, your dad. Before he started preaching. A mix of different ideas, religions. He was obviously just fine-tuning his skills of persuasion."

"What do you mean? Is that what you meant by a cult? It sounds so sinister, but my dad's a good man. He literally spends his days helping people."

"Look, I'm not here to tell you he's evil. That's not what I'm here to do. But god, it's more complex than that, isn't it? It's a lot of power he wields so casually . . . to put in one person's hands even if the intent isn't malicious. We felt so safe, so included, but it ended up being messed-up. He did some questionable things back in the day. Does that mean he's a bad person?"

"What bad things?" My voice was small.

"Well, he . . . he always had something about him, didn't he? Something about the way he talked—people listened. I admired that. He was into Eastern philosophy, religion. Interested in questioning the world, the status quo. That's what drew me in. We all smoked weed, dabbled in other drugs, trying to expand our minds, understand the universe. He was young too, but older than me. And the police, they got wind of it, and I was taken in, arrested for growing and dealing marijuana. He could have told the truth, but he let me take the blame."

My mind was reeling trying to piece together this new picture of my father smoking weed, doing drugs. All those times he'd punished us for smoking cigarettes. He seemed so strict, so closed now. Of course, I knew intellectually that he'd been young once, but it had always felt like he hadn't really existed until I did, and I'd always assumed he'd been conservative, the sort of person who was above reproach his whole life.

"I did time in prison—eighteen months. I guess at that age I didn't think it was such a big deal, but it threw my whole life off track. I wanted to be a serious academic. I was living, breathing Poet Boy when I met your father, taking a gap year from uni to travel, and planning to one day do a PhD . . . and I ended up with a criminal record."

"What do you mean he let you take the blame though?"

He laughed. "Can't put much past you, Paige White. Just like your dad. Smart. Shrewd. Beautiful. Ridiculously charismatic. I worshipped your dad. I wanted to protect him. I told them it was me who grew the drugs when it was Stephen White who had the little setup."

I stiffened. "So, you have only yourself to blame."

"Do I? Or was I manipulated? Sucked in by his charm."

"Why would you say that?"

"Because I wanted to be loved and admired by him. I wanted to fit in with what he'd created. And Stephen White, well, he got his cult in the end, didn't he? All his loyal followers. His acolytes. And the rest of his perfect life."

"No one's life is perfect," I said.

"At Paige White would beg to differ."

"Would she? You know how much I . . . struggle." I hated the hurt in my voice.

"You do have a lot more than people realize going on beneath the surface."

"You completely lied to me." There was venom in my voice now.

"Did I lie? I used a photo of myself, I was me. I just didn't tell you my age."

"It's a pretty big oversight. Lying by omission."

"Isn't that what we're all doing? Showing some details of our lives, omitting others . . ."

"Now you're talking like a philosopher."

"Touché," he said, holding my eye.

I couldn't believe it; we had that same weird, messed-up chemistry. But no, I thought, it's not that simple. "God, it's no wonder you seemed wise beyond your years. I thought it was the philosophy. My dad didn't force you to join that group or to use drugs. We all have free will."

"Do we though? What if we're merely acting out our genetic sequence."

"Well then, my dad's not to blame for your life being screwed-up then, is he? Maybe it was inevitable."

There was a beat where we just stared at each other. I thought he might say something awful, but he smiled. "Have you written any poetry lately?"

I shook my head. "Look, I don't know what you want from me. Why you've told me all this. I'm not here for a casual chat. I'm sorry if you feel hard done-by after what my father did or didn't do to you, but it was a long time ago. It sounds like you were all young. Doesn't everyone do stupid things they regret when they're young? Everyone's moved on. They're not tracking down people's daughters online." I said the last part under my breath.

"Sometimes people find it hard to move on from what happened a long time ago," he said. He laughed then but there was a cynical edge to it. "God. I've been sucked in by another White, haven't I? Drawn to you in the same way I was to him. Why do I do this to myself? I've got to stop." His fist met with the arm of his chair, and I jumped. "You're cut from exactly the same cloth as he is with your easy charisma. All that power, all those followers. The high priestess of your pretty online world. How could I be so stupid? Been so obsessed."

He hissed the last word and my skin crawled. I took a step back from him, noting the distance between us, the distance to the stairs. The sun had gone behind the clouds and the lake had turned into a dark mirror. Birds screeched in the trees. I fought the urge to run. I kept my voice calm, steady, pleasant.

"Look, I'm just trying to live my life. I appreciate you telling me all this, but please don't contact me again."

He stood abruptly and I felt fear pitch through me. I made for the stairs. Every molecule in my body was waiting to feel him grab me. But it didn't happen. He didn't follow me, or call out. But I could feel his eyes on me as I walked away as fast as I could without it looking desperate. The muscles in my legs burned, my chest hurt. I was shaking. I didn't breathe properly until I got into my car and locked the door.

# CHAPTER 43

# Jane

It was still early but the sun was already hot on her arms and legs as she followed the path around the lake. That clinging mist seemed like a strange and faraway dreamscape, but the leftover humidity hung on her skin. She didn't know where she was going. Not back to the Whites', but not back to her dad's either.

Her phone buzzed in her pocket. *Jackson calling.* She stopped and looked at his name. Silenced the call. God, what was she going to do with Jackson? He was going to want this new intel about Andy being taken in, coverage of the memorial tomorrow. She'd promised him that. She had slipped so far from who she was. Put-together Jane in her suit and heels, sitting at her desk diligently reading the newspapers by 8 a.m. Now here she was with sticks and sand in her hair, her body still bearing the imprints of a man who was being taken in by police to be questioned about the suspected murder of his wife.

*Who are you?*

The voice that had been getting louder.

*You know who you are.*

She pushed the dark thoughts away, wiped the sweat from her brow, and quickened her pace. She felt bereft, pulled apart. How had she ended up here? Caught again between two houses, two families? Neither feeling like her own. Behaving like Janie.

She reached her car. It was still piled with her father's junk. The sight of it sent pain shooting through her, the beginnings of a headache needling at her brain. What was she going to do now? Part of her wanted to get in her car and drive the single-lane highway through the forest until it met the freeway. Get out of here, away from these vast reflective lakes, throwing up too much light, too many memories, disorienting her. What did she have to stay for? She was angry with Paige for bringing her back here to face parts of herself that she'd buried.

*You are a horrible person. It's not her fault she's dead.*

She was ashamed of her dad. But mostly she was ashamed of herself. What the hell was she playing at with Andy? He was Paige's husband. His wife hadn't even been buried. What the hell was he doing? Was he grieving? Acting rashly because he was in pain? Or was he a cold person who could somehow detach? God, she seemed to attract them.

*You are playing a dangerous game.*

Her phone buzzed in her hand. Jackson.

*Call me.*

It was also a game that could endanger her job, her livelihood. It was hard enough to even keep her job in the media with the redundancies ripping through newsrooms. Would Jackson care if he found out she'd been with Andy? *Yes,* she thought, *of course he would.* But some small part inside her whispered, *But he's cheated on you. You know he has, more than once.*

"*Shut up. Shut up. Shut up.*"

She realized she'd said it out loud. Her mind was so loud, her thoughts tangled. She needed to equilibrate. To go somewhere to

think straight. She got into the car. It smelled musty—a pungent re-
minder of the house, her father, her guilt. She cracked the window, but
it hardly helped. She began to drive. The parking lot was deserted. She
got out of the car and walked into the dense, dark foliage. She followed
the track until the clearing opened out. With the morning sun filtering through the canopy above, illuminating the tops of the trees, it
really did look like a cathedral.

She sat down on a pew fashioned from the trunk of a tree and
closed her eyes. She gripped the log beneath her legs. It felt steady,
heavy, cool. *Andy.* Andy was why she was still here.

She felt shame and longing collide inside her at the thought of his
body. This wasn't just about finding out what happened to Paige. It
was about Andy now too. She took her phone out of her pocket.

*Let's find out what was really going on,* she thought.

Jane used the password Andy had given her. She was into Paige's
account within seconds. It felt like entering another person's head,
like unlocking a key that opened the secret cupboard of the mind.
Here were all the odd socks, things that were too baggy or tight. It felt
wrong, shameful, as she looked at Paige's pretty face in the round circle, but she told herself she was doing it for Andy. There were hundreds of new likes and follows and unread messages.

She went straight into Paige's messages. There were a lot of messages from men with handles like @max222356. How on earth was
she going to find the one who had been Paige's stalker?

*God, people loved you, Paige, didn't they?* she thought. She clicked on
the first message. It was from @kittyporridge.

*You'll never read this but, you were beautiful. Ethereal actually. I'm sorry
this happened to you. Hope they find who did it.*

There were more in this same vein, the same as the ones written
on her last post, dated after Paige's death had made headlines. Written
as though they could contact her through the ether. As though she
were checking her messages in death.

Jane scrolled through until she reached the messages that dated before her death. She expected more of the same, but her breath caught.

*Fucking bitch. Die.*

*I hate you and your oat milk lattes. I hate your perfect asses. Go away. You make me feel like shit.*

*Don't try to pretend your normal. Your nothing like us.*

*It all fake dude.*

*I'm gonna come to that lake of yours and kill you.*

*I know where you live.*

Jane felt sick. She knew how bad, how cruel people could be online—she'd seen it firsthand on news posts—but this was so personal. She scrolled and scrolled. The tone only softened after Paige had died. She felt tears in her eyes. She wondered if these people had felt bad after writing those things, finding out she did die after all. She heard Andy's voice, *She was in a bad place.*

*I'm sorry, Paige.*

The tops of the trees rippled in the breeze and Jane shuddered and stood up.

Paige couldn't have taken her own life the way Shep had described, on that lake, could she?

It was no wonder the police hadn't found her stalker. It was like looking for a needle in a haystack. There was message after message filled with personal attacks. What did it mean?

She clicked back to the main page. Next to Paige's name at the top of her account was a red dot and an arrow pointing downward. What was that?

Another account. @poet&paige. A picture of . . . the lake.

This grid wasn't filled with pictures, but with words. Poems. Had Paige written these? Jane felt a shift inside her. This was not the Paige she knew. Had the police seen this other account?

But this wasn't just Paige's account. It was a shared account with someone called @poetboy.

There were messages between them. *Ah, here we are,* Jane thought. *Here's the Paige I knew.* The last were dated in the days just before she died.

*Tell me there wasn't something between us when we met. You felt it. I know you did.*

*Is this the life you really want to be living, Paige? On a treadmill of other people's admiration?*

*Please, just leave me and my family alone.*

Her last message.

Jane was already calling Shep. He picked up just as Jane was about to hang up.

"Shep, hi, sorry to call you again, I know you can't talk about the case, but I've been doing some research. Did you know Paige had another account with this Poet Boy? That they met in person just before she died? Was he her stalker?"

Shep cleared his throat, and she could hear a squeak, as though he was moving through an office, opening a door, shutting it.

"Yeah, Janie, our intel team has got all that. They've accessed all her accounts. Listen, we know the guy, who he is. He was staying in one of those dinky little caravan park cabins on the lake for a while. We've actually found him and questioned him. Look, it's not him. He has a strong alibi the morning Paige died. Everything he told us we verified with what was in her account. He's telling the truth."

"What?" Jane's head was spinning. "But her last message . . . she was clearly scared of him."

"I know. But there's more info that's come to light."

"What?"

There was a pause on the line.

"Please, Shep. For old times' sake." She felt bad, felt like she was manipulating him when she knew he shouldn't be telling her, but she needed to know what was going on. "This is Paige," she said quietly.

She heard the intake of his breath. "Look, the person whose alibi seems to be flimsy is Andy's. He said he was at the Whites' house that morning with Viv, but a woman living at one of the permanent places at the caravan park has come forward to say she saw him at the tree cathedral with Paige and Viv early, at approximately six thirty that morning. The lady was walking her dog. Paige's estimated time of death is between then and nine a.m."

Jane felt like someone was tearing strips off her. She felt raw, exposed. She could still smell Andy on her skin. She looked toward the path leading to the caravan park. She could feel her body moving toward it without input from her mind. "What does that mean?"

"Well, it means he's lied about where he was."

"But the Whites saw him at the house that morning, didn't they?"

"The Whites, as you know, are very honest folk and they may have just assumed he was at the house when he said he was. It was very early in the morning."

Everything was spinning but she kept walking. She didn't know where she was going, or maybe she did. "But I know Andy, and he didn't hurt Paige. Some creepy stalker is far more likely, surely. And Viv was there that morning too?"

"Look, Janie, I know this is hard, but we're still questioning him. We're not sure what's gone on, but don't you want justice for Paige? Don't you want Viv to be safe? Surely you of all people want to know the truth?"

The truth . . . *the truth*. She had based her professional life on the search for the truth. But really, she had been running from the truth her entire life. It was funny how life worked in circles, how things returned again and again, like refractions. Everything felt more entwined than you'd first realized. But maybe all it was, was that you could never escape yourself.

## CHAPTER 44

# Paige

I'm agnostic. I fell away from my father's teachings, but I've been
having second thoughts about the faith I grew up in since being
here. I haven't prayed in twenty years. Actually, that's not entirely
true. I prayed just before Viv came out of my body. I prayed that she
would be okay, and that the pain would stop.

I've always told myself I worshipped Gaia, the goddess of nature,
her forests and beaches and lakes, but now, in this limbo place, those
things seem just as flimsy as the idea of a god did to my teenage self. It
feels like it's all made of the same stuff—hope. A balm to the despair. I
don't know who to exactly, but I have started to pray again.

*I'm sorry. I'm so sorry for all the people who I hurt during my life. Maybe
part of me is like Dad. Maybe people handed over their power to me for some
reason I don't really understand, and I wasn't careful with what I did with it. Because I liked having that power and they were willing to let me have it. But they
resented me for it. Maybe I had no idea that out there were people whose lives I*

had ruined, who were sitting with that pain. Maybe Buckley felt like this—in limbo—never living his proper life because of regret that things didn't end up as he'd hoped. That he hadn't achieved his potential. And it had made him stuck, unable to move forward, be free.

I don't care if there's only blackness, obliteration after this. I just can't be stuck here anymore. Please, please, if you are the merciful deity my father spoke of, instead of the vengeful and judgmental one I came to reject . . . please . . . I can't be here watching images of my daughter play out like a nostalgic movie. Because I know deep down that I've been deluding myself this whole time. I've been pretending that she's alive—maybe those images are my thin hope, my subconscious protecting me. The truth is (and I'm sorry I haven't been totally honest but I don't think I've been able to be honest with myself) . . . the truth is . . . I just can't face it. Because I think I am dead, and I think Viv might be dead too. And I can't bear it if she is, if I was the cause of that. Because it's starting to come back to me, that final day . . . what happened on the lake. Please, if you are a loving god, have mercy on me, let me out of this place. Let me find oblivion. Let me find peace.

# CHAPTER 45

# Audrey

Mom was waiting for me when I got home from meeting Janie at Ed and Daisy's. Mom was always waiting for me. She told me once that she never truly relaxed in life until I was in the house. She had wiped the flour from the countertops and was sitting on the old brown couch with the record player whining out Eva Cassidy songs, a cocktail glass in her hand.

Her eyes closed with relief when she saw me. But I could tell that she'd been crying. And somehow, despite this, I resented her. I resented how I was everything to her now that Dad was gone. I resented that she had everything invested in such a faulty person. Maybe I resented her for not being able to keep him, or myself for not making him love me enough to stay. And I resented that a small part of me was already feeling bad that I was going to abandon her. But her pain was so palpable. I could feel it pierce me as soon as I walked into the room. She patted the spot beside her for me to sit, but I couldn't go close, or I knew I wouldn't be able to leave her. I said I was tired and just wanted to have a shower and go to bed.

She said, "Audrey, I want to talk about what's happened between me and Dad. I'm sorry if I was a bit spaced-out before. I think I was just . . . processing things. Sit down. Sit. Want me to make you a hot chocolate?"

But I couldn't sit. It felt so claustrophobic, with the smell of sugar still in the air, the mournful vocals and the whiff of spirits. All I wanted was to escape it all. It felt suffocating. I told her, let's talk tomorrow. I'm so tired. And she nodded.

I went into my bedroom and it was as though I was seeing everything objectively for the first time. As though because I was finally escaping, I could now admit how shitty it all was. The sagging mattress of my bed, the hole in the plasterboard of the wall that I'd romanticized by putting my finger through it, the carpet that looked like dog's vomit. I went to the wardrobe and pulled out a bag and started filling it with clothes. I did it fast, like I'd seen characters in movies pack to run away. And to be honest, there was something in this depiction—in just throwing stuff into a bag quickly without thinking about it too much. There was something freeing about it—not caring for material stuff, but just feeling the call of freedom.

On my bedside table sat my journals. There were ten of them in all. I'd been keeping them since I was a little kid. I didn't bother hiding them. I thought Mom wouldn't read them. I talked to her so much, she wasn't going to be shocked by anything she read in there anyhow. But I guess I hadn't told her about the past twenty-four hours, about how my world had fallen apart.

So, I sat down and I wrote about the whole school rejecting me, Paige rejecting me. It hurt to put it down on paper, but it felt like I was leaving that version of myself behind, writing her out of my system. I wasn't going to school anymore. I wasn't going to be the one who never fitted in anymore. I wasn't going to be the person who even a father couldn't love and stay for. I wasn't going to be hopeless anymore. I wrote all of it down. I wrote that I'd contact Mom when Janie and I were in Sydney, and told her not to worry. That she could build a new life without me. She was free of me, and she could literally go anywhere, do anything with her life now, just like she'd probably always wanted, instead of being tied to some shitty gas station life that wasn't her dream.

When I had written it all down, I came out to find her curled up on the couch like a child. It's funny, but I noticed then, perhaps for the first time, how tiny she was compared to me with my big, bulky body. She looked so young and beautiful and fragile lying there, and I felt a surge of anger that my father had left her. I also wondered: If the person she had most loved had left her, what hope in the world did I, who was so much less lovable, have? But then I remembered Janie.

I took the empty glass out of Mom's hand and gently pulled a blanket over her. I kissed her cheek and left the room.

# CHAPTER 46

# Jane

Jane stood in front of a row of mobile homes. They were like replica houses with their metal walls and striped awnings. Dead leaves had collected on the window rims and rust was eating away at the metal around the doors. A few had annexes with outdoor table settings. There were colorful potted plants at the entrance of one, and a hammock was strung between two trees, a child's bike. A little cooker had been set up, with bright mugs drying on a wooden rack. The simple pride in such a modest establishment formed a lump in Jane's throat. The view was far from modest, though. All the homes looked out through a screen of dappled light, through red gums and palm fronds as big as satellite dishes, onto the lake.

*Why am I here?*

All those times she had knocked on strangers' doors over the years. She'd hated it, but it had felt like she'd had the weight, the legitimacy of the paper and usually a photographer behind her. Now she

was just a girl in the middle of nowhere with a tip-off from a police-
man who fancied her, about the possible guilt of a man she'd wanted
to sleep with, neither of whom was her boyfriend.

*Full Janie.*

She swallowed back the shame and nerves and approached the
well-kept home. A woman opened the door before Jane could even
knock. She was holding a box of breakfast cereal and was wrapped in
a faded pink robe.

"Can I help you with something?" There was cool wariness in her
voice.

Jane's work persona clicked into gear. "I'm so sorry to knock on
your door so early. My name's Jane . . . I'm a local, from The Lakes . . .
and I'm a friend of the girl who passed away on the lake a little over a
week ago . . . in the kayak . . . I'm not sure if you . . ."

She saw a flash of recognition in the woman's eyes.

She went on. "And I heard there was someone at the caravan park
who saw Paige on that last morning over at the tree cathedral." She
pointed west. "Who's helping the police with some information."

The woman's eyes narrowed at the mention of the police and Jane
could see herself reflected back in them. She probably looked crazy.
She didn't have her journalist armor on—her suit. She probably had
leaves in her hair.

She put up her hands. "I'm sorry. The police said someone from
the caravan park had helped them with information . . . and I just . . .
I'm desperate to know what happened to my friend."

The woman's face softened. "Yeah, I heard about it. Pretty full-on."
She lifted her chin in the direction of the other mobile homes. "Katya's
the one you want. She manages the place. She should be up in reception, opening up. I think she was walking her dog that morning and
she saw them."

*Them.*

Jane knew she had to keep this woman talking, but she had to stay cool. Journalism 101: More often than not, people actually want to talk. It was human nature to want to pass on information, to gossip. That was the raison d'être of newspapers, social media, everything that came after.

The woman stepped closer, looked behind her, and lowered her voice. "To be honest, Katya thought she was dead when she saw the girl lying there on the sand like that . . . It scared the bejesus out of her and then it gave us both chills when she really did die."

"Lying in the sand?"

"She was just like lying in the water and then Katya realized she was posing for a photo. A man and a little girl were there. They were taking a picture of her."

Jane felt a chill down her spine. *Andy. Viv.* Why had Andy lied to the police about being with Paige that morning?

"They had a whole setup, a little picnic. It all looked so nice, so perfect. And the little girl was there too. Katya said it was like something out of a film set . . . She said it was weird seeing someone posing like that, but she supposed that was what the young ones did now, for social media. Set up things to look perfect in photos. But of course . . ."

Jane waited. The woman moved closer still.

"But then when she was coming back around the track a bit later, she heard shouting. They were really getting stuck into each other about something. She didn't know if she should say something, get involved, but you know how it is with domestic stuff. It was early, there was no one around, and she didn't want to get involved . . . so she just kept walking. They hadn't seen her so . . . But when she read in the paper, what with the police asking for information, and well, being a mother herself . . . She was hesitant at first, but I told her to go to the cops. That poor little baby girl of hers."

Jane's mouth was dry. "Do you think she'd speak to me? Was the man threatening Paige? Does she think he did something to her?"

The woman shrugged. "I've told you everything she knows. She's pretty upset about it, to be honest. I had to pretty much make her tell the cops. But they were pretty happy she talked to them, that's for sure. Anyway, love, I've got to get my boy to school." She shook the packet of cereal still in her hand. "But I hope you find out, I hope they get him."

Nausea washed over her as she thanked the woman and left. Andy had lied to the police, to her. What the hell was he playing at? Part of her didn't even want to know. It was too awful. She thought back to the moment she saw him throw something in the water. What had it been? Some sort of evidence? Where was Paige's phone? Was he really capable of strangling his wife in front of his daughter? God.

What was she even thinking? No. She'd just shared a passionate moment with this man. Her insides felt like they were rearranging themselves. It was only a week or so since Paige had died. It was a crazy outlet, grief attraction, right? Was there such a thing? She'd google it later.

No, Andy had loved Paige, but more so, he loved his daughter. She knew she had to talk to him. Give him the right of reply. Everyone deserved their story to be heard. Innocent until proven guilty. She had to give him a chance to explain.

# CHAPTER 47

# Paige

Why do we turn to religion when things are bad? Is that all the promise of god is? A panacea for our very human pain? In a way I felt bad that I'd rejected the faith of my parents for so long, and then when my life started to fall apart, I turned back to what was familiar. I guess that was it. It was a comfort. It was what I knew. I started praying, even before I got trapped here in limbo. I started about the same time as I started getting all the messages from people telling me to kill myself. It's hard to describe what it does to you, reading those things. I told myself rationally that they were just empty threats. People who had too much time on their hands. That it wasn't real. That they didn't know me. But at night, when I woke and everything was dark, all I could think about were those hateful words.

Maybe if I hadn't built my self-worth on the adoration of people I'd never met, it wouldn't have affected me so much. But fame, or my version of it anyway, came with love, and so I don't know why the balance of life would be any different here—of course it came with hate. It's unhealthy to live always in the shadow of small red hearts, of others' opinions. A silent mind, being in nature, was the only way I could cope. That hour of meditation—skimming the still morning skin of the lake and then drawing my kayak onto the white sand to sit under the trees—felt like the only thing keeping me alive.

But after I went to meet Buckley at the caravan park, I was too nervous to return to the tree cathedral alone. It's not that I really thought he'd do anything to me. He'd pretty much left me alone after our encounter. But it was no longer my sanctuary.

Then on the morning of my birthday, I made a decision.

I'll tell you everything I remember . . . even though I'm scared to face it.

I woke early as I always did, and moved quietly through the house. I kissed Viv's tiny sleeping body. I took a moment to look at how beautiful Andy's face was in repose. I didn't bother to get into my kayak clothes. I kept my lacy silk camisole on and pulled on a pair of legging shorts. I didn't even look in the mirror when I went to the bathroom. It felt important that I didn't look in the mirror somehow.

I dragged my kayak into the shallows. The water was colder, choppier than usual, with a sea breeze rushing in through the channel. It didn't deter me. Instead of going across the middle, I skimmed the edge of the lake, hearing the birds rouse in the trees. A shoal of fish broiled beneath the surface of the water. The sun was a pale ball hovering low, only just rising. Everything seemed muted. I had been thinking about what it would be like to leave. What it would be like to see no more mornings. I didn't think I was the kind of person who would ever consider taking my own life, but I understood that it was really just about making the pain stop. When it hurts so much, all you want is for it to stop. And I had been trying to find ways to make it stop. There was one last thing I knew I could do.

My arms were aching by the time I reached the tree cathedral. It seemed apt that this would be the place to make my last post into the ether. Apt that it was my birthday. I knew that if I was to survive, I needed to leave @paige_white behind once and for all. I needed to be reborn into the real world. But as I drew my kayak up onto the sand, I saw them.

Andy had laid out a picnic rug, just back from the shore on the soft white sand in front of the altar. Dawn light filtered through the paper-barks. There was a bottle of champagne, croissants, orange juice, fresh flowers.

It felt like all the sadness inside me slid away. Viv rushed to me, still in her pjs, her hair a mess of curls, and Andy took my hand. I said a silent prayer, to God, to nature, because it felt like being saved.

"Happy birthday. I was hoping we'd catch you here. As you can see, we came straight out of bed," he said.

He pulled me into a hug.

"I'm sorry." I whispered it into his ear, and he tightened his grip on me.

"I hope you like our little surprise."

"When did you . . . ?"

"I had it all ready in the car last night, so as soon as you left, we jumped up and came. I know you come here to meditate."

"I love it."

"Come, sit."

I hesitated. "Andy, I came here to do my final post. I'm giving it all up, forever. It's too hard to be between worlds. I want to be in the real world now, with you and Viv."

He took his camera out of its bag on the rug, smiling. "I was going to offer to take a photo of your birthday picnic for the gram."

It was the first time he'd offered since everything had fallen apart. We smiled at each other and laughed a bit. We had somehow found a way back to each other, we'd met halfway. A mutual peace offering. My heart ached with love for him, and I kissed him.

"It seems fitting that you're the one to take my final picture."

"I just want you to enjoy your birthday." He drew me onto the rug and poured me a glass of champagne. Viv sat in my lap and gave me my flowers. They were in a half-moon crown, flowers threaded through branches and tied together with long, pale silk ribbons.

"Thank you, my darling." I kissed the top of her head, and in that moment I knew that I could never leave. Because it would mean leaving her. It didn't matter how bad the pain got, I would endure it.

"This is beautiful," I said, placing the flowers in my hair, fingering the long ribbons.

"It was on the front doorstep this morning. You didn't see it?"

"I went out the back door. Was there a note or something?"

"No. I thought maybe someone delivered it, you know, one of your Instagram people, for your birthday." He put air quotes around "Instagram people."

An unsettling feeling moved through me, but I dismissed it. Andy didn't know about any of it. The hate mail, Poet Boy. I guess I didn't want to let him think he was right. That was my stubborn side. I was resolved to enjoy this surprise.

"Momma pretty," Viv said.

"I don't want you to take a picture of this perfect setup, though. I just want you to take a photo of me without makeup, raw, in nature, you know? Can we do that?" I passed him my phone. "Nothing fancy. I'll just upload it, so it's done."

I walked to the shoreline. I don't know why, but I lay down in the place where the foam and scum collect, all the washed-up sticks and seagrass and bits of plastic. All the flotsam and jetsam of life. I wrote one word in the sand with a stick: *Adieu.* I dug my fingers into the sand. Felt the water lap at my wrists, the smooth ribbons on my shoulders. I closed my eyes. I could smell salt and flowers and sun-dried seaweed.

I opened my eyes to see Viv standing there with my phone.

"She wants to take the picture," said Andy, shrugging.

I realized I didn't want her to grow up like this, with this thing attached to her, and it felt serendipitous somehow that it was she who would take my final photo for the grid.

# CHAPTER 48

# Jane

Jane's car was still full of trash bags. The musty smell had intensified in the heat. She felt a pulse of shame, but it was overrun by the adrenaline leaking through her. She needed some time and space to think. She needed coffee and a shower. She was still wearing the same shorts and T-shirt steeped in lake water and Andy. *Andy*. How had she kissed and nearly slept with this man? She had never done anything like that before. She had to wash him off her skin, out of her hair. But part of her didn't want to. Her mind's eye kept replaying the moment he had eased her onto that sand. The desire. The tenderness. She'd never felt anything like that with Jackson. With any man.

She shook her head. She needed to think. She picked up a coffee and drove to the beach, where she walked and sat in the car until it was early afternoon. Then she did what she should have done as soon as she'd arrived at The Lakes—she drove to a motel.

Jane pulled into the parking lot. It had the bones of a 1970s motel, all boxy architecture and concrete, but it had been given an Insta-worthy gentrification. The red brick façade had been painted navy blue and white. The matching umbrellas completed the retro look. She could see the wavering reflection of a pool, potted palms, plastic sun loungers. Jane was sure she'd seen an image of Paige here on those lounges drinking cocktails with Andy. She pushed the thought away.

She got out of the car. She wasn't unfamiliar with staying in road-side motels. She would sometimes be away from Sydney with a pho-tographer on a job, usually a stake-out trying to get someone to talk, and they'd be told by the news desk that they had to stay overnight somewhere and return to the stake-out in the morning.

*Try to think rationally,* Jane told herself. *Try to think of this as any other news job. Use your reporter's skills to get to the bottom of it.*

The woman behind the motel counter was cheerful and dressed as though she were manning the desk of a five-star hotel in Sydney, tap-ping a fingernail in the same shade as the pool umbrellas as she scruti-nized the screen in front of her. She gave Jane a room overlooking the garden. It felt good to close the heavy door behind her, the crispness of the air-conditioning greeting her. She took a hot shower, wrapped herself in a fluffy bathrobe, and ordered pasta and a glass of wine. But when the food arrived, it was hard to swallow. The carbs seem to lodge in her throat.

That woman's words came back to her. *Really getting stuck into each other.* Why would Andy lie to her, to the police, about being there that morning Paige died? She needed to hear his side of things. But a tiny part of her whispered that maybe she didn't want to hear the truth, and that maybe the police wouldn't let him go. But his wife's memo-rial was early tomorrow.

Last night Mr. White had asked Jane to say something, a short eulogy, anything she wanted, to remember her friend. Jane had told him that she didn't really feel up to it, but he'd placed his hand on her back, steadying, warm, making her think of the laying-on of hands, of healing, and she'd relented. God, why hadn't she just said no? But he was also Pastor White, and like Paige, wasn't someone it was easy to say no to. And now she had to think of what the hell she was going to say tomorrow.

She eyed the hotel-issue pen and pad on the desk but didn't get up. She knew what they all expected. *Paige was wonderful. Paige was beautiful. Paige was my childhood friend.* She ran her hands down her face. There were plans for everyone to arrive at the tree cathedral at 6 a.m., just before the sun rose. The family had decided not to put details on social media. It would be word of mouth only. There would be prayers and flowers sent out onto the lake. Surely Andy would be there.

*He's innocent. He has to be.*

She looked down at her phone. Her thumb scrolled to Shep's number. She wanted to text him, but she knew it was unfair to push him to reveal more to her when he'd said he wasn't comfortable doing so. She felt the knot inside her gut pull tighter. She had three men—what? Interested in her? Were they? Was that what it was? She didn't even know how to characterize it. She had never thought of herself as someone who could use her body to get what she wanted. That was Paige White kind of behavior, and she wasn't like the Whites.

As though intuiting her thoughts, her phone buzzed to life. *Jackson. I have new info from our police reporter. Call me.*

*Ugh.* She did need to call him. They'd only spoken on the phone once. He was sure to know about the memorial. Her two worlds felt like they were colliding—Janie being asked to deliver a eulogy she didn't want to deliver, and Jane being asked to write a story she didn't want to write. But she needed to know what this new info Jackson had was.

He picked up midsentence. "Yeah, get it to him ASAP." There was a rustle as he put the phone closer to his mouth. "Masters, talk to me. What's going on? Have you been screening me?"

"I um . . . I've been—"

"You don't have to answer that. So, the latest . . . do you want to hear?"

She said nothing.

"The husband, Andy, he was taken into custody for questioning but then released without charge."

Jane let out a long, slow, silent breath of air. *Thank God.*

"Don't know all the details yet but they're definitely treating Paige White's death as murder."

Jane's gut churned. There was a part of her that wanted to say to him, "I know, I knew," but she resisted.

"You've got good instincts. We both knew there was something odd going on. What's the feeling like there anyway? Have you been in touch with the family?"

"A little. They're obviously in shock."

"Dare I ask if you have any other leads about this stalker from your guy?" *Your guy.*

"Hmm, he's gone quiet." It wasn't a lie. "Jackson . . ."

"Yes, Masters." There was a hint of flirtation in his voice.

She thought about Andy's hands on the back of her neck. She thought about the last time she and Jackson had made love. The way he always got up afterward and pulled on his pants and how there was never any stillness, any true tenderness between them. She thought about how Jackson knew nothing about her—about who she used to be. And how Andy had seen those trash bags in the back of her car.

It felt like she was hovering over a yawning rift in her life. *Jane, Janie.* It felt like it was getting wider. It felt like taking a step into the ether.

"What are we?" she asked. She felt sick as soon as the words left her mouth.

"In what context exactly?"

"I don't know, you tell me."

She heard him, *felt him* hesitate. "If this is about . . . Sarah . . ."

The pasta she'd just eaten rose in her throat. "Sarah from the office?"

"Masters . . ." His voice softened. "Jane. I'll take you out to dinner when you get back. We can talk."

She hung up. She pressed her palm against her chest. It felt like a bruise was blooming under it, or maybe it was just the fucking pasta. *Damn it, don't cry*, she counseled herself. *He's not worth it.* She remembered all those times she'd waited up for him, excused him. Excused his lack of intimacy. And for what? For whom? Her instincts had been screaming and she'd ignored them.

Is that what she was doing with Andy? *Why? Why do you end up with these questionable men? Because you can't be alone. Alone with yourself?*

The tears came. She was too tired. Too overwhelmed. She closed her eyes and sank down into the bed.

———

Her phone alarm startled her awake. Her mouth was sticky. Her head hurt. It was dark outside—she hadn't even drawn the curtains. Her empty plates and glass were on the end of the bed. What time was it? She found her phone. Five a.m. Paige's memorial. Shit, she must have fallen asleep. She hadn't prepared anything.

She dragged herself out of bed and looked in the mirror. Her conversation with Jackson came back to her like a hard slap. She'd silenced her phone. There was one missed call. He hadn't even tried that hard to save things between them.

There was a message from Andy.

*I'll see you at the memorial? Can we talk after?*

Her fingers hovered over the phone. It felt like she was on a tightrope. There were so many ways to fall. Should she reply? She thought about it for an inordinate amount of time before she just liked his message.

She only had the same clothes as yesterday to wear, no hairbrush, nothing but some concealer and a bit of lip gloss she found in her bag. Not exactly memorial attire. But she had to go, and she had to see him. She pulled her hair back, washed her face, and dressed. She'd have to hope that the early hour meant that people would be dressed casually.

The cloak of night had not yet lifted fully. They came in tracksuits, bare feet, carrying surfboards, candles. It was raining lightly. There were two photographers and a local film crew. It could have been much worse. The word of mouth had evidently worked—no one from Sydney. And maybe the news cycle had moved on.

Jackson's text came through at 5:45 a.m. *Her memorial is this morning. Will you be there? Can you file something? Add in anything you've picked up from the family.*

Anger knit tight in her chest. The sheer arrogance. He'd seen her collapse in the office after writing that first story. He'd all but admitted he was sleeping with the entertainment reporter. But the gloves were off. No special treatment for her now. He was treating her just like any other journalist.

She silenced and pocketed her phone as she followed the mourners down the track. Andy stood with the Whites at the front, his head bowed. She stood at the back hoping that maybe they'd forget about her saying something; it wasn't like there was an order of service printed out or anything. Pastor White addressed his congregation as the day broke high in the trees above them. Light cracked over the lake as he made sweeping, sad gestures at the altar. Ethereal music mixed with the cries of waterbirds. At one point he closed his eyes and went silent, and his effort not to break down nearly undid Jane. But he went on. Others got up to talk, said poems and prayers. Jane let it all drift over her, gems, quotes that she knew she should be scribbling down, ready to file to Jackson to save her job, salvage her relationship with him. There were a lot of words about how beautiful Paige was, inside and out. Jane was just starting to feel her shoulders drop, sure the service was close to finishing, when she heard her name.

Her head and heart were pounding. Why had she said yes to this? What on earth was she going to say? She felt eyes on her, and she moved through the bodies to the altar as if in a nightmare. Her mind was racing but nothing intelligible was coming. She stood stiffly in front of this group of people, the expectation on their faces making her squirm. *God. Say something, anything.*

"Paige was my friend." She swallowed, cleared her throat. "Ah, we'd known each other a long time, since we were kids." *Oh my god, say something meaningful.* "Anyone who knew her, knew that she would light up a room. Paige was always charismatic. Everyone loved Paige. Maybe that's why she was so popular on social media . . ." That last image of Paige's face lying just a few yards from here in the shallows. *Why did you say that?* "She had . . . that X factor . . ." Her voice trailed off. Jane felt her face flush at the superficiality of her words. *Say something about her character.* But she couldn't. Her chin wobbled and her hand went to her mouth. "I'm sorry," she mumbled.

She stepped away from the altar, mortified, but Mrs. White was there, patting her back. Pastor White returned to the front, and a hymn started up and people began to sing. Andy and some other men picked up a surfboard covered in flowers by the water's edge and pushed it out onto the lake. The singing finished and no one spoke, everything and everyone seemed to still, the trees, the water, as they watched the board drift slowly away. The only movement was the raising of phones to take photos.

*I wonder how long it will take to end up on Instagram,* Jane thought. *Or in the papers.*

She melted back into the crowd, still lightheaded and embarrassed. *I'm grieving,* she tried to tell herself, *people will understand.*

As the crowd dispersed, Andy caught her by the elbow. "Hi," he said.

She wanted to reach out and hug him, but she stopped herself. He must have seen it because he scratched the back of his neck, awkward. For a moment she thought that maybe she'd dreamed it all, what had happened between them.

"I'm sorry, I couldn't . . ." She bowed her head.

"It's okay, Janie, everyone's emotional. I couldn't even get up there. You did your best."

"I don't know," she said under her breath.

"Come on, let's walk," he said.

He led the way along the track that went west around the water instead of back to the parking lot like everyone else. The lake was turning to gold as the sun rose; the rain had cleared.

When they were alone, he slowed. "I'd suggest we sit on a log but . . ."

Jane laughed quietly. They were silent for a bit.

"I wanted to apologize for—"

"No, no, it's okay. You don't have to," she said.

"No, I think I do. I'm . . ." He took a deep breath, and she could see his jaw working to contain his emotion. He blinked in the bright sunlight. "I'm all over the shop, and Janie, I'm sorry. I know we probably shouldn't have . . . I just feel like . . . I know you, weirdly, like we've got . . ."

Their eyes met. She felt it, whatever it was. And she could see in his eyes that he did too.

"But everything is so complex and mixed up, and obviously I should be mourning Paige, not . . ." He pursed his lips and made an awkward sound. ". . . with her best friend."

Everything felt raw, scrubbed, the air, the lake, her emotions. "We weren't best friends, Andy. There was old unresolved stuff between us."

"Oh, okay, I didn't . . ." He rubbed his cheek.

"I wasn't that clear with you. I don't know . . . what you said about

the Whites, about how Paige came as a package with her family . . . I
guess I could really relate to that."

He nodded.

They were silent, the only sound the wind in the she-oaks and the
distant buzz of a motorboat.

"I know you loved her, though," he said. "I could see it on your face
when you spoke just now. I hope you believe me when I say I did love
her."

Jane felt embarrassment and shame collide inside her, but she nodded. "I do believe you, Andy. And the police obviously do too."

He took a deep breath, bracing himself. "They questioned me for
what felt like hours yesterday. I didn't ask for a lawyer, even though I
could have, probably should have."

"But they let you go."

"Yeah, but I don't know . . . They said they had more questions for
me. That I was a person of interest and that I could be charged later for
hindering a police investigation. They told me not to leave town.
Maybe they just let me out to go to the memorial."

"You lied about where you were that morning." She said it with a
voice that felt more steady than her insides.

"How did you—"

"I'm a journalist, Andy. I know how to get to the truth."

He kicked at a stick. His hands slipped into his pockets. It felt like
he was closing off to her.

"So, do you want to tell me your version of events? I assume you
finally came clean to the police?"

"Janie, you've got to believe me—I didn't harm Paige, I swear on
Viv's life."

Jane flinched, and he saw it. "I spoke to a woman. She lives in one
of the mobile homes in the caravan park. A woman saw you yelling at
Paige right before she died. Viv implied that you'd made her sad too.
You can imagine how that looks."

"We did yell. We had a fight, but did this woman tell you that before that I'd surprised Paige for her birthday? That I'd brought Viv to the tree cathedral and set up a special breakfast to surprise Paige? It's just, we had issues, and they all came to a head that morning."

"And then Paige ended up dead."

"Yes. No. Yes, but I don't know how she died, I swear it. I know the police think there were signs of a struggle, that she had bruising around her neck but . . . but I know how she was . . . She was irrational, angry . . . hurt. Janie, she'd been hurt by other people, what they'd written online . . . She'd been hurt by me."

"So, you think she killed herself because of that?"

"She wasn't in a good place. I think the fact that it was her birthday . . . it made her more emotional."

"How do you explain the bruising then? You were the only one there, Andy. Why did you lie to the police about that? To me? Why wouldn't you just tell them the truth?"

He looked at the ground. "After they hauled me into the station the first time, when Viv and I went up to my parents' place, I got scared. I thought they'd immediately just think it was me. I don't know what happened out there on the lake." He put his head in his hands. "I can't handle the fact that I might have caused her to take her life, okay? That I was there, and I did nothing. That it's all my fault . . . I thought it was just easier, safer, to say I didn't know what happened on that lake, that she just went out like normal, because, Janie, you have to believe me, I don't."

"I saw you throw something into the water, the day we met on the track for the first time. I don't know, it was . . . strange."

He looked at her now, but his eyes were unfocused. "I don't know. God, what do you think I was throwing . . . some evidence away? It was probably a rock. I throw shit in the lake all the time. God, she'd only just died. Those first few days are a total blur."

"Why do I feel like there's something you're not telling me, Andy?"

She put her hand on his arm, softened her voice. "I want to believe you, I really do. I can sense your anguish. But you have to help me. Is that really everything? What were you two fighting about?"

He ran his hands over his face and closed his eyes for a moment. "There's something else. I didn't want to tell the cops because of what happened afterward . . . I thought they might take my daughter off me if they knew what really happened. And I couldn't, I just couldn't lose her too."

Jane waited. The sky was shot through with dawn, gold and red, as though the lake were on fire. It was shining right in their eyes.

"Because of what happened with Viv."

# CHAPTER 49

# Paige

I posted the photo as soon as Viv took it. I sat up, the silk of my top sticking to my body, and uploaded the first photo on the camera reel. I didn't skim for the best one—my daughter had taken it—I didn't even know if it was in focus, if I was properly in frame, and I didn't care. I could hardly see the screen in the dawn sun. But it was the symbolism of it. I guess I'd grown up in a family obsessed by symbolism. I didn't write anything, I didn't hashtag. I pressed Share. Andy pulled me to my feet.

It felt done. Finished. A clean slate. So I knew I had to be completely honest. I had to tell him I knew about Tam. I wanted us to be honest. I wanted us to start again.

"It's done. My last post. I'm living in the real world from now on." I felt light, I breathed deep. "I've been dealing with so much online hate. There was a guy who actually came here, to The Lakes, to find me."

"A stalker? What the fuck, Paige? Why didn't you tell me?"

I shook my head. This wasn't how he was meant to react. He was meant to embrace me, tell me everything was going to be okay now that I'd disentangled myself from that all-consuming world.

"No, I think he's harmless, really. I'm not that scared of him, he's left me alone. I've just had enough. I want us to go back on the road, get the caravan, and go up north with Viv. I want to be happy, like before, but this time let's not catalog it for the world, let's keep it for us."

He came and wrapped me in his arms then and it felt so good. I felt my body relax into his. I almost, almost felt safe. I drew away from him, looked him right in the eyes. "But, Andy, I need to know that you're not emailing her anymore."

His grip slackened and he took a step back. "Her?"

"Tam, from the shop." I said it straight. No particular emotion.

His face contorted into something unrecognizable. "I—"

"Please, please don't gaslight me about this, not again. I know. I've seen some of your emails . . ." A lie. I'd seen all of them. But who among us tells the whole truth? Is there even such a thing?

"You've been going through my emails?" His eyes flashed and his mouth twisted.

"I just stumbled on one on the iPad, you'd left it open. And I may have checked a few more times."

"What the hell, Paige? She's a friend, so what? We've talked about this."

"Really? Are we really getting into this again? Can you just admit she's freaking in love with you, and you liked that attention."

"I hope you're joking."

"No, really, I know how it feels . . . to have all that love and attention, and admittedly maybe you weren't getting enough from me. But, Andy, it's not healthy."

"You've lost it, Paige."

"No, I haven't actually, I've actually finally, finally found my way.

And I just want—need—you to come clean with me. Admit you've been having an emotional affair with this girl, and you can apologize and we can move on. I know it's been hard between us lately."

"There's nothing to admit." His face was hard. He was looking out onto the lake.

My head began to spin, and I sat down on the pretty picnic blanket and wondered how moments ago things had felt so perfect. "You're a fucking liar, Andy."

"I'm not the one who had a fucking stalker and didn't even tell her husband about it."

"You have no idea what I've been going through."

"Maybe that's because you didn't tell me."

I felt my eyes fill with tears. "How could I tell you when I didn't trust you?"

"Fuck. I don't trust you either. I don't know who you are anymore. You're so worried about image, about how you appear, it's like there's nothing there anymore. All I wanted was someone real."

And there it was.

I thought of Tam—plain, simple, and uncomplicated. Or was she? I thought about all his protestations about her not being good-looking—as if that mattered in the end. I'd thought I wanted to discuss it, that I could handle teasing out his emotional infatuation, but now faced with the depth of his betrayal, I felt destroyed by it. Tears burned my eyes.

"I was having an emotional affair too, Andy. With a poet online who turned out not to be who he said he was. So, I just wanted to say, we're even. Okay? We're even. And I'm sorry, even though it was never real. It was never real like you and Tam."

"*Real?* What the hell does that mean? You don't exactly have a firm grasp on reality, Paige. I don't know where you're getting all this."

I laughed darkly. "I knew you'd do this. I'm getting it from your own words, Andy, and hers. It's not all in my head so don't tell me it is. Don't do this to me. To us. I took screenshots for god's sake. I just want you to be honest."

His hands went through his hair, and he turned away from me.

"Did you sleep with her?"

He didn't turn around. I watched the rise and fall of his shoulders, how quick his breath was. "Andy. Did you sleep with her?"

He turned around then and looked at me, but it felt like he was looking through me, as though I weren't even there anymore. And I knew his answer. It felt like a great weight was on me. My clothing was still waterlogged and my eyes were clogged with tears. I saw in a moment of aching clarity just how far my life had veered away from me, away from the ideal I'd been playing. I realized that I was probably going to be a single mother with no immediate income. But at least I had my parents, at least I had Viv.

I picked her up and kissed her soft cheeks then walked to the water's edge. I waded ankle-deep and pulled the kayak off the sandbank. I sat down and placed her carefully in front of me. I just wanted to get away from him. To go home.

Andy stood in the shallows. "What are you doing? She doesn't have a life jacket, Paige. Don't."

I looked at him. His eyes were squinted against the light coming off the water and I thought how beautiful he was in that moment. "Do you love her?"

I saw on his face the truth, but it didn't make me get out of the kayak. I couldn't go to him. I knew in some deep, gutting way that he had ruined us, ended us.

How is it that someone so close to you, whom you know so well, can be so far away at the same time? That's how I felt about Andy. It was how I felt about myself.

He reached out for Viv, but I hugged her tight. She was in between my legs. The place she'd come from. She was mine, she'd come out of my body.

My voice was cold. "Don't you touch her."

I used the paddle to dislodge the kayak and push away from the shore, from him. My arms, my body, felt strong, capable, and at this moment I was so grateful for this lake, these mornings of quiet solitude because I knew what was coming was going to be harder and more lonely, would require more strength, than anything I had ever experienced.

"Paige. What are you doing? Don't do this. Come back," he called out, but he didn't stop me. He stood there with his hands on his head. He could have waded deeper, come after us, but he didn't. I guess that was because doing so would have meant answering my questions, owning what he'd done.

The sun had turned the soft peaks of the waves silver and the slosh of the water against the hull, the dip of the oars calmed, lulled me. I looked back to see him on the shoreline, the cathedral of trees rising behind him. I looked ahead of me, my little girl ensconced close to my body where she belonged, the open water a fractured mirror.

# CHAPTER 50

# Audrey

The next morning when I opened my eyes, I felt a strange mix of hope and dread. I poked my finger through the hole in the wall above my bed as a sort of farewell to this sad little reality. It felt like I was finally going to stop hiding in the imaginary worlds of my books and start my own real-life adventure, where I'd get to be myself rather than always having to find ways to avoid myself. I dressed in my school uniform so Mom would think I was going to school as normal, but I'd hidden my packed bag in the garage. I knew she wouldn't go in there because it reminded her of Dad. The dirt bike was propped against a wall, and I gripped the grooved handles, remembering the way my father had shown me how to rev the engine, to brake, even while my legs were too short to reach the ground. I wasn't sure how I was going to take the bike without Mom noticing, but I knew I needed to be ready.

I expected her to still be in bed, emotionally flattened by what had happened, but she was in the kitchen wearing another sundress. She'd showered and her hair was wrapped in a towel. She was making French toast. The news radio was on.

"Only three days left of the school year and then we've got the whole summer. What shall we do?" She put a plate in front of me.

I felt guilt slice through me. "You didn't have to make French toast."

"It's fine. I woke up with a craving."

I wondered if this was just an extension of her manic baking phase yesterday.

She sat down and poured maple syrup into a dark puddle on my toast. "We could go camping. Find a little spot by a beach or river and cook over the campfire and swim."

I could see what she was doing. We'd done this with Dad when I was younger—ridden the bikes into the bush with a tent and a week's worth of tinned food strapped onto the back.

"What do you reckon? Beach or river?" Her eyes sparkled. It felt like she'd decided to move on with her life.

"Maybe river," I said, taking a bite of the sweet toast. It hurt my teeth. I could picture us somewhere up the coast, sleeping in the little blue tent that leaked when it rained, lighting fires in the afternoons, toasting marshmallows, our hair getting knotty with salt and smoke. It nearly made me abandon my plan.

"I'll drive you this morning. I know you weren't feeling great yesterday."

"No, no, it's fine, I can walk. I want to." There was no way I was going back there, even for three more days.

But her enthusiasm wouldn't be dampened. It broke my heart.

"I'll just put my face on, then we'll go, okay?"

Strapped into the car, it felt like being driven back to the scene of a crime. Mom dropped me off at the front gate and I slung my bag onto my shoulder and waved with as much cheer as I could muster.

Swaths of kids swarmed around me. The feeling of Christmas holidays was in the air. Excited chatter, that long stretch of summer. I thought that maybe yesterday would be forgotten. Maybe everyone could move past the rumors and the drama and that it was a new day.

And then I saw them up ahead. Paige and Yas and Janie. They had their arms linked and they were laughing. The sun filtered through the leaves above them casting them in a soft, dappled light. They all wore light, filmy, flowing dresses, as though they had coordinated their outfits, and perhaps they had. I felt a cold sweat prick my body. How could I have forgotten? It was casual day for the senior school. I would be the only one in uniform. There was no way I was going inside the school. I turned to cross the road and then head to the lake, to Daisy and Ed's, to safety, but a voice called out.

"Auds, you dag! Did you forget?" Paige indicated her clothing.

I felt a cascade of relief at her warm, familiar tone. I remembered the feeling of standing under freshwater falls to shower when Mom and Dad and I camped by the river. The purity of the water that came from the melted snow off the mountaintops. And in that moment, I thought that maybe I would go camping with Mom, stand under icy falls and collect kindling for fires. That we could stay here and build a life without Dad. That I did have friends.

Paige linked her arm through mine and it felt like coming back into the fold. Like a sheep that had been out all night being sealed into the safe pen.

Janie flicked me a small smile. I let them lead me into the school. I'd overreacted yesterday, read too much into tiny things, of course I had. That's what I always did. They were talking about their summer holidays. The Whites were going to their aunt's place in Sydney. She lived at Bondi Beach and had a pool that overlooked the water. Paige was talking about sneaking out to go to the city. I suddenly saw how absurd my plan had been to go on the dirt bike with Janie to Sydney. Why had I thought things would be any easier there?

We turned into the hallway, and my heart felt like it stuttered to a halt. There was a group of kids around my locker and I knew. It was like an animal instinct. I just *knew*.

The sea of people parted as I approached them. I heard their whispers, their embarrassed laughter before I saw why they were laughing. Someone had broken the crappy lock to get into my locker. The front and inside were covered with the torn pages of books. Dread thickened my blood as I dragged my body closer. Someone had used yellow highlighter to highlight the text. I knew even without reading them that they were the sex scenes from Ed and Daisy's books. Shame crashed through me. I could feel all of their eyes on my back. I could hear their snickers, the squeak of their sneakers.

*Why?* I wanted to ask. *Why have I been singled out? Why me? What did I ever do to any of you?*

Someone made a high-pitched moaning sound, and the hallway erupted with laughter. It felt like being in the middle of a circus, and I was the clown. The laughter echoed around my head, which felt strangely hollow. I looked to Paige and Yas huddled among the crowd, their hands over their mouths. They didn't move to comfort me. My eyes met Janie's and they were full of sadness, but she didn't step forward. Why would she, when doing so would be social suicide?

I ran. Out of that corridor; out the front gate of the school; I ran along the deserted roads until I met the track to the lake. I stopped to catch my breath, my lungs burning. When I reached Ed and Daisy's I was sweating, thirsty. I let myself in and gulped water from the bottle we left there. I checked Daisy's bookshelf. Was there a gap where several paperbacks had been removed? I couldn't tell. Nothing else was amiss.

*It's okay,* I told myself. Make a cup of tea. Maybe Janie will still come after school like we planned. Maybe we can still escape this place. A small part of me wanted to run home to my mother, to tell her everything, but I knew how relieved she was that I'd finally found friends.

She'd be ashamed of me for this new failure, this new humiliation. She'd pretend not to be, but really, she would be. Because I was shameful, ugly, worthless.

I busied myself so I wouldn't cry. I was past crying. I felt like a numb, hollow shell. I put the kettle on. I looked out the window to the calm surface of the lake and tried to tell myself that the world went on. Nature wasn't concerned with this petty human shit. Then I realized that I was brave, that even if Janie didn't come, I could still leave this place. I felt a surge of defiant, hot, thick anger.

There was a novel lying on the tiny table. I wanted to throw it out the window, but it hadn't been there yesterday when we left the caravan. Maybe this was Janie's note to me. There was something lodged inside. I opened the book.

# CHAPTER 51

# Jane

Andy walked right to the edge of the lake. He put his hands on his thighs and dropped his head.

Jane came up behind him. Kept her voice soft, calm. She could see that he was having some kind of breakdown. The emotional toll all this was taking on him was apparent in the hopeless curve of his back. "What happened with Viv, Andy?"

He straightened and wiped his eyes, but he wouldn't look at her. He looked out onto the water and shook his head. "She only did it because she was desperate, she didn't want Viv to witness what she was going to do to herself. Or she never would have just . . . done that to our daughter." His voice broke. "I can't believe I was so angry with her, Janie. So angry. But it was all my fault, you see. And I put our daughter in so much danger. I'm so ashamed. I'm scared if the police knew they'd take Viv from me. I can't lose her too."

Jane grasped his arm. "Andy, what are you talking about?"

He turned to her, and his face was white, his eyes full of remorse. "I hurt Paige so much. It was all my fault."

Jane felt a chill run through her. Something moved in the bush behind her, and she swung around. She pressed her hand against her chest in relief as she saw that it was Mr. White coming toward them on the track.

"Ah, there you are, mate. Everyone's looking for you. We're heading back to the house." He sized up Andy's state and placed a hand on his shoulder. "Come on, it's been a rough morning. You too, Janie. Come join us for breakfast at the house. It would mean a lot."

"Yeah, yeah, okay," said Andy, wiping his hands down his face.

Mr. White put an arm around him and guided him slowly along the track. Andy didn't turn to look back.

Jane nodded absently, but she said nothing, didn't move. She couldn't. She couldn't go back to that house, so full of her past, so full of Paige, and now with the added humiliation of her horrendous speech, and her feelings for Andy.

She stared after them. What was Andy suggesting? What had Paige done to Viv? Was this guilt about their fight before Paige died? His words rang in her head. *I was so angry. It was all my fault.* She looked out onto the lake and drew her arms close. But the police had let him go. He was broken, yes; he was flawed. But surely, he hadn't killed her?

*You couldn't feel this way about someone who had done that.*

Her phone rang in her pocket, startling her. It was Jackson again.

*God.* She knew what he wanted. She took a deep breath, willed herself to focus. She had been so caught up in this family the last week that she'd completely lost track of herself, her own life. She really needed to pull it together. Forget the personal stuff between her and Jackson. She couldn't put her job in jeopardy. A career in journalism was fragile as it was. She couldn't lose everything she'd worked so hard for.

*My life is in Sydney, not here. It can't be here.*

There was a noise, a stick cracking. She looked behind her on the track, but no one was there. Her heart was racing.

She picked up the call.

"Jackson, hi."

"Masters, there you are."

"Here I am." Her voice sounded strangely defiant.

"I take it you went to Paige's memorial?"

"I did go to the memorial." She said it through her teeth. She could barely control the emotion that had risen suddenly in her throat.

"Look, Masters . . . Jane, I know you're upset. I don't like how we left things."

"I don't think you can really presume to know anything about me."

"Okay, Masters, I get it, I get it."

"No, actually, I don't think you do, Jackson."

She realized how little she had ever called him by his name. And he always used her name. God, the power had always been entirely in his court, hadn't it, right from the start. She thought about all the ways in which she'd just handed it over to him willingly. How had she just blindly ignored and repressed it for so long?

*You are good at giving over your power, and blindly repressing things.*

"Can we keep things on track though, just for now?" His voice was crisp.

She laughed darkly. "You seemed pretty fucking happy to veer off track all those other times. After the pub every Friday night. That time in the bathroom just before deadline. That didn't seem very on track."

"Okay." His tone was condescending now. She could just imagine him holding up his hand, his way of interrupting. Of telling her she'd gone too far.

"I'm not writing your story, Jackson."

There was a pause.

"Come on, Masters, you're stronger than this. Let's not let our personal stuff get in the way."

"Yeah, well, the personal stuff *has* gotten in the way. And yes, I am stronger than this. I don't want to write about this. I thought you might have gathered that when I was on the floor crying the first time I wrote the story."

"Okay, well . . . I don't have time for this." He hung up.

"Fucking coward," she hissed. She realized she was shaking. Her head throbbed. She looked around. Everything was very quiet. She was totally alone, just her and the lake. It felt like the past was pulling her under now that she might have destroyed her future. She had tried so hard to keep it at bay. To stay buoyant. But being in Paige's bedroom . . . Andy's body so close to hers . . .

She knew she needed to face this. If she wanted the truth, concrete evidence that her gut instinct was right—that Andy was innocent, and that Paige didn't take her own life—she needed to rip open the barely healed wound of her and Paige's joint past.

She had intel that no one else had. *No one else knows the significance of those flowers around Paige's neck. Not the police. Not Andy.*

Her phone was perilously close to dying but she opened Instagram. How would she approach this if this *was* a story she was covering for the paper? She would work systematically. She'd carefully check every single like and comment on the last posts Paige had made.

Then she saw it: a face so tiny she might have missed it. In profile. Smiling. So hidden in her past, her subconscious, that her mind could barely register it.

@nature_lover was the account. A single like on one of Paige's pictures of the lake at dawn. Jane's fingers skipped over the keys so fast she dropped her phone. The police would have never made this connection. Jane knew she was the only one who could. It was the thread of her past that she had spent so many years trying to sever from the knotty tapestry of her life. And yet, here it was again.

She expected to find a private account, but she clicked on the profile, and it was like a portal opening into someone's world. But it wasn't any world. It was the lake. The lake that had defined their child-hood, that sat in the center of everything, like a blinding mirror. There were only five pictures. A fire roaring in a grate. A glass of white wine sweating against a sunset. A mug of tea and a paperback novel with the lake in the background.

Jane straightened, her mind sharpening. Where was this picture taken from? Where was this house? Then, in the final image, she saw it. A rope swing that they'd used as kids to propel themselves into the cool green water. It was a big old timber house, right on the south end of the lake—the sort of place large families would rent for the summer but abandoned otherwise. She knew exactly where it was.

A chill ran through her. The police had been looking at the wrong cabin.

# CHAPTER 52

# Paige

As we got farther out onto the lake, the sun went behind a cloud and the water turned pewter. Birds whipped across the sky and the wind howled through the trees. My arms ached with the effort of steering through the rough water. *It's okay, just get to the other side. Just get home.* Sometimes when I paddled, words or phrases would stick in my mind. Rowing a boat felt like poetry. They were linked somehow. The rhythm. The repetitious pull of the paddle. And this was what was in my mind like a song. *Get to the other side. Get to the other side.*

My muscles, honed on this lake, pumped hard. Viv was wriggling between my legs. I'd never taken her out deep in the kayak, only in the warm shallows, always with a life vest. The kayak's nose slapped against the waves and I felt a twinge of fear. It's the fear every mother has from the moment they bring life into the world. And I thought, *Damn it, Paige, why did you have to react so dramatically?* And the regret hit me like the wall of water over the kayak. I pivoted, steadied the vessel, using all my strength.

And I thought about Andy's face, his stillness in the shallows, his passivity and weakness, his deception, and a new surge of anger filled me.

I rowed harder, right, left, right, left, but I couldn't seem to catch my breath; I knew I was starting to panic. I knew I had to stay calm. It was still quite a distance to get home, but there was no way I was turning back. I looked behind and he was no longer standing there. I stopped paddling for a moment and we drifted, the wind clawing at my back, my muscles burning. I closed my eyes, forced air into my lungs, willed my heartbeat to calm.

When I opened my eyes she was slipping over my salt-slick legs. It was so fast, so silent, so sudden. She was like a glistening, slippery fish. And I dove, I dove in after her.

# CHAPTER 53

*I don't know if I left it there to spook her. To be honest—maybe, a little bit. Or maybe I wanted to make something beautiful for her. I was watching her, that was the truth. That's what she wanted, wasn't it? To be watched? But that morning was different. It was her birthday. You can find out anything online now. I left the flower crown on her doorstep in the hours when even the insects are asleep. There were always random people at that house. Even if someone had seen me, no one would have thought much of it. But I'm sure no one saw me. I'm very good at being invisible. I'd fashioned it from the wildflowers that edged the lake, along with two flowers picked from her garden in the dead of night. Maybe I just wanted her to wonder who had left it there, and why. Birthdays have a strange effect on me.*

*It seemed significant, that it was her birthday. That's the thing about birthdays, they're always the hardest. I was waiting for her, but it wasn't all that different to any other morning—or so I thought. I was always glad to see her out there on the lake. She had become part of my day, like my morning coffee at dawn, my afternoon book, my evening wine. She was on the water later than usual. And the lake was messier. No glassy reflections of tall green trees. No bell-like bird call from the shore. The roar of the wind tore across the surface.*

*I had spent so many mornings watching her kayak slice through the water, I could see, even from a distance, that something was off. It was an instinct more than anything. There was something erratic about the way she was paddling. Or maybe it was just the inclement weather.*

*I was sitting on the veranda with a cup of tea. I got up to pull a cardigan around my shoulders and picked up my binoculars from the ledge where I kept them. I trained them on her. She was wearing the flowers in her hair, and I didn't know what to feel about that. Was it arrogance or had she forgotten? Maybe she didn't care. Maybe she just thought they were pretty flowers.*

*And then suddenly, she was gone. I lowered the binoculars, strained to see with my naked eye. Where was she? The kayak was still there. I felt a pulse of panic. I threw off my cardigan and looked into the binoculars again. Without her weight, the kayak lifted and fell in the water like a leaf. I couldn't see her.*

*I don't know why I did it. I think the lake felt like it was part of me by then. I could almost feel its swift currents, its cold channels, and the churn of its agitation that morning. She wasn't too far out but the water was rough, deep. I knew I could get there fast. My arms were strong, honed by hours swimming this vast body of water. When you do anything long enough it changes you. It changes the shape of you.*

*I stripped off to my underwear. The cold was like a baptism. I saw spots in my vision as my head went under. The going was much rougher than usual. The waves tossed me around as though I were sea foam. But I knew I had weight, strength. I focused on my breathing. I wasn't thinking, I was just moving. I saw something, someone, surface and then go under. I quickened my pace.*

*I reached the kayak—the nose was submerged. It had taken on water. I scanned for her between the dip and peak of the waves. I took a deep breath and went under. The color was like tea, greenish brown, and I could see the glow of pale limbs through the gloom. Her face, straining toward the surface. She was only a few yards from the kayak, but it may as well have been a mile. As I swam closer, I saw there was something attached to her. Another body, but smaller. A child. I felt it like a blow to my chest. I swallowed water and surfaced. Coughed. Her child. I had never seen her child in real life, only in pictures. Her child. Her perfect child feeding chickens. Swimming in the sea. Smiling. Eating ice cream in the sun.*

*I wondered in that moment about the deeper reason I had come here to this lake. Why I'd returned to this place of relentless pain. Was it to torment myself? Was it to torment her? Is that why I'd left the crown for her? Had I somehow caused this? As I swam closer, I saw that she and the child were entwined. There were long ribbons trailing in the water. I had tied those ribbons around that crown. They were pale tendrils, like silken hair, like seagrass, and I saw that she was entangled in them. I saw this child of hers, its will to live, clawing to the surface, to life. Gripping her long hair, the ribbons around her neck, in its fists. Pulling itself up, and her under.*

*And I thought of my child, and I wondered what it had been like for her in the end, in those final desperate moments, when the body fights for survival even if the mind has made a decision to give up. I wondered if she fought, if she clawed and hung on to life and wished she had made a different decision.*

*I saw so clearly what I wanted to do and I knew I only had moments, seconds, to act. I knew I could only save one of them. And how I wanted to save Paige. To pull her body to the surface, let her gasp sweet air. Save her life. Because in doing so, she would know my pain. To lose a child and to live. That was what she deserved—the searing unfairness and pain of that. I wanted her to feel the loss of her daughter every second of every goddamn day. To be suffocated by it when she woke in the morning and then again in the moments before she slept. I wanted her to live like a zombie for the rest of her life, never feeling anything fully—not love, not pain. Not allowing herself any pleasure because she was alive and her child was dead. Never being able to forget. Always blaming herself. Because what is a mother, if not the one person who should be able to keep their own child safe.*

*But I could see that Paige didn't blame herself. That she had forgotten. When she put that flower crown on her head, it showed me that she had forgotten what she did to my daughter. What she did to Audrey.*

I moved toward their flailing bodies. I took a deep breath and went below. The little girl had her eyes squeezed shut, every molecule of her fighting, gripping her mother from behind. Paige grappled at her throat, her arms and legs scrambling. I saw the whites of her eyes. Neither of them could get traction.

I thought about the day I packed up and drove to this lake. The day I found her account. How I spent hours looking at her perfect, beautiful life. Thinking how she got to live when my girl died. The hate I felt for her was like spitfire. Then when I arrived on the lake and I saw Paige so alone in its vastness, so vulnerable against the elements, my anger cooled to something I couldn't articulate. The swimming helped. Nature helped.

But now, seeing her gasping, taking in water, struggling to survive, the anger is back. I want her to feel the worst possible pain. It would be so easy, so so easy to reach out and grasp her around the shoulders, kick hard to the surface, sling my arm about her chest, and let her live. Let her child die.

But as I get closer, I hear a voice. It's soft, a whisper that sounds like the trees on a warm summer evening. It has been nineteen years since I heard her voice. I thought I'd forgotten the sound of it. The voice, its nuances, is the thing you forget first. But here it is, loudening in my waterlogged ears, and she's telling me something I don't want to hear.

I think of that time we got in the car and drove north—on a whim, only days before she was gone. Of how we jumped into the sea in our clothes, of all the hope we had for our lives. Of how often I thought back to that day and treasured the fleeting beauty of it. And she's telling me I can't do this to another mother. That is not who I am.

I want to scream at her, What would you know? You left me. She was so young. She'd hardly learned about the world yet. But I know my girl. She had a heart that was too open for the cruelty in this world. This is not what she would have wanted. She would not have wanted it to end like this.

I'm close now. Paige has seen me. There's nothing but panic in her eyes, on her face. She already looks like a ghost. In that look, there is all the love and fear a mother holds. And I reach for her daughter. I pry her mother's hair, the ribbons, from her curled fists, feel her little body squirm and rage, and I kick up, away, my legs powerful. And we're on the surface. Viv gasps, coughs, but I know I don't have much time. I hook my arm around her tiny chest and I'm at the kayak in four swift kicks. I hoist my arm over it and the little girl clings to the side. I know I can't leave her here on this half-submerged vessel. She's too little. I can't go back for Paige.

I wonder what her face looks like now, knowing it's over, that the world has ended forever for her, but knowing that her daughter will get to live.

## CHAPTER 54

# Jane

Her phone had died. But she didn't need it for where she was going. She got in the car and drove to the southern end of the lake. She parked on the street and joined the track that they'd walked as kids to the old swing. It was still early. The dew clung to blades of grass, the clouds moved in slow communion across the sky. It was a perfect autumn morning. The heat was only a dim promise.

She found herself in front of the cabin. There was no movement inside. On the veranda facing the lake were an empty mug, an ashtray with an unsmoked cigarette, a towel, and a pair of binoculars. She felt a cool breeze bite at the backs of her bare legs. Maybe the Indian summer heat had finally broken. Goose bumps spread across her skin. Why was she here? A reporter's hunch. No, it was more than that. Was it really to save Andy?

*Maybe it's to save yourself.*

What was she going to do? Walk up and knock on the door?

Suddenly the link between this solid house, these everyday objects, and that tiny photo in the ether seemed tenuous, ridiculous. Was there even a link? Or was she chasing ghosts? Her blood turned cold at the thought. A voice inside her said that this wasn't even her issue to deal with. She had been miles away when Paige died; she hadn't even known Andy then. Or Viv. She hadn't made any pretense of being close to Paige. She wished suddenly that she'd just stayed away. They had only been children themselves. It was nineteen years ago. What did she hope to achieve by being here?

But something louder, deeper inside her said that maybe this was everything. That things had come full circle. She thought of the years she had spent running from herself. Hiding behind her job. Behind lonely, empty relationships. How funny that she had chosen a profession dedicated to probing the truth.

She stood there, suspended, feeling strung between two worlds. The real world and that online place that Paige had inhabited. The world of the living and the world of the dead.

She heard movement behind her and she turned, heart thumping. A woman was standing there. Her silver hair was slicked back from her face and her body was brown. She seemed solid, strong. She had a towel wrapped around her at her chest. She'd been swimming. Jane tried to marry her with her memory of the pretty, delicate woman in the retro dresses at the gas station.

They stood there in silence for a moment, longer than was socially polite.

"Jane, isn't it? You still look the same. I thought you might find me." Her voice wasn't unkind, but it wasn't warm either. "You were always the smartest of them. Not as smart as Audrey, but not too far off either."

It had been so long since she'd heard that name. It was buried deep inside her, like a jewel—precious, hard, and sharp.

"You'd better come in," Charlotte said, walking past her and up the stairs of the veranda. Her voice sounded resigned. Or maybe, Jane thought, that's just how a woman's voice sounded after losing a child. "I need tea to warm up."

Jane instinctively reached into her pocket, but her phone wasn't there. It sat lifeless in her car. A quiver of panic went through her. The way this woman had been expecting her. They had unfinished business, and Charlotte knew it. *You don't know what she might have done to Paige.*

But then she thought of Audrey. Of her mother's face that day at the funeral, the face that had haunted her for so many years. She had looked so frail, as though all the life had been sucked out of her body, not just her daughter's.

Jane climbed the stairs slowly, cautiously. From up here the lake looked a deeper shade of green, trimmed by white-trunked gums under a horizon of clouds.

"It's a very pretty view," Jane said, and felt sick at her flippancy.

"It's grown on me," said Charlotte. "I didn't mean to stay for so long, but nature moves to a different rhythm."

Jane thought of the handle @nature_lover. That tiny photo of Audrey at age sixteen that her mother had used as her profile picture. She thought suddenly of all those suspended accounts. Those lives cataloged in such minute detail until the day they stopped, and the account became a kind of strange tombstone as it had done for Paige. But Audrey had died in a time before the endless catalog. When things weren't recorded forever in the ether, not in the way they were today.

"Would you like a cup of tea?" Charlotte asked, her hand on the doorknob, about to go inside.

Jane's breathing was shallow. It felt difficult to swallow. *It's an innocent request*, she told herself.

"Thanks, okay," she forced herself to say. *How could she know?* Even the police had never found out.

"Take a seat. I'll just be a moment."

Jane sat down. Her legs, her hands were trembling. She pressed her sweaty palms into her knees. *You have to be here. You have to face this.*

Charlotte returned with two mugs. They looked handmade, misshapen, cozy. She set them down on a timber table between Jane's chair and a rocking chair, which she eased herself into. She moved the ashtray, put it on the ground. Jane wondered why the cigarette was unsmoked. She felt like a detective. It seemed integral to her survival that she pick up on the tiniest of clues.

Charlotte held her steaming mug, blew on it, and took a sip. Jane picked hers up and felt her insides burn, as hot as the ceramic in her hands. She didn't know how to drink this, what to say, where to look, where to start.

"You became a journalist," Charlotte said. "I've watched your career."

Jane felt a cold numbness spread to her extremities. *No one knows I'm here*, she thought. *I don't even have my phone.* She cleared her throat, tried to steady her voice. "Yes. In Sydney." She stared at her tea.

"I think it's a thing parents who've lost children do. It's a kind of exquisite torture I suppose, to see where your child's friends end up. To track the passing of time in that way."

Jane felt hot tears in her eyes. "Charlotte, I'm so sorry. I know it was a long time ago, but I've never, never forgotten Audrey."

"It feels like yesterday. But it was years ago, and you're a woman now. And you're good at your job. That's why you're here. Being a journalist is really like being an investigator, I imagine. Piecing together people's stories, crimes."

The last word rang out into the stillness. It was deathly quiet. Jane put the mug down. There was no way she was drinking the tea.

Charlotte ran a finger over her lips. "I can see you don't want your tea, and I'm sorry . . . I didn't do it as some kind of a test. Or maybe I did . . . I found it, you know."

Jane felt the blood drain from her face.

"The note." Charlotte laughed softly under her breath. "The police just thought she'd accidentally poisoned herself. Just run-of-the-mill risk-taking sixteen-year-old behavior. She'd wanted to get a bit high, you know? And it was true, she had a lot to escape—the bullying at school, those horrible pages stuck to her locker. Her dad running off with another woman. And I know I didn't deal with that well, I wasn't strong enough for her. But I knew that it was more than that. A mother always knows."

Jane felt like she was going to throw up. The blood rushed in her ears. She considered getting up and running but her body wouldn't move.

"But I don't think I knew a hundred percent until you didn't touch your tea."

Jane felt like someone was squeezing her throat shut. She thought of those strangulation marks around Paige's neck. The flowers in her hair, how they had ended up around her neck. The flower in Audrey's tea . . . how it must have felt when that poison went down her throat, seeped into her blood. Jane couldn't breathe. Should she run? No, this woman looked stronger, fitter than her. She was ages away from the nearest house. Could she jump into the water and swim?

*Definitely not.*

"The police returned a pile of stuff from that caravan you girls had made your own. Lots of tea, romance novels. Audrey did like to read, didn't she? And inside one was a note. It seemed innocent enough on the surface.

Jane closed her eyes. It felt like waiting for a blow.

"'Tea for one?' Written in blue pen."

There was a metallic taste in Jane's mouth. She couldn't speak.

"You and Audrey had lots of tea in that caravan, didn't you? It was your thing. They found jars and jars of it. And lots of teapots. But the toxicology report confirmed it when they found her. She'd steeped that dried flower you left her in hot water and drank it as a tisane."

*It wasn't me, it was Paige,* Jane wanted to cry. *I was an innocent bystander. It wasn't my idea. I was coerced. I was not the charming, charismatic Paige White. I was just plain Janie.*

"I thought at first that Paige had written that note." Charlotte looked onto the lake as she spoke. "I knew Paige had made the dream catcher with Audrey for an assignment. I was there, they talked about it at my kitchen table. I knew about the angel's trumpet flowers they used in it. I imagined it was Paige who picked it from her garden and dried it and stuck it in the book for Audrey to find. But the handwriting . . . I knew I'd seen it before. You two used to write each other letters."

Jane's sixteen-year-old self rushed back to her. The terror she'd felt when her mother had left her. How the only place she'd felt safe was the Whites', with their prayers and their warmth and their offer to all but adopt her. How ashamed she'd been of her dad, his decaying house that had so repelled her mother that she'd left.

*I had to choose,* she wanted to say. *I had to choose between Paige and Audrey. And I wanted with all my heart to choose Audrey, to run off to Sydney with her. But I was so scared. I was only a child. I had to choose the Whites. I had to choose Paige. I had no mother.*

"It was my writing," Jane said.

Charlotte looked up from her tea, but Jane couldn't meet her eye.

"I've spent my life blaming beautiful, privileged Paige White for Audrey's death, but I'm the one who wrote the note." She shook her head. "We both thought . . . I don't know, that it would be a silly joke. I did it to show my allegiance to Paige, because she knew I loved Audrey better than her. But I had to make sure she and her family kept me safe. Because I couldn't go back to live with my father. I was so ashamed of him because my mother left us, she left me. I never thought Audrey would actually do it. That she'd make the tea and drink it. Or that it could possibly . . ."

Charlotte smiled, but it was filled with so much sadness Jane wanted to avert her eyes. She made herself keep looking. "Audrey never would have made that tea if she thought Paige White had written that note. Paige meant nothing to her. It broke her heart that you were the one who wrote it."

Jane felt herself keel. A sickening grief overtook her, and she let it. It felt like years of keeping a wave at bay and finally letting it break over her. She let herself be dragged into its depths. She had been so cruel, so selfish. She was living a lie. Telling herself that she was somehow better than Paige White, when really, she was exactly the same. Made of the same stuff. Or worse. She'd used people to get what she wanted. Maybe it wasn't as obvious as Paige, but she still did it. She did it in her job. She'd done it with Shep. She told herself that she was plain, sensible, smart Jane, but really she was manipulative, selfish Janie. Maybe, just maybe, she was exactly like her own mother. And now maybe she was doing the same thing to Andy.

Jane wiped her face, tried to compose herself. "I'm so sorry. I'm so sorry. I've thought of Audrey every day of my life. Not understanding how I could have written that. How I could have been so cruel. I've never regretted anything more. I've wished I could undo what I did."

She glanced over at Charlotte. The other woman was very still. She wasn't looking out at the lake now, she was staring down into her lap. Jane was struggling to catch her breath. It felt like she was the one drowning. She wished Charlotte would scream at her, tell her she hated her, pummel her with her fists, but she just sat there.

Jane felt like she was babbling now. "I don't know what happened out there the morning Paige died, but you see, it wasn't all her fault . . ." Her voice broke. "I don't think Paige deserved to die. If anyone deserves that, it's me."

Jane put her hand over her mouth, squeezed her eyes shut. Had this woman harmed Paige? What if she had? Did that mean she was going to harm her too? She thought of her first words. *I thought you might find me.* Maybe this was all calculated. Maybe Jane had walked straight into a trap.

*This is what you deserve.*

Charlotte looked up. She nodded slowly. "You're right. Paige didn't deserve to die out there that morning. She wasn't a perfect person, but are any of us? She didn't deserve to die like she did. My daughter didn't deserve to die like she did. Audrey ... she'd been struggling with her mental health for a long time before we came here. It's why we came here. A fresh start."

"I'm sorry. She was the most real friend I ever had."

Charlotte smiled. There were tears in her eyes. "I tried to save her, to save Paige. I swam out there, but her daughter was struggling too. They'd both come out of the kayak and I could only save one of them. I chose her daughter."

Jane gasped. It felt like coming up for air from the turmoil of her feelings. "Viv was in the water?"

"Yes." Charlotte nodded, then shook her head, remembering. "I swam her back to shore, to the Whites' property. There was a deck chair there by the water with an old towel on it. I wrapped her up. She curled up into a little ball. She was so quiet ... She was clearly in shock. I was torn about whether to take her into the house. But then I heard a car and her father came around the side of the house. I think he was looking for Paige, scanning the water. He was distressed. I watched to make sure he found his daughter, took her safely inside."

Jane's mind was racing, thinking back to what Andy had said. *Or she never would have just ... done that to our daughter ... I was so angry with her ... but it was all my fault ... I put our daughter in so much danger.* He must have thought Paige had just abandoned Viv, left her there on the shoreline alone, where he found her. Then when Paige's body was found, his guilt, blaming himself for it all after their fight.

Jane looked over at Charlotte, who was holding her cup to her chest, her eyes lowered. "You didn't tell anyone?" Jane asked.

"I didn't . . . I didn't, I don't want to get involved. Because of every-thing that happened. Because of what they might think. The police came by once, but I didn't answer the door."

"Andy thinks Paige left Viv on the shore because she was going to take her own life. The police think Paige was murdered because of bruising found around her neck." Jane's hand went to her own throat. "She was tangled in the flower crown. It was wrapped around her neck."

"It got caught around her neck and her daughter was pulling her under. But . . . I left her that flower crown, on her doorstep. I don't know why I did it. It was her birthday. Birthdays are always the hard-est for me. Audrey didn't get any more birthdays. I guess I just wanted to see if she had any remorse for what she'd done to my daughter. I don't know. Maybe she didn't understand the significance. Maybe she didn't notice the angel's trumpets I'd picked from her garden. Maybe it was just another flower crown to her."

Jane shivered. *But I understood the significance and I couldn't admit it, even to myself. Especially to myself.*

Charlotte took a deep breath and looked out onto the lake as though steadying herself. "It was an accident. I didn't mean for that to happen to Paige."

"I didn't mean for Audrey to die."

Charlotte was quiet for a long while, her head bowed. "I believe you, Jane," she said.

Their eyes met. Something ran between them. Something un-nameable, something unknowable, something terrifying, but also beautiful. Like a vast body of water. Like nature. Like life and then death.

Jane picked up her mug. She hadn't drunk tea in nineteen years. She closed her eyes and took a sip.

# CHAPTER 55

# Paige

I remember nothing after jumping in after Viv.

I was just here suddenly, suspended in this caravan. I thought it was about this place having the most likes. I'd convinced myself that it was because this was once a place of peace and comfort, my sub-conscious buffering me. But that's not entirely true.

There's another reason that I'm in a caravan. It's a reason I've tried not to think about, that I've pushed down, that I've repressed inside me for a very long time. I haven't been entirely truthful. With who? Who am I talking to, after all, but myself? There's no longer an audience in this pretty echo chamber. No, it's myself I haven't been truthful with. Because really, that's the hardest part. But the truth is that I am capable of great sacrifice for my daughter, but I'm also capable of great cruelty when I'm threatened.

There was another caravan once. I'm so ashamed. Not ashamed in a simple way, but in a way I find difficult to even acknowledge. So it was easier to forget this other caravan, its meaning. Why it might be there, actually, that I'm stuck.

I never allowed myself to wonder what she went through in those final moments before she died. Did she hallucinate? Did she feel good before her body began to give up? Or was she terrified the whole time? Was it slow or fast? Was there a moment when she realized what she'd done and regretted it, but it was too late?

Because I don't know how it was for me after I dove into the lake after Viv. Maybe our brains block out those last horrific moments. Maybe there is at least some mercy at the very end.

I don't know what made me cruel. I always blamed being so young, but it wasn't just that, was it? It was the power. The way it made me feel when I saw her suffer. It made me feel better about myself. Everyone blamed the locker incident for what she did to herself. But it wasn't just the locker incident. I picked the angel's trumpet from the garden and pressed it flat inside one of Dad's heavy religious books. Maybe I was angry, hurt that Janie and Audrey had something so special. I could see it. I knew they were planning on leaving me and I couldn't bear that. I was so jealous. I wanted her out of the picture, but I didn't actually want her dead. At sixteen you don't even have a real concept of death.

I guess Janie blamed me and I blamed her for what happened. It was easier that way. I remember when we heard. It was the last day of term, with that magical stretch of summer holidays before us—beach days and lake swims and watermelon and summer crushes on tanned boys. One of our teachers came into class and told us that Audrey Lucas had died. Janie and I looked at each other and deep down we knew. But we never said another word about it. I think we thought if we never ever spoke or thought of it again, it would mean that it didn't happen.

The rumor was that she was doing drugs and she overdosed. But we heard the whispers of the adults who knew the truth. *Such a strange thing to do. Who knew a flower that dangerous was in the garden? Must have been depressed. What with her dad leaving them.*

She was thought of as a bit wild, so that suited the narrative just fine. People talked about her as though they'd liked her, loved her even. How she had been cool because she didn't care what anyone thought, and she was her own person. But really, she cared very deeply about what everyone thought. Because is there anyone among us who doesn't? We are social animals. We're made for connection. We all want to be loved by others. That is so very clear to me now, in this place, alone.

Janie and I spent that last summer together. She lived at our house. We drank a lot. We wiped ourselves out. We wanted to forget. Willed ourselves to. Then it was the HSC year and she got serious, much more serious than me. She wanted to be a journalist. She moved to Sydney part way through the year, stayed with her grandmother, but only until the moment she finished her HSC exams at TAFE.

What I did to Audrey was the worst thing I ever did to anyone in my life. And diving into the water after my daughter was the best thing. There have been so many everyday, forgettable in-between things, tiny slights, moments of benevolence, but these are the moral book-ends of my life.

I don't know if there is a god who hears me. I've stopped praying, but I close my eyes and press my hands together, as I was taught as a child.

When I open them, the feed has stopped. Everything has gone very quiet. Now there is nothing. No pictures on the makeshift screen outside, no movement of the trees. It is just me. I was lonely before, but this is something new. The world, or my access to it, has gone now. Everything is fading. Everything is going dark. I don't think I'm in limbo anymore.

I am in a different caravan. It smells like tea and old books. A blackness moves around inside me. Fear grips my gut. And I see her there, sitting on the bed, surrounded by books, alone. She has one open. I want to tell her that she should close it. That she shouldn't take that pressed flower out and hold it to her nose. She shouldn't get up and walk to the tiny kitchen and put the kettle on.

She should get away from this place—go to Sydney as she intended. That life is so much bigger and longer than this single moment of excruciating pain, and that if she can just get through it there will be happiness again, I promise. But she can't hear me, she can't see me. I am, as I suspected, a ghost. I see her put the dried flower into a brown teapot, pour hot water over it. She watches the desiccated bloom swell back to life.

She sits there and watches it for a long time. Her eyes are dead already. She is resigned. I want to shake her, but I can't. I scream at her, but she doesn't hear me. She takes a sip and then another. I can see her frustration in the grim pull of her mouth. There are tears running down her face. Nothing is happening. She rips a piece of petal and stuffs it into her mouth, chews. I look away as I see her eyes roll back in her head. I don't want to see this, her end. There is a howling, shrill like a kettle boiling. I don't know if it's coming from her or me. I'm so scared. But I know I must look at her, and I do. What I see makes the final hope in me die.

My voice is a whisper. "I'm so sorry, Audrey. I know you can't hear me, but you were loved. You were special. You didn't deserve this. I'm so sorry. Forgive me."

I close my eyes and I feel like I'm floating. The caravan, its hard edges, its musty smells, dissolve. I am in water. There is green all around. My hair is in my face, and my arms flail. It feels like it's choking me but there's something else. I claw at my throat, but something is dragging me under. I see a flash of white-blond hair. My darling, my Viv. She clings to my neck, my hair, her little limbs scrambling for me, her mother. The will to live is so strong, so wild and pure, and I try to lift her away from me, up, toward the light, but my lungs are burning, and I tell myself, *Don't breathe, you mustn't breathe*, but the burning is so bad and so I do. I breathe in. Water fills my lungs. It's not a sensation I have ever felt. And I realize with a strange detachment that it will be my last feeling. That this is it.

Then there is a strange, absurd sort of calm. And I see it. Someone is there, a shadow hovering above us, human or godlike, I cannot tell. And they're reaching down, powerful, strong, grabbing us, and I have a singular moment of hope. We're going to be okay. Of course we are. Then I see that they have Viv. I feel her disentangle from me, the sting of hair ripped from my scalp. And it's like she's flying above me, light as a bird, lifted to the surface. There is sunlight up there; there is life. There is air. But the surface is getting further and further away. I am going in the wrong direction but there is nothing left in me. I can feel myself liquefying. And I know as I sink, away from the flowers that float above me on the surface, that I didn't survive. But it's okay, because my little girl . . . she did.

## CHAPTER 56

# Jane

The lights were on, and the house looked oddly beautiful, like a lantern in the early evening light. She sat in her car full of trash bags in the driveway. She didn't know what was morally right anymore, what was wrong. She didn't know if she should reply to the message she knew would slide onto her screen from Andy when her phone charged. She didn't know if she deserved to be alive while Audrey and Paige were gone. All she knew was that she hadn't been able to bring herself to take the bags to the dump.

He came out of the house. He was bent with the labor of carrying a stack of papers, and she saw that he was very frail now. He dropped the stack onto a new pile of junk by the fence. There were the computer monitors that had lived in the hallway, the newspapers that had been stacked by the TV, the bags of clothing from the spare room, old pillows, lamps with broken shades, supermarket bags overflowing with cords.

She got out of the car.

"Janie," he said. He walked toward her, with effort. "Doing a bit of a throw-out."

She could see on his face the toll it was taking, cleaning out, letting go of all this stuff, when his whole being was primed to want to keep it. But she could see that he was doing it for her.

"I'm so sorry, Dad. I'm sorry I took your stuff. I had no right."

He nodded. "No, Janie, you were right, you were right. It's about time, I reckon."

"I couldn't throw out any of it," she said, indicating the bags still in the back of her car. "I'm sorry I just took it all and left you."

He looked sad. She wondered if he was thinking of her mother. But he stepped toward her and drew her into a hug. He smelled like dust and sweat and salt air and still water. He smelled like the lake. He smelled like home.

# Epilogue

*I look at the teacup, empty on the table. I take it to the sink and rinse it. It would have been easy. I knew she'd be the only one who would come. Who would know. Who would remember. And she did. But you would never forgive me if I hurt her.*

*I don't have much to pack. I throw everything into the one bag I brought.*

*I don't know where I'll go. I'll find another body of water. I'll swim. But it will feel different now. I close the door of the cabin. And as I drive away from the lake, I feel myself getting farther away from you.*

*I know this is what you want for me—to be happy, to be free, to let you go. I never will. But I'll try, I promise, I'll try.*

# Author's Note

I worked for many years as a print journalist covering news and the arts. But at one point I was a social media editor for an online parenting website. The things I saw people write to each other and about each other, both under the cloak of anonymity and overtly, dismayed me and really stayed with me. I felt compelled to explore and interrogate this on a deeper level through fiction.

In my research I read many accounts of harassment, bullying and mental health disorders connected to social media and living in our increasingly ubiquitous online world. This included the painful experiences of those in the public eye, and the sometimes tragic experiences of teenagers who did not feel they could escape their online bullies.

For those who may have had some difficult emotions come up while reading this story the following may be helpful:

988lifeline.org

stopbullying.gov

# Acknowledgments

This novel was written on Guringai land and I pay respect to the Traditional Custodians, Elders past and present.

It has been an absolute dream working with Lori Kusatzky and the team at Crown Publishing. Their care, passion, and attention to detail at every step of the way has been so inspiring. Lori, thank you for understanding my vision for this story, championing it, and bringing it to a wider world. I feel so lucky to work with you.

Anna Valdinger, your editorial insight always astounds me. Thank you for guiding me through five books. And thank you Scott Forbes, Kate Butler, Taylah Massingham, and the publicity and marketing teams at HarperCollins for all they do to bring a book into the world.

Thank you to the art departments of HarperCollins and Crown for their incredible cover art.

Di Blacklock and Pam Dunne made this book so much better with their excellent editing and proofing.

I'm indebted to my wonderful agent, Tara Wynne, for always having my back and broadening my horizons.

A huge thank you to Liane Moriarty and Mikki Brammer for their incredible endorsements.

I owe Ali Lowe many cocktails for beta reading and for getting me out of the house and bringing so much laughter and inspiration to the author life.

Thank you to my local author network: Karina May, Maxine Faucett, Ber Carroll, and Petronella McGovern. Knowing you're all around the corner for a coffee or a wine is the best.

Karina Ware, Kirstin Bokor, and Danielle Townsend, thank you for being my first eyes on a manuscript before I even know what I've made. I always trust you to read with honesty and care. And thank you for being such amazing friends and sharing my love of books and writing.

Thank you to the amazing Sydney authors who I see almost weekly at events. You are too many to name individually, but you know who you are. I love our honest chats, our shared passion and our obsession with our craft.

Bec McSherry and Janneke Thurlow, thank you for the coffee and lunch catch ups.

Shoba Rao, your early help with the journalism content was crucial.

Enormous gratitude to Jill, the detective who answered my endless questions with patience.

Part of this manuscript was written at Varuna, The Writers' House and their incredible support for Australian writers is much needed and so valued.

Thank you to my family for their love, and to my mum for her generous support in innumerable ways.

To Ben and Sophie, you see the ups and downs of the writing life and always encourage me and keep me sane. Love you.

To the passionate and indefatigable booksellers who hand sell and the librarians who champion and keep books alive, a heartfelt thank you.

Finally, to the readers who reach out to tell me what my words mean to them, you are a big part of what keeps me writing.

# ABOUT THE AUTHOR

**VANESSA McCAUSLAND** studied English and Australian literature at Sydney University and graduated with honors in theater and performance studies. She worked as a journalist for nearly twenty years, including as a news and arts journalist for *The Daily Telegraph,* and her writing has appeared in numerous other publications. She has published five novels in Australia and lives in Sydney with her husband and daughter.